HEARTS POUNDING TO THE CADENCE OF LOVE

"So how many horses do you have now?" Sam asked.

"A few. The sorrel I rode the other night. Another couple of mares I'm training for *charreada* riding. And then I have the most incredible new black stallion. *El Tigre* is still half-wild."

"Like you."

A quick glance at Sam told Louisa he admired that in her. "But I'm getting him to settle down," she replied.

"I'd like to meet this *El Tigre* sometime. Maybe ride him myself if you'll let me."

"Hah! You couldn't even ride Defiant," she reminded him.

"I might have learned a thing or two about ornery personalities in the past six years."

The way he was staring at her made Louisa think he meant her as well as the horse he had once owned.

By Roslynn Griffith

Pretty Birds of Passage
The Wind Casts No Shadow
Heart of the Jaguar

Available from HarperPaperbacks

Heart of the Jaguar

≫ ROSLYNN GRIFFITH ≪

HarperPaperbacks
A Division of HarperCollinsPublishers

HarperPaperbacks   *A Division of* HarperCollins*Publishers*
10 East 53rd Street, New York, N.Y. 10022

Cover illustration by Diane Sivavec

First printing: December 1994

Printed in the United States of America

HarperPaperbacks, HarperMonogram, and colophon are trademarks of HarperCollins*Publishers*

❖ 10 9 8 7 6 5 4 3 2 1

Heart of the Jaguar

Prologue

Spotsylvania, Pennsylvania—May 1864

The odor of death filled the air.

Captain Beaufort Montgomery sniffed with distaste and steeled himself as he gazed down on a field of ragged, bone-weary men gathered in small groups around half-drowned, smoking fires. Some men stretched tents over their shoulders seeking protection against the rain; others rolled themselves in the canvas and lay close to the logs, trying to sleep. Most merely huddled within themselves, having no shelter at all against the raw, inclement weather.

A pitiable scenario.

Beaufort sighed, fingering the medallion he wore beneath his gray wool coat. He envisioned the comfortable library in his home in New Orleans, the retreat where he'd spent most of his time before being called to war. Aged texts in Spanish awaited him there, along with fragile codices in Aztec hieroglyphics. He'd paid dearly for the materials and made more than one arduous journey into Mexico to obtain them. Enthralled, intrigued, fully enraptured by the past, he'd waded through two languages to write papers about the ancient Mexica, had viewed his servants' knocks on the door as gross interruptions.

The war with the Union had disrupted his studies completely.

Disruption. That was too kind a word.

Staring down at men who'd been forced to descend to the level of animals, Beaufort now understood that his world itself was at stake: that the South was being destroyed. Even if he lived to return to New Orleans, nothing would ever be the same.

He would never be the same.

Once a scholar fascinated by bloody ceremonies that took place in the safety of the past, he'd been forced to kill in reality, to send men to their deaths.

The elegance of ritual sacrifice had lost most of its luster as he'd seen numberless undignified, bloated corpses.

Beaufort shuddered as a cannon boomed somewhere nearby. He could barely remember a time when the stench of gunpowder didn't fill the air, when smoke didn't float and twist on the wind like writhing serpents.

Writhing Aztec serpents, fierce fangs dripping.

He'd dreamed about serpents the night before and saw them now, before shaking his head and determinedly turning away.

He was so tired, so disheartened. Sometimes reality and imagination merged. The medallion he wore was believed by some to be magical, a token that could call up the gods. He fingered it, wondering if he only imagined that the metal gave off heat.

Dawn came. Behind the heavy cloud cover the sun rose, and with it activity renewed. Divisions of Union soldiers swept over a barrier of interwoven limbs and branches.

"Fire!" came a cry from a Confederate officer.

Men in blue uniforms pitched over the hastily built breastworks to land face first in the marsh grass. But others escaped this fate. Union men kept forging through the rain and mist and smoke, downing Confederate soldiers in a bloody hand-to-hand combat.

Hour after hour the warfare continued, until the battlefield was littered with bodies.

From his vantage point on a hill, from whence he sent more of his men to their demise, Captain Beaufort Montgomery watched the carnage helplessly.

The world was ending, just as the priests of the Mexica had predicted. The sun would be swallowed up by darkness . . . unless the gods themselves deigned to intervene.

Below, disheartened young Confederates raised pieces of shelter-tents above them in truce. They wanted to give themselves up and live. Enemy fire slacked off.

"C'mon in, Rebs!" came a shout from behind the Union line.

Twenty or more young soldiers—boys, really—stood with weapons lowered, and for a moment panicked as they got a better look at the slaughter around them.

That moment of hesitation signaled their deaths. Before they could surrender in fact, gunfire renewed and the men in tattered gray dropped to the mud. Most looked dead. A few crawled toward the Union line on their bellies, crying and screaming for mercy.

Beaufort turned away from the sight of cowardice, raised his face to the sky. Surely the gods would take action with the proper sacrifice.

At that moment a ray of sunshine somehow managed to slice its way through the misting gray.

The gods.

They had answered! He inhaled the pungent smell of blood and stopped fighting death, let it seep into his pores . . . let it imbue him with power.

When Beaufort gazed at the battlefield again, he saw it through new eyes. There were serpents writhing among the struggling soldiers. He smiled as he withdrew his sword.

"I *am* death!" he roared, sweeping down the hillside against orders. He had a higher task now.

No matter that many of his men lay still, eyes staring, mouths gaping.

"Beaufort! Where the hell you think you're going?"

Beaufort's eyes glazed over; he barely recognized his cousin Lamar, separated from him by a field of bodies covered in mud and blood-spattered blue or gray.

"I shall honor my warriors!" he shouted, holding his saber high. "And bring back the sun!"

"Beaufort, don't be a damned fool! You're gonna get yourself killed!"

But Beaufort was beyond reasoning. He had nothing to fear. He plunged forward, muttering in Nahuatl, the ancient Mexica language. Though bullets whizzed by, none found him. They couldn't kill him.

He was invincible.

He was a god himself—Quetzalcoatl.

His gaze fastened on a Union officer even younger than he who fought ferociously alongside his men. The sandy-haired lieutenant saved one of his own soldiers from certain death. Then another. He ignored a flesh wound, a bright red slash across his left shoulder, and continued to do battle, his newest target one of Beaufort's own—a boy with straggly black hair and bronzed skin who fought back like the devil himself.

"A brave heart!" Beaufort cried, charging toward the combatants.

He flew at his enemy and, surprising him, shoved his saber through the Union officer's chest. The boy in gray fell back, breathing hard, wounded but alive.

His expression astonished, the lieutenant swayed on unsteady feet, then sank to his knees, and, finally, his side. His breath wheezed harshly through an injured lung. Beaufort tossed aside the weapon that had downed the officer and knelt beside him, ripping open his uniform to bare his already bloody chest.

Pain-filled hazel eyes were fixed on Beaufort's face. "Finish me," the wounded man begged, his rasping voice no more than a whisper. "Make it quick. . . . Please . . ."

Drawing his knife from its sheath, Beaufort felt power surge through his limbs.

The serpents danced. He inhaled fire.

In his mind, the captive lay on a slab of stone rather than on a muddy field. He himself wore a cape and headdress of fine feathers rather than a worn woolen uniform. And his follower—the half-breed boy—stared at him, black eyes wide.

"Die with honor and pride!" he intoned, the knife flashing in a lethal arc.

A gurgle of sound escaped the lieutenant's lips. Then he went still, eyes and mouth open in a silent, endless cry, but not before Beaufort grabbed his prize— the brave if nameless officer's bloody, still-beating heart.

1

Northern New Mexico—October 1886

Louisa Janks flirted with the massive stallion as if he were one of the ranch hands on the de Arguello spread where she lived and worked the horses. The difference was that the stallion would get closer to her than any cowboy.

"You'll do this for me, yes?" she coaxed, running her hands delicately along his neck and back. Beneath the red dust and brambles, his coat was as black as her own waist-length hair, which she'd pulled over one shoulder in a single thick braid. "It's in your own best interests, you know. Better gentled than dead."

She'd moved the stallion before daybreak, before Adolfo's orders could be carried out. Consort to a herd of wild mares, the stallion had stubbornly refused to let his harem be taken and tamed without a fight. He'd already come for them once before and slashed the new pasture fence to ribbons with his mighty hooves. He'd led the mares to freedom. The men had gone after the herd and recaptured all but the stallion, who once more had returned to claim his ladies a few days before.

This time he'd been caught and confined.

Though Louisa had insisted she could gentle him if given enough time, both Adolfo and Chaco had agreed that the stallion was bound to cause too much trouble meanwhile. He wouldn't let anyone get near him, much less break him. He would have to be destroyed.

That was when, her Comanche blood protesting the destruction of such fine horseflesh, Louisa had decided to steal him.

She'd known she was taking her life in her hands in doing so, for the stallion was the wildest, bravest horse she'd ever gotten close to. And it had taken some doing. Nearly an hour to lure him to the fence, his reward food laced with a calming herb. She hated to drug an animal, but if she hadn't, she wouldn't have been able to handle him in such a short time, and she wouldn't have gotten him safely out here to her hideaway in the foothills at the edge of the de Arguello spread.

Now, the drug was wearing off and the stallion was becoming his own surly self. He bared his teeth and nipped at her arm. She moved away fast, then tapped him firmly on the nose, keeping him controlled and on the ground when he might have reared.

"I bite back," she warned, narrowing her thick-lashed brown eyes. "Besides, you don't really want to hurt me. You're just scared, aren't you?" Her voice and hands were gentle and soothing as she moved her head close enough to his so that her warm breath fanned his flaring nostrils, a Comanche trick to make the stallion hers. "Let's walk around and use up some of that energy of yours."

Normally she wouldn't tack a wild horse until it was calm in her presence, but she'd haltered the stallion to get him off the ranch. Now, using a short lead, she walked him around what was actually a tiny box canyon. The natural corral, cut into striated, multi-colored stone dotted with sagebrush and stunted juniper, had walls that went practically straight up. Its fairly narrow opening had been easy to secure with a bunch of split logs, some removable for access. She seldom used the place since it was so far from the main buildings, but now she was glad she'd had some of the boys set it up for her last year, as an alternative to using the ranch corrals when some of the horses came down sick.

Her big bay gelding, Defiant, stood tied on the other side of the crude fence, watching, rolling his eyes so she could see the whites. He neighed and snorted indignantly when they approached. The stallion answered, legs dancing.

Louisa kept walking, stroking the horse's neck. "Calm down," she said soothingly. "Defiant's a little jealous, is all. He doesn't like me paying so much attention to such a fine-looking fellow as yourself."

She circled him several more times until he quit spooking. Then, stopping him at the far end of the corral from Defiant, she used an *ayate*, a coarse fiber bag, to groom the stallion. His flesh rippled at the new sensation. He gave her what she considered to be a filthy look, which made her grin, but he didn't move away.

When he whinnied, Louisa laughed. "I knew you'd like it. Feels good, huh?"

The stallion tossed his head and looked straight forward as if refusing out of spite to agree. Still grinning happily—for this was a better beginning than she'd hoped for given his unpredictable temperament—Louisa continued working, placing more weight on his back for short periods of time, careful to stay out of kicking range of his long legs as she circled him to work on his other side.

Not that he even tried to stomp her.

She had a way with horses. Some called it magic—the ability no doubt inherited from her father, Red Knife, who'd died before she was born. Even though her mother had tried to make a lady of her and sent her to an assortment of finishing schools from which she'd been expelled, Louisa had always known she would be happiest surrounded by her treasured horses. When she finally finished the education Belle Janks had been so anxious for her to have, Louisa had firmly stated her intentions for the future. No drawing rooms and fancy getups for her.

Thank goodness Chaco and Frances Jones had given her the job she'd begged for more than three years ago. Gentling, grooming and feeding horses while wearing a skirt, split or no, was a ridiculous proposition, so she happily adopted men's attire while working. And she'd enjoyed shocking everyone in Santa Fe that time she rode to town wearing men's trousers, too. But, giving in to Ma's histrionics, she'd promised to change into something more ladylike before heading into town thereafter.

Louisa was just finishing up the grooming, which at least removed a layer of dust from the stallion's thick coat, when she heard hoofbeats approaching the canyon.

"Uh-oh, you're on your own until tomorrow morning."

Removing the lead, she gave the stallion a firm, light pat on his rump. He scooted away from her and rolled his eyes. She left him straw, a bucket of feed, and another of water, which she hoped he wouldn't kick over. With a big sigh, she went to face the two undoubtedly angry men who were fast approaching the small canyon.

Chaco Jones, natural son and sole heir of Armando de Arguello, ran his ailing father's *estancia*. Even from a distance, she could see the dour expression that made his rugged face look hard and mean. While she had the utmost respect for her boss, he didn't scare her like he did a lot of people. So what if he was a reformed gunslinger. As for Adolfo, a tough knife-wielding companion of Chaco's who worked as his ranch foreman, Louisa thought of the Mexican as the older brother she'd never had. He'd looked out for her when she'd visited the Blue Sky Palace, her mother's business, for years before going to work for Chaco and Frances.

The coming encounter was certain to be more irritating than alarming.

"Looking for me?" she called as she neared the fenced side of the corral.

"You got a lot of nerve, Louisa Janks," Chaco said as he brought up his buckskin next to Defiant. "You know what they do to horse thieves in this territory."

"You gonna hang me, then?" she asked, grinning.

"Some respect for your employer, *chica.*"

Reining his paint next to Chaco's mount, Adolfo glared at her, and Louisa forced herself to hide any signs of amusement. She wouldn't be smiling much longer if she couldn't talk the men out of destroying the stallion, anyway.

Almost to the fenced area, she heard the thunder of hoofbeats following. Fast.

"Louisa, look out!" Chaco growled.

She flew around to see the stallion heading straight for her. He appeared indignant and determined to run her over. A flutter shifted her innards around, but she didn't move. Didn't run. Her hand slipped to the leather thong around her neck, and she grasped the bear claw woven with beads and feathers, the only reminder of her Comanche ancestry Ma had saved for her. The token had kept her safe for twenty-two years, and she didn't doubt it would do so again.

Even so, she couldn't help the thrill pumping her heart hard and choking off her breath as she faced down more angry horse than she'd ever dealt with before. She felt as if a powerful locomotive were bearing down on her.

"Girl, what the hell's wrong with you? Get over here!"

She ignored Chaco and concentrated her energy on the stallion who was fast closing the gap between them. Her heart climbed into her throat, but she didn't move. She heard Adolfo mutter a prayer for her soul in Spanish.

"You will not hurt me, *El Tigre,*" she said aloud and fairly calmly as the stallion rushed her.

But Louisa felt his heat before he swerved to the left, his big body barely missing hers, his coarse tail whipping her in the face. He'd taken a coup off her, that was all. Just to show her he could.

And just to show him he hadn't intimidated her, Louisa turned her back on the circling stallion and calmly walked toward the two angry men who were about to open the corral.

"Don't you dare," she warned them. "If he gets away, you'll have to help me catch him again!"

The men stopped as if they worked for her rather than the other way around. Both their gazes fixed on a spot over her shoulder and Louisa knew the stallion was making a second pass. She refused to look his way, and, indeed, she heard him turn while he was still some distance from her. She reached the fence and climbed through an opening, only then checking to see what the wild horse was about. He continued to circle, but at a less frantic pace. She couldn't wait to feel that power under her when she finally got to ride him.

"He's showing off. Isn't he the most beautiful thing you've ever seen?"

"*Dios,* you have a stomach of iron," Adolfo muttered.

"But a soft heart. I couldn't let you destroy him."

"That wasn't your decision to make," Chaco reminded her, his spooky gray gaze on her.

He wasn't any better at intimidating her than the stallion was. Louisa stood her ground, arms crossed, staring up at him. "You gonna fire me?"

"I oughta."

"What you oughta do is give me the time to work with him just like you would any of the other horses."

Chaco scowled, hardening his already rough-edged features. "Let me get this straight. You want to be paid to work with a horse that was supposed to be destroyed?"

She nodded.

"Your head is as hard as his."

He hadn't said no, Louisa realized. "And when he's trained, I'll buy him from you."

"Oh, you will, will you?"

"It would only be fair, since he was caught on your spread by your men."

"I'm right glad you're willing to be fair."

"Of course," Louisa went on, knowing she was

pushing her luck, "I'll need some help to bring out a decent supply of straw and feed and water. . . ."

"Can we talk about this on the way home?" Now Chaco sounded downright irritated. "Frankie figured you got into trouble again. If I don't get you back fast so she can see for herself that you're in one piece, she'll have the vapors."

"You're the boss."

Louisa was unable to hide her grin, especially when Adolfo made a rude noise trying to cover a laugh that made his sparse mustache quiver. Frances Jones had never had the vapors in her life, but Louisa wasn't about to argue the point. She'd won, after all. Quickly mounting Defiant, she pulled the horse between the men's.

"*Chica.*" Beneath his fall of dark curls, Adolfo wore a serious expression. "You must stop taking such crazy chances. You may not always be so lucky as to walk away unhurt."

A flush of irritation shot through Louisa. "I always know what I'm doing."

Not in the mood for any lectures, she kept her gaze on the surrounding mountains and foothills while urging Defiant to take the lead. Her life was her own and she would run it any way she saw fit.

She didn't fear being hurt.

She didn't even fear death itself.

"Louisa's downright foolhardy," Belle Janks lamented. The former madam paced the length of the Blue Sky Palace bar that was empty in the middle of the afternoon but for Jack Smith, the silver-haired bartender. "I swear she's trying to get herself killed."

Frances Jones watched from the small table where she sat and nursed a sarsaparilla. Having inherited half of the Blue Sky from her first husband, Nate Gannon, she'd sold her share to Belle upon marrying Chaco. Since a few of her girls had either married or changed professions, Belle had closed The Gentlemen's Club and now relied on the income from the hotel and casino. In town to pick up supplies for her students, Frances had stopped at the Blue Sky to catch up and been distressed to learn Belle had already heard the details of her daughter's latest escapade.

Hoping to reassure her friend, Frances said, "Louisa is merely spirited."

"Hah! When she was a kid, she was spirited." The tops of Belle's breasts quivered above the lace-and-bow-trimmed green bodice that set off her dyed red hair. "Now Louisa's plumb wild. Not the way I feared, of course. Not with men. Damn it all, I didn't mean to make her hate men, Frankie."

"She doesn't."

"Or be afraid of 'em. I only wanted her to have something better'n me. I always hoped she'd meet some nice proper young man who'd marry her and give her a good home and babies. But it don't seem like that's ever gonna happen. Ain't nothing I can do to put sense into the girl's head."

"If you want, I'll try talking to her, try to find out what might be bothering her."

"Would you, Frankie, honey? You've always been able to reach her."

Not always. Frances supposed Louisa had set such store in her because she'd been the young woman's teacher in Boston. Louisa had gotten herself expelled from Miss Llewellyn's School for Girls and Frances fired with her—both unfairly, of course, the whole thing having to do with Louisa's "heathen" ancestry. But that was a long time ago. More than six years. It was equally long since Lieutenant Samuel Strong had been transferred to Fort Sill, Oklahoma.

Louisa had never been forthcoming about him.

As if she could read Frances's mind, Belle asked, "You don't think she's still in love with that Strong fella, do you?"

"Louisa told you she loved him?"

"A mother knows some things. Just 'cause I didn't make no fuss when you and Chaco brought them two back from the desert don't mean I'm stupid." Belle wrung her hands. "I saw him the day he left town."

"You talked to him?"

Belle shook her head. "Just watched. I was glad he was riding outta my little girl's life. I wanted to protect her from the terrible things that happened to me when I was young. . . ." Her voice had a catch in it. "I didn't know he was gonna take part of her with him."

"I'm sure she's over him by now," Frances said, though she wasn't certain of any such thing. She merely wanted to make Belle feel better.

"Maybe you're right."

Frances truly hoped so, for she doubted Lieutenant Samuel Strong even remembered Louisa Janks. If he had cared for the stunning, wild, pure-hearted young woman as Frances believed at the time, surely he would have written, if not returned to Santa Fe years ago. If he'd truly been a man in love, she couldn't imagine anything stopping him.

*   *   *

Fort Bowie, Arizona Territory

"Strong, you've got to stop this nonsense before it's too late." Major Eli Hart's full mustache bristled; his beefy face reddened. "Think before you throw away your career. You're a West Point man, for God's sake."

As was Major Hart.

Sam Strong thought about the horrors he'd seen over the past half a dozen years, the atrocities against the Indians—primarily the Apache—that he'd participated in as an officer in the U.S. Cavalry. Nightmares drove him to give up his commission, nightmares caused by nagging guilt. He sure as hell didn't want to rack up more black marks on his soul. He could hardly live with himself as it was.

"I'll settle on a new career," Sam said tightly.

One that took him far away from the stench of blood and death.

For a moment, his tortured spirit returned to the mountain stronghold where his unit had trapped several dozen Apache, mostly women and children and old men. He could hear the death screams of the innocents as clearly as if the incident had occurred yesterday rather than several years before.

"What would your father say about this?" Major Hart was still trying to talk him out of resigning. "He was so proud of you."

Only because he never knew how low I've sunk, Sam thought.

"My father's dead. I guess he won't have anything to say, now, will he?"

He expected an explosion from the major, but it never came.

Instead, the man shook his graying head. "I guess

I'll have to accept your decision, much as I dislike it." He asked, "But first, can you find it in you to do me a personal favor, one last job for your country? I've received word that there's some madman stirring up trouble on the Mexican border, a fellow named Montgomery who's leaving a pile of bodies in his wake. The army wants to investigate the matter."

"Since when does the army go after murderers?"

"Since the man in question is a former Confederate officer. Seems he's acting like he's some sort of god and is gathering up followers. Could be he's really gathering troups."

Sam understood. Many former Confederates had escaped south of the border and had schemed to invade the country they'd lost. Even after twenty years, such plans were taken seriously.

"If we don't watch out, this Montgomery could start up another war with Mexico," Hart went on. "Major Anderson at Fort Marcy would be the one to fill you in."

Fort Marcy . . . New Mexico Territory . . . Intriguing, though the things he'd fallen in love with about the area, especially the young woman with wild dark eyes and a spirit to match, were sure to be long gone. Besides, how could he face her with this blackness in him? . . .

"We need a special man, a good man, one with plenty of experience," said Hart, referring to the accolades Sam had received for the Apache Wars. The major rose from behind his massive desk. "You'll be doing me a favor with Anderson if you'll go. Will you do this one last thing for me?"

Reluctantly, Sam nodded. "For you." He only hoped he wasn't making a mistake.

"Then good luck to you, son." Hart held out his hand

for a vigorous shake. "Tough world out there, away from the army. Maybe this'll change your mind."

"I doubt it."

Sam returned to his quarters to pack the few belongings he would take. The heliograph equipment he'd bought himself and an extra uniform would be his only reminders of his seven years with the army. He wondered if he could leave his nightmares behind as well. He hoped so, for surely that would leave him free to dream again.

He picked up a Bible, hesitating putting it in his leather satchel. He wasn't worthy of God's love, not anymore. And yet he couldn't leave the present from his mother behind. His long fingers flared over the leather cover, and he allowed the book to fall open where it would.

Caught in the binding was a small feather, dark and tattered with age.

A rush of longing shot through him as he touched the reminder of a certain bear-claw necklace—and the night that he'd obtained the feather from it. Louisa Janks had been the best thing that had happened to him in his twenty-nine years. He could still see her mocking smile as she challenged his stuffy pretentions. She'd loved taunting him, calling him a pretty tin soldier.

Well, he wasn't so pretty anymore, inside or out.

Memories flooded him. He could still feel the silk of Louisa's hair . . . taste the sweetness of her mouth. . . .

He snapped shut the Bible and quickly stuffed it into his satchel.

Louisa Janks was Mrs. Somebody Else now, another man's wife and mother to the unknown man's children. Several, probably. He needed his head checked if he even imagined she remembered more than his name, Sam told himself.

He wasn't going to Santa Fe to see her.

Startled, he realized the wind would have no say. He'd made up his mind. With all the options he had open to him, he would return to the one place he never wanted to forget.

He wouldn't think about the woman.

2

Nuevo Laredo, Mexico

He couldn't think about the past.

Beaufort Montgomery put the last twenty-two years behind him as easily as he did Texas. His raft cut across the waters of the Rio Grande, bringing him once again to the haunting land he knew as his real home.

Mexico.

The Mexica. A dozen or so brown-skinned people gathered at the bank, several pointing—no doubt at the oddity he presented: a lone man, pale-skinned, white-bearded and white-haired, traveling from the east on a raft teeming with snakes.

Surely they'd recognize his divinity. Beaufort had finally received a sign after too much time spent on the other side of the border. This, the portents had told him, was the momentous occasion to return to his homeland. His band of followers were on the opposite bank and would soon follow.

He gazed at the people before him, mainly peasants. But there would be true believers among them.

"Keep warm, my little brothers," he told the serpents as his light craft rushed the bank.

Then he leaned over and with each hand grabbed a rattlesnake behind the head. He held them high and spread his arms in greeting while other reptiles crawled over his feet.

On the bank, the natives huddled, chattering, appearing ready to run. He was ready to take them in hand—to instruct them, lead them and, ultimately, to save them.

"Behold, I am Quetzalcoatl!" he thundered in Spanish, then repeated the phrase in the Mexica's older language, Nahuatl. He propelled himself from the raft even as it touched land.

Not that he much looked like the plumed serpent of the Aztecs. Yet. Even so, a few wide-eyed individuals immediately fell to their knees. More laughed and muttered amongst themselves as their numbers swelled.

How dare they? Didn't they know that Quetzalcoatl had been predicted to return from the far east on a raft of snakes? The ones he held wound their bodies around each of his arms and rattled their tails in annoyance. Others slithered off the raft, no doubt seeking a warm, dry place to sun themselves.

"I am the incarnation on earth of the great god!" he shouted. Just as priests had been in more ancient times. "I can lead you safely through the earthquakes that will destroy the fifth empire of the sun!"

"Fifth empire? What is he talking about?" asked a woman.

"Do not concern yourself with his nonsense," one man said.

Another demanded, "Do you really think we would follow a lunatic?"

Curling his lip, Beaufort sought the man who'd uttered the question. His gaze narrowed. Burned. He was incensed by the smile that quivered below a thick, drooping mustache. "Sacrilege!" he intoned. What did this dirt-streaked native know about gods and what they expected of mere humans?

"If you are Quetzalcoatl or any god, then show us your magic." The man's mocking grin revealed rotting teeth.

Beaufort held out the snakes. "These creatures who travel with me do me no harm."

"Bah! You have removed their venom."

"Then you will not be afraid to take one of them from me and fondle it so." Beaufort demonstrated, rubbing his cheek against the reptile's head even as it flicked its fangs.

The man paled, but others pushed him forward, urging him to respond to the challenge. Beads of sweat that had nothing to do with the blazing sun gathered on his broad forehead and his breath came harshly, lungs pumping in his barrel chest. Trying to hide his fear, he strode forward and snatched the rattler Beaufort had used for the demonstration.

"You see!" the man cried, holding the snake away from him. "Anyone could do this."

Seemingly gaining courage, he turned the rattler's head toward his face and grinned. His mistake. As Beaufort had known it would, the irritated snake struck out, its fangs meeting the man's fleshy neck.

"A-a-ah!"

The man tossed the snake aside. It slithered toward

the dusty town awaiting Beaufort. His burning eyes turned on the doubter, who was sinking to his knees.

Though he still gasped for air, he was as good as dead.

A small gift for the gods, Beaufort thought, dreaming of far greater as he looked into the faces of several new converts.

Northern New Mexico

"I shall die if I do not have one of your smiles," Javier Zamora told Louisa with an exaggerated sigh as he watched her fasten the gate of the pasture where she kept the wild mares. "All I do is think of you."

Finished working with half a dozen of the new horses—and that after spending more than an hour following sunrise further cultivating *El Tigre*—Louisa had just let another mare loose to join the rest of the small herd. The pretty little pinto kicked up her heels as she loped toward her companions, a few of whom greeted her with welcoming nickers.

Oddly enough, the hot-blooded black stallion was coming along faster than his brood, due, no doubt, to the fact that she'd isolated him so completely. He depended on her for everything. Food. Water. Companionship. He couldn't help himself. She'd caught him watching for her arrival by the gate that morning. And though he immediately turned his back on her once she entered his corral, Louisa figured he was merely playing hard to get.

Now, taking her cue from the stallion, she said airily, "And what kind of things do you think about me, Javier?" reflecting only a mild curiosity rather than a passion she couldn't feel.

"Your beauty haunts me day and night," the good-looking young Mexican went on.

Truth be known, she didn't care about Javier romantically, but she really did like him, in addition to the other half-dozen ranch hands who seemed to adore her. They were all honest, hardworking young men with respectful attitudes. Any one of them would be her devoted suitor if only she would indicate her willingness to be courted by him. Sometimes her lack of serious interest in any of them made her feel guilty, but she couldn't help but enjoy the attention. The pretty words. The flirtation. For that was all she allowed herself: a few smiles. A carriage ride into town. Perhaps even a dance. Having her heart broken once had been enough to put her off getting deeply involved in another relationship.

So far, no one man had tempted her to change this attitude, and Louisa sometimes thought she was destined to be alone forever.

Javier's dark eyes looked as sad as those on that old hound Ma had let her keep when she was a kid. "Say you will allow me to escort you to Don Armando's fiesta, please," he begged, referring to the *estancia* owner's eightieth birthday celebration to be held the following weekend.

There would be a dance and tables of food following the *charreada*. Louisa would perform in the exhibition of horsemanship and, if the truth be known, it would be her favorite part of the evening. She could be herself, not have to pretend. . . .

"Say yes, Louisa, and put me out of my misery."

"I'll put you outta your misery, Zamora," Ben Riley threatened as he stomped toward them, "with my trusty Colt here." He slapped his gun for emphasis. Belying his freckle-faced boyish looks, Ben was a bit hotheaded and therefore no one to mess with when aggravated. "Louisa's going to the fiesta with me."

"My heart, you have betrayed me?" Javier mourned.

Looking from the bulldog back to the hound, Louisa forced herself to hide a grin. "Not exactly—"

"Whyn't you get to work before Adolfo comes lookin' for you," Ben told Javier. "Louisa and I got plans to make."

"Ben Riley, don't you be starting trouble," Louisa admonished him, keeping her tone sweet. "You know very well I did not accept your invitation."

A ghost of a smile touched Javier's wide mouth. "Then there is a chance for me, yes?"

"No," Ben insisted.

"Let Louisa decide for herself which of us is the better man."

"You insulting my manhood?"

Javier gave him a contemptuous glare. "You call yourself a man?"

"Why you—"

Before Louisa could stop him, Ben swung out and landed a fist on Javier's jaw, making the Spaniard's head snap back.

"Cut that out right now!" she insisted, but the rivals ignored her.

Javier came back swinging and popped Ben a good one. His nose spurted blood.

"I'm not going to the fiesta with anyone!" she protested, appalled.

Not that it seemed to matter, so intent were the men on besting one another. Both went flying and landed in a tangle on the dusty earth mere inches from where she stood. They'd been growling at each other for weeks over their interest in her, and now they seemed bound and determined to take their frustrations out on each other physically.

Well, let them.

Most of their punches missed their target, but they kept at each other like two rabid dogs.

Louisa stood back and fumed. Why couldn't they get it through their thick skulls that she wasn't some damn prize to be won? Surely they couldn't think she would go to the fiesta with the winner of this brawl. As was her way of keeping things light with the young men who wished to court her, she had promised not only Javier and Ben but several other ranch hands some of her time and a dance at the fiesta. She could hardly make good on her promise if she arrived with an escort. But try to get that notion into their thick heads. She hoped they were both black and blue and sore when they finished. A little physical misery would serve them right.

"What the hell's going on here?" came an angry bark that made Louisa jump.

"Chaco!" Not wanting the two young men to get into trouble with their boss over her, she smiled in his scowling face and said, "Oh, they're just having a friendly disagreement about branding or some such."

"Friendly, my eye," Chaco muttered, already entering the fray, grabbing both men by the backs of their clothing and hauling them to their feet.

Javier was the first to realize what was happening and immediately straightened out, while Ben took one last wild swing that landed smack on the side of Chaco's head. Louisa winced. Now he'd gone and done it.

"You through, Riley?"

Finally seeing through his haze of anger, Ben went slack. "Y-yes, sir." With blood from his injured nose trickling down to his mouth, he looked about ready to choke.

Chaco had that effect on most men.

"And what about you, Zamora?"

"Anything you say, Señor Chaco."

"What I say is . . . get back to work before I bust your heads myself."

Ben whipped off, while Javier moved more slowly, giving Louisa a last, lingering look that assured her of his undying love. "Your eyes reveal your soul to me," he said softly as he passed her, "and the wildness waiting to be savored."

Louisa started, but immediately pushed away thoughts of another man who'd said almost those exact words to her. . . .

Figuring on going while she had the chance, Louisa started for the neat cabin that was her home. A mistake. Chaco's hand, wrapped firmly around her upper arm, stopped her midstride.

"So what was this all really about?"

"Don't make more of it than there is," Louisa begged, fearing for Ben's and Javier's jobs. "They work real hard. You know that. They were just letting off some steam." When Chaco continued to aim that spooky gray gaze at her, she finally admitted, "It's my fault. Something I said. Please, don't blame them."

Letting go of her arm, Chaco shook his head and sighed. "Louisa, what am I gonna do with you?"

She sighed, too. It was going to be all right. She should have known. Chaco had always been more than fair and tolerant.

"There's nothing to do . . . unless you're not satisfied with my work."

"You know I am."

He'd better be. She was the best at gentling wild horses, as opposed to breaking them. Better even than Adolfo, who'd taught her everything he knew long ago.

"Mind if I go now?" she asked. "Thought I'd wash up before supper."

Aiming a look at her that would quell most people, Chaco said, "Don't dawdle. I'm starving."

She took the opportunity to escape to what had been her home for the past three years. Her cabin awaited her opposite the Joneses' adobe hacienda on the other side of the pastures and corrals and outbuildings, situated beneath a couple of old cottonwoods, backed by hills and juniper-dotted rock striated with colors that changed with the position and intensity of the sun. She imagined it might have been a bit cramped when Chaco and Frances had lived there while their house was being built, especially after Phillip, their firstborn, came along, but Louisa felt the snug single room was perfect for her, giving her glorious privacy and enough space to spread out. And she was close enough to her beloved horses if one of them needed her and far enough from her ma so she wouldn't be nagged about her chosen life on a daily basis.

An hour's hard ride north and west of Santa Fe, the de Arguello spread was one of the largest in the mountainous northern half of the territory. Though his health was failing and he was now mostly confined to a chair with wheels because he had such difficulty walking, Don Armando, Chaco's widowed father, still ruled the original *estancia* his family had built, and he did so with an iron fist. The living areas of father and son were nearly fifteen minutes apart.

Entering her cabin, Louisa figured that was because Chaco didn't like to be nagged any more than she did.

She and the former gunfighter had a lot in common, starting with their ancestry, her father being Comanche and her mother Anglo, his father Hispanic and his mother a half-breed—half sister to Geronimo.

Little more than a month before, Louisa had mourned with Chaco when Geronimo and his small band, the last of the free-roaming Chiricahua Apache, had been rounded up by the army and sent off to some god-forsaken swamp in Florida, far away from their mountain desert homeland that encompassed northern Mexico as well as the southern parts of both the Arizona and New Mexico territories. She'd had more than a taste of separation from home herself, having been shipped off to finishing schools in various parts of the country. Every time, she'd grieved and vowed she would never leave home again.

As she poured water into a washbasin, Louisa allowed her mind to wander away from New Mexico Territory, all the way to Fort Sill, Oklahoma, where Sam had been transferred from Santa Fe's Fort Marcy—and all because he'd come along to protect her when she'd run away. She wondered if he was still there. If he was happy. If he ever thought of her.

Damn Javier for making her remember!

It had been that last comment of his, the one about her eyes revealing the wildness of her soul. . . .

"You're a wildcat," Sam told her, his blue-green gaze intense as he took her in his arms. "I knew it the first time I looked into your eyes and saw your soul."

"You can't see a person's soul!" Louisa protested, laughing. He might be a pretty tin soldier, but Sam made her heart pound wildly as no other young man

had done. But then, he wasn't like the others. "Only God can see that."

"You're wrong, or how could I know you so well?"

He accepted her for who she was, didn't care if she was a half-breed, didn't care that she'd been accused of murdering Eusebio and Enrique Velarde, that half the town thought she was a diablera, *an evil witch. Louisa had liked him from the first—stuffy and by-the-book as he could be, he was a superior horseman, able to ride almost as well as she, which in her mind made up for a lot.*

Now, with the way he was standing by her, accompanying her on her flight from a lynch mob that would hang her for horrible murders she hadn't committed, she was certain she loved him.

So when he kissed her, Louisa didn't quickly end the embrace and move away, as she was wont to do with other young men who'd tried the same. Blood rushed through her and her head went all woozy and she held on to Sam Strong like she might fall if she didn't.

That she liked his tongue invading her mouth surprised her. When Eusebio had tried as much, she'd bitten him.

But she allowed Sam to do what he would, and with enthusiasm she sought to learn the things her mother had sheltered her from and that she herself had thought to reject. Because she knew too much about what went on between men and women— though she was only sixteen, Louisa had no illusions about The Gentlemen's Club Ma ran—she'd vowed never to let any man get too close unless she someday chose to marry.

Now here she was, moaning, begging for more when Sam touched her breast. . . .

Louisa's breasts tightened as if Sam had stroked them a moment ago rather than six years before. She hated this torture, hated remembering. She tried not to. Sometimes it was harder than she could bear. She was twenty-two and only one man in her life had ever engaged her heart, her body and her soul.

One man who had abandoned her.

The transfer might not have been Sam's idea, but he hadn't fought it. He hadn't fought for her. He'd left town and hadn't looked back. Hadn't even written.

She could almost see him now, sitting straight and proud in the saddle, blue uniform spotless, golden curls bright in the sun, handsome face almost too perfect. She remembered the very first time he'd kissed her, after she'd won a horse race she forced him into.

Unexpectedly, her eyes pooled and twin tears rolled down her cheeks. Angrily, she swiped them away. She wouldn't cry for Sam. Never again.

Never for any man.

She had her horses. And they would be enough.

Leading a roan packhorse loaded with the remainder of his supplies and bedroll in addition to his leather satchel, overloaded saddlebags and a case containing the heliograph equipment, Sam rode into Santa Fe looking for changes and finding few.

The central plaza was exactly as he remembered—an open square of paths and trees with a gazebo, a modest covered pavilion used as a bandstand. The Palace of the Governors, a sprawling seventeenth-century adobe fronted by a great portal—an overhang spanning the length of the building—sat on one side of the plaza and still housed the offices of the U.S. Territorial government. The army occupied buildings north of the Palace, while a virtually empty Fort Marcy lay beyond on a hill overlooking Santa Fe.

He headed down a familiar narrow side street laid out in a *trazo* pattern. The structures built around small courtyards, or *placitas,* had common walls that formed a continuous facade on either side. A pretty young mestizo woman carrying a basket glanced up at him. Her eyes widened slightly and she averted her face as she rushed away. Though used to an occasional like reaction from the fairer sex, Sam tightened his jaw and got down to business.

First thing after looking up Major Anderson in his office, Sam asked, "Why me?"

"This Montgomery fellow is stirring up Mexicans on the border." The middle-aged Anderson hunched forward, hands fisted on his desk. "And running off cattle on the U.S. side. Specializes in quick ambushes, seems to disappear like smoke. You've dealt with that sort of thing a lot . . . with the Injuns."

Smoke? It sounded like Montgomery was building up a reputation bordering on the supernatural, like Geronimo. Sam pointed out, "You could say the same for any number of men stationed in this part of the country."

"Not all have your experience. The Rangers are having a hell of a time tracking this man in West Texas. The army wants one of its own to look out for U.S. interests, unofficial-like, that is. I was told you could work pretty much alone and fast. And that I could trust you to make whatever decisions were necessary."

Like killing if he had to? That was the implication. "I thought this was only an investigation."

"I suppose that's what Hart thinks. He sent me a telegram, saying this was your swan song." He added,

"Since this situation is a bit more than you expected, there'll be some extra pay in it for your retirement . . . if you survive."

"It's that dangerous?"

"Could be deadly, I won't lie. That's why I want you to look up a man named Monte Ryerson in West Texas. He fought for the Confederacy, saw Montgomery's work firsthand. Even testified to get the man committed."

Major Anderson went over the details of Montgomery's crimes, obtained in a special hearing after the war was over. Some of the specifics threatened to make Sam sick. Someone had to stop the bastard. Might as well be him. Nothing more to lose but his life.

"Take a couple of days," Anderson said. "Get yourself a room at one of the hotels. We'll pick up the bill. I understand a man needs a little rest and recreation before starting on an assignment like this one. Just don't take too long and keep me informed. We need to go over a list of my men, so I can recommend the ones I think will do for your purposes."

"Thought I was going alone."

"You'll need some support, won't you?"

"I'll think about it."

Sam saluted and left the major's office, taking his horses to a nearby stable the moment he struck sunlight.

Impulse drew him to the Blue Sky Palace. Though his men had frequented the place when he'd been stationed at Fort Marcy, he'd never stepped foot in the hotel-casino himself. But he remembered well enough who owned it. Or who had.

Not everything could be the same as it had been six years before. He certainly wasn't.

Saddlebags over one shoulder, satchel in one hand, heliograph case in the other, Sam crossed through the *placita* and negotiated the hotel entrance with difficulty. Exhausted from his week's ride without enough sleep, he was happy to secure a place to unload his belongings and a bed on which to rest his weary bones.

Before trying to sleep, however, he dug out the half-empty bottle he'd carefully wrapped in a shirt and stored at the top of a saddlebag. He caught a glimpse of himself in the round mirror set over the chest and for a moment was startled. Anyone who knew him would have thought a stranger occupied his room. The harsh-featured, scarred soldier with greasy, stringy hair surely couldn't be him.

Chasing away the chill that shot through him with a long slug of whiskey, Sam excused his poor grooming to the harshness of travel. He just needed sleep and a bath was all. Nothing he could do about the scar, but the rest was a matter of catching up, which he would do in short order.

The potent liquor fast warmed his gut and relaxed him. He hesitated before taking another slug.

He wasn't a drunk, Sam told himself.

He merely needed enough whiskey to help him sleep. To help him forget for a while.

But the bottle was empty before he shut down . . . and when he awoke, the first thing that niggled at him was the craving for another drink.

He needed something to chase the cobwebs from his muzzy mind. Right away. And his stomach was so empty it echoed. The room was dark until he lit a lantern. He must have slept for hours. Music and the muffled sound of voices reached up to him through the floorboards and enticed him to hurry. He could use some lively company.

Pouring water from the pitcher on the chest into its matching bowl, he splashed his face, ran damp hands back through his hair. That would do for now. He ought to shave, change into clean clothes, and he would do so. Later. When he had the energy.

When his insides stopped shaking so bad he had to clench his jaw to keep his teeth from rattling.

He traded his room for the common areas downstairs, which were nearly full. On a stage situated so customers both from the bar area and the casino could see, three young women in brilliantly colored satin costumes with matching plumed feathers in their hair danced to a tune plucked from an old piano.

The first drink helped. The second steadied him enough to order dinner, *posole*—a pork stew made with hominy—and fresh tortillas.

"Haven't seen you around," the bartender, who'd introduced himself as Jack Smith, commented.

"First time here. To the Blue Sky, that is. Been in Santa Fe before."

"And you came back," the silver-haired man said as the music ended and the dancers left the stage, "so you must like it. Meaning to stay?"

Sam shrugged. "Depends."

"On what?"

Noting a dark-haired dancer in red satin coming their way, imagining for a moment that hers was the face that haunted his better dreams, Sam honestly said, "A woman."

"We don't run The Gentlemen's Club anymore," Smith told him. "But you can go over to Burro Alley and find whatever you're looking for."

Sam hoped to God he wouldn't find Louisa there. He hadn't found her here, either. Meeting the pretty young woman's hazel eyes, he experienced both a pang of regret and profound relief. He didn't know what the hell he was doing here in Santa Fe. Whether she was married or not, he wouldn't want Louisa to see him looking like he did now anyway.

The dancer was looking, and she didn't seem at all put off as the woman carrying the basket had earlier.

"Can I buy you a drink?"

"Sure, caballero." After flicking her eyes over the scar that was a souvenir of the Apache wars, she turned to Smith. "Tequila, straight."

When her drink came, Sam refilled his glass and made a toast. "To the prettiest woman I've seen in a long time." He touched his glass to hers.

She gave him a sloe-eyed look and a sultry half smile. "Here's to your seeing more of me."

Downing the whiskey, Sam wondered how literally she meant that. Before he could ask, the bartender set his food before him. Sam dug into the fragrant, spicy stew. Only when the bowl was half-empty did he attempt to make conversation with the dark-haired woman who waited patiently.

"You were doing some mighty fancy dancing up there."

"I didn't think you were watching."

"I saw enough."

Enough to know she was entertaining. And pretty. And eager to get to know him better—though why, he couldn't say. He'd seen that look in dozens of eyes before, though not in a long time. Not for nearly a year. The Gentlemen's Club might have been shut down, but he didn't have to hear it from her lips to know she was available.

"What's your name?" he asked, pouring another

drink and indicating that the bartender should do the
same for her.

"Nina Chavez. And yours?"

"Captain Sam Strong."

"Strong, huh?" His name barely more than a murmur,
she moved closer and slid a hand up his forearm. "I like
strong men," she said with a throaty laugh.

"What else do you like?"

Her smile was wanton. "Take me someplace private
and I'll show you."

Unable to remember the last time he'd had a woman,
Sam wasted no time. He downed his drink, threw money
on the bar and took the bottle.

"Hey, what about your food?" the bartender asked,
indicating the half-eaten stew.

Sam pointed to the money. "That'll cover it. Right
now, I'm hungry for other things."

Activities that would make him forget some unpleasant deeds that haunted him . . . and take his mind off
the pleasant ones, too.

As he started to leave the bar, he realized another
woman was watching him as well. A middle-aged red-
head who wore a low-cut emerald green dress and a
puzzled expression. She was wandering around the
casino, talking to customers, but her gaze kept stray-
ing back to the bar . . . and to him. Or maybe it was
the dancer.

"Who's that woman?" he asked.

"Belle Janks, the owner."

For a moment, Sam's heart raced. Louisa's mother?
He hesitated, his gaze flicking around the place. No
Louisa.

"She keeps looking this way. Maybe she doesn't
approve of the company you keep."

"Now, that's none of her business," Nina said, pressing closer to his side and urging him toward the door to the hotel lobby. "Belle's a little strange, anyhow. She's been okay with me, but I've seen her lose her temper. . . . Well, some say she's not quite right in the head."

Drinking straight from the bottle, Sam forced Belle Janks from his mind and concentrated on Nina, who'd prompted thoughts of Belle's daughter.

If he didn't look too hard, he might be able to imagine he was making love to Louisa.

3

"Make love to me, Sam," *she pleaded, her fingers caressing his neck and shoulders with a strength akin to that of desperation. Her heat burned through the material separating them.*

"Are you certain?"

"No," she whispered, following that with, "As sure as I've ever been about anything."

Her confusion touched him. He looked down into her sun-kissed face, into the dark eyes all warm when they met his. Wild eyes. Like her. She was the most spirited, most exciting female he'd ever met. And she wanted him.

Too staid for his own good, he hesitated. But only for a moment, for how could he resist the vibrant woman who begged to be taken.

On the floor of a cave that felt as cozy as any bed he'd ever known, he helped her remove her clothing,

*one garment at a time, lovingly kissing each new area
of flesh revealed to him. Yes, lovingly. For love rather
than mere lust drove him. She made him forget caution
and convention, especially when she touched him.
Boldly. Intimately. Drawing from him a response that
went beyond the physical . . .*

. . . the hand stroking him drew forth a tentative
response that roused him from sleep.

Sam opened his eyes and in confusion focused on a
naked dark-haired beauty who was not Louisa. Dawn
filtered through the curtained windows, revealing her
perched above him, doing her best to seduce him with
her hands, her breasts, her lips . . . but rather than
growing harder with her increased efforts, he went
flaccid.

Nina frowned down at him. "For a moment, I thought
I could renew your interest in me."

Renew. Did that mean they'd engaged in the act?
He couldn't remember much more than her name and
the way they'd met, and his body certainly wasn't
telling. Trying to force the issue, he was rewarded
with a pounding head. He groaned and squinched his
eyes against the pain.

"You shouldn't drink so much," she said, rolling over
to her side of the bed and pulling the sheet up to cover
her breasts. "Liquor makes a man . . . less of a man."

"Had a lot on my mind." And now he was hungover
again. Muzzy and disoriented.

"Obviously not me."

"My fault, not yours. I apologize. Any whiskey left?"

"You drank nearly the whole bottle last night before
we even got to your room," Nina told him. "I poured the
rest out the window for your own good. You probably
feel like hell this morning, huh?"

His head sure did, not to mention his mouth, which tasted foul. "I deserve to."

He'd been drinking too much off and on for months, but this time he'd gone beyond reason. He didn't even remember climbing into bed with Nina.

The dance-hall girl sighed and asked, "So what's her name?"

"Who says it's a woman?"

"Experience."

Maybe being in Santa Fe and thinking about Louisa had been the catalyst, if not the cause. He admitted, "My hell goes a lot deeper than a lost love."

"We all got problems, caballero." Her hazel eyes connected with the scar and she frowned. "Guess you're right—yours do go deeper than most. You want to talk about it?"

He never talked about it. Not with anyone. "Why would you want to hear? What's in it for you?"

"Cynical, too." Though she didn't sound offended. "Maybe I like you."

"You don't know me."

"What if I'm just plain lonely?"

Which sounded like the truth, though he couldn't picture a woman who looked like her being alone for long. "You could have had any man in that bar last night. Why me?"

"'Cause you looked like you needed company more than most."

Pity? Sam hated the thought. Had he sunk so low that a woman would sleep with him because she felt sorry for him?

"I don't know whether to thank you or kick you out of my room," he grumbled.

"At least that's honest." Nina rose, allowing the sheet

to slip from her voluptuous body. "But don't exert your-self. I can take a hint."

Sam grabbed her wrist and avoided staring at the breasts that practically swung in his face. "Let me apologize again. I don't usually act like an ass."

She smiled. "Don't worry about it."

"You won't get in any trouble because of me, will you?"

"With Belle?" She shrugged, freed herself and pulled on a lacy, beribboned camisole. "Considering how she used to make her living, the one thing Belle Janks doesn't do is judge anyone else's morals."

An odd sort of exhilaration sweeping through him at the prospect of getting information about the young woman he'd once loved, Sam played dumb. "I'm sure I remember her being at the Blue Sky last time I was in Santa Fe. That was, oh, about six years ago."

"Belle was only half owner back then," Nina volunteered, now slipping into her red satin costume. "And she ran The Gentlemen's Club as well."

Sam propped himself up on his elbows. "Right, and she had a daughter. . . . What was her name?"

Nina's brows shot up. "Louisa?"

Too casually, he said, "I suppose she helps her mother run the place."

"You suppose wrong."

Her denial hit him hard. "Married, huh?"

Nina laughed. "Committed to one man? Not hardly. That girl's a hellion and a heartbreaker." Her expression knowing, she laced up the front of her bodice. "She acts like she's some virgin goddess."

Not hardly . . . at least not the virgin reference . . . though he believed the hellion and heartbreaker parts.

Not that Sam was about to share any of that information with Nina.

"You seem awfully interested in Louisa Janks. I'm thinking I should be jealous."

Now that Nina was fully dressed and Sam's head had cleared a tad, he was more appreciative of her assets. "You don't need to be jealous of any woman."

As it seemed he had no need to be jealous of any man.

"I wanna horse, too!" three-year-old Amelia Jones insisted from her perch on the split rail fence. A protective Frances stood behind her.

"You're too little," pint-sized Phillip stated with the authority of an older brother. "You gotta wait till you're five like me." To Louisa, he whispered, "She's jealous."

She bit back a smile lest the boy feel she was laughing at him. "You could tell her you'll let her ride Spangles"—an Appaloosa gelding Louisa had picked out for him because of the horse's gentle nature.

"But he's s'posed to be mine!" Phillip insisted.

More than his golden brown hair and hazel eyes reminded Louisa of Frances. He also had a dose of her friend's stubbornness . . . as well as her good heart. Pretty little Amelia not only looked like Chaco with her black hair and gray eyes, there were times when she could be nearly as tough.

Meeting Frances's gaze over the heads of her children, Louisa whispered to Phillip, "Spangles still will be all yours even if you are nice and make your little sister happy."

"Oh, bother!" He kicked a booted toe into the loose earth and raised a cloud of dust. Then he tromped over to Amelia. "Promise not to cry, an' I'll let you ride Spangles next week."

"Now!" Amelia insisted, her eyes already filled with tears.

Phillip made a frustrated little-boy sound. "Tomorrow, then. Spangles is my horse and I get to ride him today for as long as I want!" But when his sister's lower lip quivered, he caved in. "Well, maybe later."

Amelia's smile was bright enough to light up the sky. And it came so quickly . . . as if she'd purposely been playing on her brother's feelings. Louisa wondered if Phillip realized it, too, when he gave his sister a suspicious look. Nevertheless, he allowed her victory graciously.

He returned to Louisa, who had been teaching both children to ride since before they could walk. "Can I try my horse now?"

"I'll hold the reins while you mount."

Phillip hated having her give him a boost—"like a baby" he said—so she'd had a couple of the hands drag an old chunk of tree trunk into one corner of the corral. While Spangles wasn't particularly big at fifteen hands, he was huge for a five-year-old. The boy climbed first on top of the log, then onto the gelding's back. Taking the reins, grinning, he placed his feet in the stirrups that had been specially altered to fit him.

"Look at me, Mama!"

"You are absolutely perfect for each other!" Frances called.

Phillip did make a perfect little cowpoke with his chaps and hat, Louisa thought with amusement. "Walk Spangles around the corral a couple of times to get a feel for him."

Louisa never took her eyes off the boy as she joined his mother. Not that she had to worry. Both children were naturals around horses and not at all scared when something unexpected happened. As a matter of fact, she thought Amelia enjoyed the pranks some horses tried to play on them.

"Phillip is so excited," Frances said. "He hasn't talked about anything for weeks but getting his own horse for his birthday. I hope he takes his responsibilities seriously."

Phillip would be expected to groom and feed Spangles, chores he had only done on occasion previously.

"I'm sure he will. He's a fine boy."

A quick pang tore through Louisa, especially when she noted how Amelia leaned back into Frances and pressed her little forehead into her mother's cheek. A very pregnant Luz was coming to join them with Raúl, her oldest, half clinging to her hand, trying to make her race faster than her condition allowed. Adolfo and his wife were expecting their fourth child.

"We came to watch," an out-of-breath Luz said.

Though the day was mild and her dark brown hair was plaited and pinned up off her long neck, perspiration dotted the Mexican woman's golden skin. She was getting very close to her delivery day but refused to modify her activities if she could help it.

"Good job!" Louisa called out to Phillip. "Walk Spangles across the corral and then circle in the other direction."

Raúl, only a few months younger than the other boy, scrambled up the rail fence and sat near Amelia. "I can ride better than that!" he bragged.

"Can not!" Amelia protested.

"Your brother rides like an Anglo."

"Does not!" The little girl indignantly defended her brother. "He rides almost as good as Papa!"

Raúl snorted and Amelia reached over to punch his arm.

"Hey!"

"Amelia!" Frances protested. "You are not to hit anyone. How many times have I told you that?"

Louisa smothered a laugh when the little girl gave her mother a stubborn look and refused to answer.

"You hurt Raúl and he'll be afraid to play with you anymore," Luz warned.

The indignant expression on her son's face was comical. Before he could protest, Amelia said, "Sorry, Raúl."

He gave her a grudging, "Yeah, sure."

"Will you play with me now?" she asked, her smile winsome.

"Thought you wanted to watch Phillip."

"Uh-uh. Boring."

Raúl was already climbing down. "We can play poker like Louisa taught me and Phillip."

"Yay!" Amelia began squirming in her mother's arms.

Frances gave Louisa a look. "Poker, huh?" She set her daughter on the ground. "Luz, would you mind looking after them? I want to stay until Phillip finishes."

"Only if Raúl promises to teach me, too. He already beat his papa," Luz said proudly, waddling off after the two children.

Louisa could feel Frances staring at her. She called to Phillip, "Jog him!"

"Now you're spending your free time teaching the children card games?"

Louisa was an expert at playing—and cheating—having learned from the best. The late Nate Gannon had been Ma's first business partner and Frances's first husband. "Only for fun."

"I'm not criticizing. It's just that you work so hard already, I would think you'd want your free time for yourself."

"I don't mind. They're great company. I like spending time with them when I can, just like you enjoy teaching every kid on the spread." After marrying Chaco and selling off her half of the Blue Sky to Belle, Frances had started a school for all the children of the *estancia* workers. "Kind of makes up for not having any of my own."

Other than when she got to play "aunt" to Frances's and Luz's children, Louisa's arms remained achingly empty, and it seemed that situation wasn't about to change any time soon.

Probably never, she thought morosely.

"You could have children if you wanted them."

Louisa remembered the one time when she'd thought she might be pregnant—had hoped she was, if only for a few days. Thank God she'd been dead wrong. Better not to have a constant reminder of Sam around to torture her . . . or to bring a child into this world without a father. She'd seen that happen to some of Ma's girls over the years, and the outcome had been pretty sad.

"I'm not about to have children without being married," she finally told Frances.

"I wasn't suggesting you should. I merely thought . . . Well, isn't there any young man who interests you, makes your heart beat a little faster?"

So that was it. "You've been talking to Ma again, haven't you?" The two women had always conspired to give her "good" advice. While Louisa knew they both loved her, she was an adult now and capable of living her own life. Trying to discourage Frances from continuing with the discussion, she yelled to Phillip once more. "Cross the corral again and keep jogging!"

But a little interruption didn't distract Frances from her purpose. "So what about it, Louisa? Half the hands on the ranch are crazy about you."

"They're boys."

"They're older than you are."

"In years maybe."

Frances tried a new tactic. "I didn't have the chance to marry when I was your age. Being a spinster can be lonely."

"Spinster? I'm not exactly innocent," Louisa reminded her. After all, it had been Frances and Chaco who'd found her and Sam in that damn cave.

"You're not real experienced, either," Frances said. "And that's not what I meant. I'm talking about sharing your life with someone."

"I have plenty of friends."

"It's not the same."

"I can't miss what I don't know," Louisa hedged, now getting irritated.

She couldn't help the ache that grew inside her every time she caught Frances and Chaco in an intimate moment. Even Adolfo and Luz, two temperamental people who were always arguing, made no secret of their love for each other. But she certainly didn't have to discuss her most private feelings with anyone, not even the woman who was her best friend.

"Don't you ever want to get married?" Frances asked, direct at last.

"Only to the right man."

One who was strong and pure-hearted. One who flaunted convention and authority to do the right thing. One who could make her feel like she couldn't live without him.

Sam Strong had been all those things.

Before she could embarrass herself by telling Frances as much, Adolfo rode up, a frown on his face. "You two see Luz?"

"She's with the children," Frances told him. "Why?"

"I'm riding into Santa Fe. I figure I better tell her I won't be home for supper or she'll skin me alive when I get back."

Louisa called out to Phillip, "You can lope Spangles now, but take it nice and easy." Then she turned to Adolfo. "What's going on? You look mean enough to eat a rattler—live."

"Ah, *chica,* your would-be lovers are acting like fools. I didn't see either Javier or Ben all morning. Then over at the bunkhouse, I heard Javier rode into Santa Fe to see his sister last night and Ben followed a while later. He'd been drinking. Said he would fix Javier once and for all. No one's seen either of them since."

If anything happened to one of those hotheads because of their infatuation with her, Louisa would never forgive herself. "You don't think—"

"I don't think nothing," Adolfo interrupted. "Like I said, I'm riding into Santa Fe to find them. And God help them, because when I do, I'll boot them both all the way back here."

"I'll help you." Some righteous anger was better than fear, Louisa decided, praying neither Ben nor Javier would hurt the other seriously. "Frances—"

"Go. I'll supervise Phillip. He can ride a while longer, then take care of Spangles just like you taught him."

Louisa was already over the fence and running

toward the small paddock where Defiant grazed. "Five minutes, Adolfo," she called over her shoulder. "Go kiss your wife good-bye."

Kisses. Love. Bah! Nothing but trouble. Louisa couldn't believe she'd actually wasted precious moments mooning over Sam after all these years. She was not only ready to knock some sense into Javier and Ben . . . she knew what she would do to Samuel Strong if she ever saw him again!

El Catorce, Mexico

"So what do you think we should do with this man who searches for us?" Tezco Baca asked his sister as they headed the column of thieves on horseback toward home. "Could this gringo named Montgomery be one of Diaz's men trying to trap us?"

Beneath the man's hat she wore as part of the trappings disguising her sex, Xosi's exotic features drew into a frown. "Not likely. This man is a gringo but not a European. Diaz has no use for the *Americanos* or for the old ways."

This madman was claiming to be the incarnation of the Aztec god Quetzalcoatl, come to see that the world didn't end, that the sun wouldn't die. Tezco spat. As if he or his sister were stupid enough to believe such nonsense.

They had received this information about Montgomery and his quest from a lookout who intercepted them as they approached El Catorce after raiding one of the trains that transported silver from the mines to *Casa de Moneda,* the mint. Their man had been very worried, therefore worrying Tezco as well.

"We should have him brought to us on his knees and force the truth from him."

"I do not think that would be the wisest course. We surprise him. Perhaps we will find the truth to be profitable."

Always interested in profits, Tezco grunted his approval. He was a man of action, with no individual he'd ever met his physical equal, but Xosi was more cunning a creature than he. They made an invincible team and had done so since their parents were killed nearly twenty years before, leaving them orphaned. Tezco had been thirteen and Xosi nine.

He gave the dozen men who rode with them instructions to bring the loot to an abandoned church at the edge of town. Then he and Xosi headed for home.

"We will transform ourselves into law-abiding citizens and then pay the madman a visit," he said.

Tezco changed into a *faena* suit, the simplest of *charro* costumes worn by ranch hands for daily chores. Brown suede chaps the color of his eyes and a shade lighter than his dark, shoulder-length hair were fastened at the sides of his legs with bone buttons; a matching short jacket topped his white shirt.

When he entered the *sala,* Xosi was already waiting for him, straightening her mahogany hair while gazing into the small silver-mounted mirror she always wore on a chain about her slim neck. Her lush body was barely contained by her skimpy, lace-edged white *camisa* and calf-length red skirt. She was also smoking a *cigarillo,* a habit Tezco abhorred in women.

She said, "Let us see what this gringo wants of us."

Montgomery wasn't difficult to find. Muffled screams quickened their steps. A small crowd of strangers waited outside a whitewashed building as a local whipped out of a doorway, cradling his arm, his face contorted in misery as he raced down the dusty street.

Glad he'd secreted a knife at his ankle, as Xosi had on her thigh, Tezco fearlessly led the way inside. Sitting near the fireplace and dressed in peasant garb was a man who appeared to be in his early fifties, despite the shock of white hair that fell to his shoulders. He held the handle of a long tool—a branding iron—whose end was enveloped in flames.

"What the hell is this?" Tezco demanded, realizing that the peasant had been branded.

Eyes that burned through the dimness turned on him. The white-haired, white-bearded man rose. "Ah, finally. Tezcatlipoca. Welcome."

The way Montgomery pronounced the name of the ancient god for whom his parents had named him gave Tezco pause. The man exuded power. Despite himself, he felt a small chill.

"Yes, you are Tezco Baca," Montgomery went on with a smile, "the descendent of Moctezuma. Your blood is sacred. You are true Mexica, a man meant to rule. I was given the title Beaufort Montgomery at birth, but I am now the true incarnation of Quetzalcoatl, returned so that we may save our people from the world's destruction."

Our people. Tezco was tempted to sneer at the gringo, though there was a myth about Quetzalcoatl being a bearded white man. "The Mexica—the Aztecs have been dead for centuries."

The white head shook. "Only the outward evidence of the empire was destroyed. The people lived to create new generations—"

Xosi came forward. "And what is it you hope to accomplish?"

"You are Xosi?" Montgomery's mad eyes seemed to burn through her. He stirred the embers with the branding iron, then spotted the plaited silver chain disappearing into Xosi's *camisa*. "May I see your mirror?"

"You wish to see my necklace?" Glancing quickly at Tezco, as if to ask how the gringo had known about her treasure, she pulled the engraved, mounted piece out for Montgomery to see. It was a small replica of a hand mirror.

"Lovely. So that you may admire your own beauty." Again, Montgomery smiled. "And so that your brother may see what is hidden, as well."

Tezco frowned.

"'Smoking Mirror,'" mused Montgomery. "That is what Tezcatlipoca means. A fierce warrior with a handsome face and the ability to appear and disappear at will. Not to mention that he steals any woman he wishes and foretells the future."

A down-to-earth man, Tezco was becoming more and more uncomfortable.

Again Xosi asked, "What do you mean to accomplish?"

"Together, you and I and Tezco will regain our thrones."

"Thrones?" Tezco snorted. "Have you not heard of Diaz the dictator?"

"I care nothing for Diaz, nor should you. We, the gods—and the earthquakes—will defeat him. But with the proper planning, with the proper sacrifices, enough land will survive and the *Mexica* will prosper. They will worship those who have saved them."

Xosi leaned forward. "The people will prosper how?"

"By receiving rains in abundance, by growing maize

the likes of which no one has seen, by finding the lost *Tesorería de Tula.*"

Tezco was familiar with the legend of the underground treasury somewhere in the vicinity of Tula, an ancient Toltec and Aztec city near the capital that was now no more than a ruin.

Caring less about rains or maize, he remarked, "No one is even certain this treasury exists."

"I am." From the folds of his shirt, Montgomery pulled a ragged piece of hide embossed with crude lines and picture-figures. "I have a map. Though the treasury was buried in a hidden pyramid many miles north of Tula, in the vastness of forbidding mountains. That is why the Spanish never found it."

Xosi's eyes glittered in the firelight. "So, one only needs to follow that map to find Aztec gold?"

Which she and Tezco would happily take from the madman as soon as they got the chance.

"If you can read the ancient hieroglyphics and utter the correct incantation that will open the massive stone door at the entrance," Montgomery said.

Bah! Hieroglyphics and incantations. Tezco's frown became a scowl. What did this crazy fool know anyway?

"But gold is only the symbol of power," the madman intoned, reaching into his shirt a second time to remove a shiny medallion. "We cannot fully live on earth again until all five pieces of the wheel are recovered."

"Wheel?"

Tezco thought the medallion resembled the Aztec calendar found in the last century. His experienced eye told him this piece was brass, though it glimmered oddly in the firelight. No, *glowed.* Again, he felt a chill. He told himself he must be witnessing an illusion.

"This is a miniature worn by the lost pyramid's last priest-guardian," Montgomery explained, sticking the spooky medallion back in his shirt. He reached down for a large leather bag from which he withdrew a chunk of gold decorated with the face of a sun god, Tonatiuh. "But this is real. The center. We must find the other four pieces."

Gold. Xosi locked gazes with Tezco. He could see both fear and guile in her hazel eyes. They connected. Montgomery was mad, that was for certain. But he did possess real gold. And perhaps he also held the key to a treasure the likes of which brother and sister could hardly imagine.

"We are interested."

"And you will be amply rewarded when we find *Tesorería de Tula.*" The man added, "Of course, you must first show your loyalty by your willingness to suffer."

Xosi's gaze was drawn to the iron Montgomery had used to brand the peasants. "I will be first."

Once again, Tezco thought his little sister had to be the bravest woman in the world.

4

Santa Fe, New Mexico

"*Never met a braver* woman in all my born days," a sandy-haired drunk told Jack Smith.

On the way to being drunk as a skunk himself, Sam relaxed at a table near the bar of the Blue Sky Palace, privy to every word of the cowpoke's lament to the bartender. The man's boyish visage was marred by a nose that was swollen and bruised from what must have been a recent fight. A dozen other men occupied tables or space at the bar, and it seemed that every one of them was listening, too.

"Sounds like you've fallen in a big way," Smith said. "Have you told the little lady?"

"She wouldn't wanna hear it. Won't even step out with me," the young man complained. "Asked to escort her to the fiesta for Don Armando's birthday next weekend, but she'd rather go alone so's she can dance with a bunch of no-accounts."

"Who do you call a no-account?"

Sam shifted in his seat to better see the man who'd entered the conversation uninvited. A tad unsteady on his feet, a good-looking Mexican glowered at the Anglo. His jaw was bruised and he had one hell of a shiner.

"Can't a man even drink in peace?" the sandy-haired one griped.

A grizzled cowpoke at a nearby table guffawed, and his buddy joined him.

The Mexican gave the men a warning look before refocusing his attention on his challenger. "That is what I intend—to have a peaceful drink. Right here." He signaled the bartender. "Tequila."

"Whyn't you find someplace else to swill your rotgut? Someplace where I'm not?"

The Mexican got all huffy and Sam figured he was ready to swing at the Anglo. A couple of other dark-skinned men—Mexicans or Indians or mestizos—seemed to take the insult personally as well. One of them shoved his chair back so hard it tipped and fell over.

"Hey, sit down!" the grizzled Anglo yelled from the next table.

His drinking companion pulled the standing man back down before he could respond.

Tightly, the young Mexican at the bar said, "You cannot tell me where I can or cannot buy my tequila, and you cannot tell me to stay away from Louisa."

Louisa?

"I can tell you anything I want. And I'll be happy to tell you where to go."

Sam thought quickly. Louisa. How many women in

Santa Fe were named Louisa? Surely they couldn't be talking about his Louisa.

Before he could ask, Smith boomed, "Boys, cool down!" He slammed an empty glass onto the bar. "This is a friendly establishment!" Nervously eyeing the room—for everyone present now seemed wired by the argument, including Sam—he opened a bottle of tequila and filled the glass. "Let's keep it that way."

The sandy-haired man cleared his throat and released the wad into the brass spittoon near his foot. "Hard to do with his kind around."

The Mexican uttered an oath in Spanish that Sam didn't quite catch, then lunged at his antagonist.

Then the whole room erupted, with chairs and tables flying and glass breaking.

"Fistfight!" Smith yelled, looking toward the casino as if for reinforcements.

Sam rose unsteadily and pushed himself away from his table toward the two original combatants. He had to know who this Louisa was. But first he had to make the room stop spinning. He halted about a yard away from where they grappled with one another and tried to get his bearings.

"Hey, boys," Sam growled, having difficulty focusing on them. The whole room seemed to be twirling around him. "Who is this Louisa?"

He caught the sandy-haired one's attention for a moment until the Mexican got both hands around his throat. Now Sam was getting annoyed, because they weren't paying a bit of attention to him.

"You weren't meaning Louisa Janks, were you?" he demanded, stumbling closer.

The Mexican glanced back, giving him a heated glare. "Louisa Janks, yes. What is she to you?"

A commotion from the casino caught Sam's attention. Several men were rushing the bar. No, the one accompanying the short, bowlegged Mexican was a woman.

Must be seeing things.

Sam squeezed his eyes shut as if to clear his vision, but when he opened them again, he still saw the soft curves in a man's pants, shirt and vest. Dark hair plaited in a single braid hung over one shoulder. He remembered the feel of that hair, the thick, silky texture of it, just as he remembered the bear-claw necklace decorated with feathers and semiprecious stones that swung between her breasts.

"Javier! Ben!" she was yelling. "What in tarnation do you think you're doing? Stop right now!"

Looking startled, they did. And as they stood apart, the Mexican named Javier turned to Sam. "I asked, what is Louisa Janks to you?"

Remembering the night in the cave, Sam knew exactly what she was to him . . . if only in his own mind. He tried to glower at the man, but since his face muscles weren't cooperating, he suspected his expression merely appeared foolish.

"Damn it, she's *my* woman!"

The last words out of his mouth before a fist closed it for him.

She was seeing a ghost. That was the conclusion Louisa drew when Javier's fist crashed into the stranger's face. For he had to be a stranger, a ghost that was a weird-looking version of the only man she'd ever loved.

"Sam?" she whispered.

It couldn't be.

But she ran to the side of the downed man anyway.

Javier tried to stop her. "Louisa—"

"Not now!" she cried, pushing him away to get a better view.

Staring down at the barely conscious man—at the grubby blue wool shirt, the stringy lackluster hair, the beard-stubbled face, the wicked-looking scar that ran from the corner of his left eye down to his jaw—Louisa tried telling herself she was wrong. This couldn't be the pretty tin soldier she'd fallen in love with.

He couldn't be.

"Sam Strong?" she choked out, hoping against hope she was wrong.

When he turned his gaze on her, she was certain of it. While his eyes might be blue-green, she saw none of the confidence she remembered, none of the pride, only a haunted expression that chilled her. Then, as he rose to his elbows, the eyes focused on her, and for a brief moment cleared.

And she knew.

"Louisa? My God, is that really you?"

Following pure instinct in answer, Louisa drew her arm back and punched Samuel Strong in the jaw as hard as she could. His head whipped back and hit the floor with a thud for the second time in as many minutes.

This time he was out cold for sure.

"*Chica,* what has this man done to you?" Adolfo demanded as he pulled her to her feet.

The bear claw swinging against her chest as she straightened, Louisa said, "He took away my life."

*   *   *

West Texas

Monte Ryerson played with the leather thong holding the bear claw he wore for courage and protection as he reread the account of the dead men.

Sitting here in his own ranch house more than a thousand miles and twenty years from the battlefield, ghosts of the past haunted him.

MUTILATIONS MOUNT read the headline in the *San Antonio Star*. The article focused on the grisly remains of a body found near the border of Mexico, the ninth or tenth body in the past few months discovered with the heart ripped out. The first had been in the French Quarter of New Orleans. Then there were four along a trail between that city and San Antonio. Now there seemed to be a bizarre murder turning up every other week, one of them even occurring in New Mexico Territory, which was only miles from the Ryerson ranch.

Monte couldn't help remembering the battlefield in Spotsylvania, twenty-two years before.

He visualized the horror as if it had happened yesterday. The Union officer would have killed him if Captain Beaufort Montgomery hadn't intervened. Only fifteen at the time, Monte had first been grateful to have his life spared, then horrified when the captain cut out the man's heart . . . while he was still alive.

The captain's cousin Lamar had led the madman away, saying he would take good care of Beaufort, who was then taken to an asylum in New Orleans. Monte never spoke to anyone of the atrocity he'd seen that day, except at a Union hearing right after the war.

Now Montgomery had escaped and was running amok cutting people's hearts out. Because Monte could identify Montgomery, who was more or less in the area, the army wanted him to help one of their officers stop the man before he started another war, his soldiers mainly Mexican peasants and Indians.

What could Monte do but agree? It seemed destiny decreed that he would once more come face-to-face with the madman who had saved his life.

El Catorce, Mexico

"Your destiny rests on the pleasure of the gods," Beaufort told Tezco and Xosi in his quarters, while his growing following gathered in the plaza. "I am Quetzalcoatl, and I will save you from destruction. Our journey starts tomorrow."

"Where are we going?" Xosi asked, her hazel eyes enticing.

Beaufort steeled himself against her beauty, a difficult charge considering he'd gone more than two decades without a woman.

"Most of the force will journey with me west to the mountains, to the site of the hidden pyramid," he said, focusing his attention on her brother. "We will pick up more converts along the way and our troops will swell."

"You said most," said Tezco.

"Some of the others, including your group, will form search parties for the missing parts of the wheel. You shall bring back the topmost section, which resides in an ancient site amidst the ruins of a pueblo appropriately named Aztec in New Mexico Territory."

"If you go west and we head north, how shall we find you?" Tezco asked.

"I have drawn out a map." Beaufort handed over a

piece of paper. "Including the path that you should take to the ruins." He pointed to an *X*. "Your piece of the wheel lies here."

An expression Beaufort couldn't read flickered over the younger man's sharp features. "This had better not be a fool's journey."

"If you want proof, look into your mirror. Believe in Tezcatlipoca, the god of the north." He was fully aware that Tezco Baca still hadn't accepted his true destiny. As an additional enticement, however, he pulled forth an ancient, ornate dagger that he'd collected long ago. The blade was obsidian, the handle a snarling jaguar formed of jade and gold. "There will be far more of this in the *tesorería*."

Beaufort could tell Tezco was impressed as the younger man examined the treasure. Once Tezcatlipoca made his presence felt, such trinkets would not be necessary.

"The ceremonies will start as soon as all search parties return. You shall take your place as leader of the sacred order of Jaguar Knights, with those warriors you deem brave as your minions. For their initiations, of course, you must personally take at least four worthwhile captives on your journey."

Tezco frowned. "Captives?"

"We need slaves, true?" Xosi said, circling Beaufort too closely for his own comfort. "Better strangers dig for this treasury."

"Not slaves," Beaufort corrected, forcing his mind away from her natural sensuality and onto the plan. "Sacrifices. In creating the world, the gods gave their hearts and their blood to the sun. Similar sacrifices must be made to appease them. We will especially need our strength to do battle with the forces of the night, so that we will see another sunrise once the earthquakes begin."

He wouldn't detail the nature of these sacrifices just yet. Even the initiated might squirm at the idea of ripping a beating heart from the chest of a worthy opponent. The thought of dividing the body for ritualistic consumption might be enough to drive them away altogether. No, this information could wait, Beaufort decided.

"How does one judge whether or not a captive is worthwhile?" Tezco asked.

"Why, you must choose the ones with the bravest hearts." An irony indeed.

His gaze encountered Xosi's surging breasts. Too bad he had to remain celibate at all costs. Giving in to his baser nature had banished Quetzalcoatl from Mexico centuries ago. He couldn't allow it to happen again, no matter how much he was tempted.

He sent Tezco and Xosi on their way, then called in a young couple who had been recently married. Settling himself in his comfortable chair in front of the fire, he told them what he wanted them to do for him.

Maybe he had to remain celibate himself.

That didn't mean he couldn't watch.

Northern New Mexico

For the first time in six years, Louisa cursed herself for having remained celibate since her one night with Sam. If she'd shared her body and feelings with other men, she wouldn't be consumed with thoughts of him now.

Luckily she had the horses to keep her busy. Working with them would help her forget the emotions that had raged through her the day before. Thank God Sam Strong hadn't come to by the time she'd left the Blue Sky Palace or she would have had to face him in truth.

Still, as she worked with the mare that was coming along the fastest—not only was she able to ride the pretty paint, she was already taking the mare through the various gaits—Louisa couldn't help wondering what Sam was doing in Santa Fe and how fast he'd be gone this time. Maybe he'd already left. He'd been so drunk, he surely wouldn't remember seeing her. Not that he cared anyway.

If he had, he would never have said what he did. . . .

Naked and a little shy, Louisa relaxed into Sam's side, more content than she ever had been in her sixteen years. She'd finally learned what making love with a man was all about. And while it had been scary, it had also been wonderful, and, most of all, inevitable. For Lieutenant Samuel Strong was her heart. And amazingly, Sam loved her, too. He'd told her so. Several times.

Sighing, she snuggled closer to his manly warmth, and though he wrapped his arm around her more fully, he seemed oddly stiff, as if something were troubling him.

"Why didn't you tell me?" he finally asked.

"I did tell you I love you." Hoping to loosen him up, she poked him in the side, but he didn't react.

"I meant that you were a . . . that this was your . . ."

"My what?"

"First time," he growled softly. "That you were a virgin."

She stiffened. "Of course it was my first time." How could he think otherwise?

Realizing exactly how, Louisa grew sick inside. No

doubt Sam had heard talk about her and knew Ma was the madam of The Gentlemen's Club. He must think . . .

"If I had known—"

"What? You wouldn't have touched me?" Refusing to look at him, Louisa pulled herself free and scrambled for the protection of her clothing. "You thought I was a harlot!" she cried, fumbling with her undergarments. Then why had he lied? Why had he told her he loved her?

His visage darkened. "I never said that!"

"You didn't have to." She was crushed, fighting tears. "You assumed you weren't my first lover. Then what does that make me?"

"A beautiful, vibrant nineteen-year-old woman with normal desires."

Reminded that she'd lied about her age, Louisa grew even more defensive. "Sam Strong, you're—you're a stupid man." As if she would satisfy her desires with just anyone! Desires she hadn't known she had before meeting him. "I wish to God I'd never met you!"

"Louisa, be reasonable . . . "

But she hadn't been reasonable. She'd been brokenhearted, and a brokenhearted sixteen-year-old didn't know how to be reasonable. She'd hurriedly dressed and spent the rest of the night huddled against the cold wall crying to herself, hoping against hope that Sam would comfort her, reassure her that he truly did love her.

Instead, Sam Strong had stayed as far away from her as possible.

And then in the morning, they'd been rescued by Frances and Chaco. Shortly after, Sam had been transferred to Fort Sill and left Santa Fe.

Until now.

As if reliving that night in the cave conjured him, Sam appeared before her, seemingly out of nowhere. He stood near the gate, staring at her. She hadn't even heard him ride up.

For a moment, she caught her breath as her gaze traced every nuance of the face that she had once loved. The face that had changed so greatly. It wasn't the scar that made the difference; Indians considered scars badges of bravery, and she guessed the Comanche in her did, too. Besides, it didn't take away from his looks. He was still incredibly handsome, but in a flawed, world-weary way that had more to do with his eyes than the scar. A healed knife wound? He was only twenty-nine, but he looked far older. His eyes held that haunted look, as if they had seen terrible things he didn't want to live with.

Or couldn't.

Not a trace of the pretty tin soldier remained.

She tried to ignore him and her own unacceptable reaction to his presence, continuing to work the mare as if he weren't even there.

Obviously unwilling to be ignored, Sam called, "You're still the finest horsewoman I've ever seen."

Her answer was stiff. "Then you haven't seen anything."

Putting a mostly tamed mare through her paces was nothing compared to what she would be doing at the *charreada* the following Saturday.

"I'd rather watch you than any other woman any day of the week."

"Hah!"

Her concentration shattered, Louisa grew sloppy. Sensing her inattention, the mare broke gait and tore around the corral as if she'd stumbled into a hornet's nest. Damn it all! This never happened to her. Cursing Sam for probably the millionth time, Louisa kept her seat and her head, letting the mare run off some steam before showing her who was boss.

"Easy now."

Louisa used her legs more than the reins to control her mount. Out on the range, a cowboy often needed both hands to rope a steer, so the horses were taught to obey leg signals. Not that this mare had them down pat yet, but she was learning almost as fast as *El Tigre.*

As Louisa regained control, they passed Sam, who said, "See what I mean?" An admiring grin was on his lips and his eyes fairly glowed.

Louisa frowned and chose to end the session early, lest Sam do something to unnerve her for real and therefore ruin her still-fragile rapport with the animal. She dismounted and led the mare to the gate.

Sam got there first.

Heart pounding ridiculously, she stared at him through the split rails. Stared into those beautiful blue-green eyes. Then she pushed by him after he undid the gate for her.

She didn't say a word, merely went about her business as though he didn't exist. But he did exist. He silently dogged her steps while she removed the mare's tack and cooled her down, then groomed her and sent her back into her pasture. Louisa had planned on working with another horse but gave up the idea as useless. Resigned, she locked the pasture gate and turned to her unexpected visitor. No matter her inclination, she couldn't ignore him forever.

So, hands anchored on her hips, she faced him down. "What exactly do you want here?"

"To see if you were real."

"I can show you," she said, holding out a fist threateningly.

He grinned and moved close enough so she could smell the liquor on his breath. Had he had to fortify himself to find the courage to face her—or did he always start his mornings with a drink now?

Louisa backed up, saying, "You smell worse than a sweaty horse. And whiskey doesn't help solve anyone's problems."

"Sometimes it does."

"Are you a drunk? Is that why you look like . . . this?"

She'd made fun of the old Sam, but right now, staring at the seedy man before her—stringy hair slicked back beneath a grimy Stetson, shirt that had seen better days—she wished that pretty tin soldier would make a magical appearance. This Sam was dissipated, falling apart. Seeing him looking like he did was enough to break her heart all over again.

"Sometimes a man has to drink to forget—"

"What? You surely don't mean me." Louisa laughed and turned her back on him.

He grabbed her arm and spun her around. "Life can be hard on a man!"

She tried to wrench her arm free. She was strong for a woman because of her work, but Sam was still stronger. She stood facing him whether she would or no, fuming, trying to hang on to her dignity.

"You're not the only one who's had tough times, Samuel Strong!" she shouted.

"You have no idea of what I've seen and done to survive the last six years."

"I didn't exactly have an easy time of it myself."

Being looked down upon by just about everyone and tortured by her classmates because she was a breed. Seeing men hanged for rustling when she was a small girl. Having half the town think she was the one who'd murdered a former suitor and his brother. Running away because she'd feared the townspeople would form a vigilante committee and hang her.

That's where Sam had come in. Didn't he remember? Had the drink erased everything she'd told him . . . everything they'd shared? Or had he done that himself, and gladly?

He looked guilty now, surprising her. Perhaps he did remember. The haunted look was back in his eyes.

Good.

This time, she freed her arm easily, though she could feel the imprint of his fingers on her flesh. Damnation! She could practically feel his hands running down her body intimately, as they had in truth six years before. She hadn't forgotten Sam or the feelings he'd stirred up in her. To her dismay, she suspected she never would.

Taking the chance of embarrassing herself good, Louisa said, "I don't understand it—how you could have gone off and left without giving me a second thought."

"I did think about you, Louisa."

"Hah!"

"Ask your friend Frances."

"What about Frances?"

"She came to see me when I was in the lockup. I couldn't do anything about the transfer, but I told her to let me know if there were any consequences."

Consequences? So he had considered that she might be pregnant. Unwilling to soften toward him so easily, she demanded, "What's that supposed to mean?"

"I—I would have found a way to come back so I could do the right thing and marry you."

Louisa stared at him, at that moment hating Sam

Strong more than she ever had during the past six long, lonely years. He could have said a dozen other things and somewhere mentioned the word *love*. But he hadn't. Truth was he would have married her out of a sense of duty, not because of any special feelings for her. Long ago, she'd realized he'd lied about loving her, so no news there. Still, she couldn't help the hurt that welled up inside her so strong she could choke on it.

"I wouldn't have wanted you," she lied.

"Yes, you would have," he said, more sure of himself than made her comfortable. "You wanted me then." He stared deep into her eyes, making her flush. "You want me now."

"How dare you!"

Furious, Louisa swung out, but this time he was ready for her. He caught her wrist.

His features softening, he said, "You still love me, don't you?" with a sense of wonder.

Despising the way her heart was pounding in assent, she yelled, "I hate you!"

"Do you?"

Before she knew what he was about, Sam jerked her arm so she went flying against his chest. Louisa tried to fight him, but it was a battle she wasn't destined to win—not against the determination she read in his expression. Though she told herself he wasn't even the man she'd fallen in love with, it didn't seem to matter.

For the first time in six years she felt really and truly alive, far more so than she did when gentling a wild horse.

And when his mouth crushed down on hers, she knew a longing so fierce it frightened her. She fought him even as she kissed his whiskey-flavored mouth back, for it seemed that she could do nothing less. Her struggle weakened as her passion grew. Not merely her physical lust—the tightening of her breasts, the heat burning between her thighs—but the hunger in her heart.

So caught up was she in the feelings only Sam could stir in her, Louisa didn't realize they weren't alone until Chaco's voice broke through her haze of passion.

"What the hell's going on here?"

Like two children caught doing something they shouldn't, Louisa and Sam simultaneously let go of each other and stepped back.

Chaco's spooky gray gaze bore right through Sam Strong. "You. I heard you were back in town."

Sam's gaze was level. "You don't sound pleased." He didn't sound like he cared.

"Should I be?"

When Chaco turned to Louisa, her unease grew and she looked away.

"I pay you to work with the horses, not with soldiers. You want to play, do it on your time, not mine."

Shocked that Chaco should say something so crude to her, Louisa glared at him. She wanted to be angry, but the concern in his expression wouldn't let her take that anger out on a man who was not only her boss, but her good friend.

She turned to Sam. "You'd better leave."

"That's what you want?"

"Yes. I have my job to consider."

Sam looked from her to Chaco without deference. "Right."

Moving to his chestnut, he loosened the reins from the split rail and mounted. Louisa had forgotten how well he sat a horse, how magnificent he looked, as if he were part of the beast he rode. The reason he'd tugged at her heartstrings in the first place. At least that one thing about him hadn't changed.

The chestnut crowded her, but she stood her ground, even when Sam's leg brushed her arm.

"I'll be back."

Louisa couldn't help the way her heart sang at the promise.

5

True to his promise, Sam planned on returning to the ranch to seek out Louisa, but not until he knocked off the whiskey and cleaned himself up. Her calling him a drunk and her disgust at his appearance had gotten to him but good. She made him feel like less of a man.

Sam didn't think he could shine in any woman's eyes, but he did his best to be presentable in his army dress blues. Thank God he'd brought them, despite his continuing determination to leave the army once this assignment was over.

It was the day of the fiesta celebrating Don Armando de Arguello's eightieth birthday. To Sam, it seemed the perfect occasion to present himself to Louisa Janks. *Charreadas* were generally an open invitation for anyone to attend, so he wouldn't be the only stranger. He wouldn't be alone with Louisa either, but at least he could set foot on the de Arguello spread without the threat of being bounced on his posterior, as Chaco had seemed inclined to do. Sam figured he would get lost in the crowd, and even if Louisa's self-proclaimed protector spotted him, Chaco wouldn't dare ruin his own father's celebration as long as he didn't start trouble.

Not that he was afraid of Chaco Jones, or any man. Or death, for that matter.

After tying up his chestnut with what seemed to be hundreds of other horses, he made for the crowd around the nearby *lienzo,* a frying pan–shaped corral made of whitewashed adobe that sat a good distance from the main house and outbuildings. One end of the large circular ring had a small grandstand, where a white-haired man in a wheelchair sat. Don Armando. Opposite, the ring opened into an alleyway a dozen yards wide and several dozen yards long. Spectators were already gathering along the walls, picking out favored spots from which they would watch the *char-reada* that would begin the evening's festivities.

"Sam Strong?"

Hearing the woman's voice, Sam stalled in his tracks and whipped around to face Frances Gannon. No, Frances Jones now. He tipped his hat respectfully.

"Ma'am."

Her hazel eyes wide, she murmured, "You're not exactly what I remembered. . . ."

Nor was she. Marriage to Chaco apparently agreed with her; it added an attractive sensuality to her features, along with soft color to her pale complexion and gold to her light brown hair. Dressed in a split skirt and fancy shirt and fancier hand-tooled boots, the former Boston schoolteacher had turned into a fine-looking Western woman, even if she was frowning at him.

". . . and not exactly what I was warned to expect," she finished.

"Who did the warning?"

"My husband."

Sam grunted. "I don't seem to be in favor with the man."

"Nor with me. Not if you've come to hurt Louisa again. Have you?"

"That's not my intention."

"What are your intentions, Lieutenant—"

"Captain Strong," he corrected her, before admitting, "Truthfully, I'm not sure what I intend to do. All I do know is that I never forgot Louisa. I stayed in the army for one last assignment knowing I'd have to return to Santa Fe to get the details. I hoped I'd get a chance to see her again."

She took his measure. "You break her heart a second time, Sam Strong, you won't have to worry about my husband. You'll have me to deal with. You understand?"

Taken aback by her ferocity, Sam said, "Perfectly."

"Now then, perhaps you'd better find a place for yourself. The *charreada* is about to begin."

Sam looked around. "Have you seen Louisa?"

"She won't be watching. She'll be performing."

He should have known.

So when the riders came out in costume and circled the arena to the music of a small marching band, he looked to the group of six young women riding side-saddle at the head of the parade. Wearing plain white blouses, red skirts and colorful striped *rebozos,* they waved to the crowd. No Louisa. His forehead pulled into a frown.

"So where the hell is she?"

Then Sam spotted her on a small sorrel mare with

one white foot and a star on its forehead. No skirts for Louisa. She wore a fancy *charro* outfit: tight black suede pants adorned with ostentatious silver buttons up the sides, short gray suede jacket, black felt hat and black leather saddle embroidered with silver, silk and gold thread.

Sam could understand her wearing pants while working with the ranch's horses during the day, but why should she be dressed like a man for the fiesta?

Then it hit him. She wasn't planning to do some pretty patterns, riding back and forth swiftly, weaving in and out—a magnificent ballet performed at breakneck speed—as was the custom for the young women. Louisa would be showing off her skills with the men.

Indeed, the first event was the *cala de caballos,* during which riders exhibited their control over their mounts. Last in the lineup of six, Louisa was magnificent as she urged the sorrel into a breakneck gallop down the handle of the *lienzo.* Just as it appeared that she would crash into the grandstand where Don Armando held court, with Chaco, Frances and two small children at his sides, Louisa brought her horse to a halt in three stages of braking action. The sorrel seemed to crouch on her haunches, sliding forward, then crouching, then sliding.

Finally, the sorrel stood erect and quiet until Louisa gave her some secret signal, for Sam discerned no movement of the left hand holding the reins or of her feet. With back legs fixed to one spot in the sand, the mare danced to her left, then to her right, then made a complete circle. Done with the capers, Louisa again discreetly signaled her mount to pace backward, neither she nor the mare ever glancing behind them.

When they reached the starting line, Sam whistled and clapped as hard as any of the other spectators.

Then, during succeeding *suertes* in which mares were roped by their hind or front feet, bulls were ridden or grabbed by the tail, dancers or lariat twirlers performed, he looked for Louisa in the crowd. No luck. She was obviously staying close to the other competitors.

And when the *paseo de la muerte,* or death pass, was announced, he realized why. Louisa was the first to appear before the crowd, a looped rope in one hand, galloping her horse at full speed, racing twice around the ring. Then she settled next to the release gate behind which a wild mare waited.

The gate was opened, the barebacked mare forced out of the chute, three mounted riders prompting it to move faster around the ring. Waiting but a moment, Louisa, too, galloped her mount at full speed, positioning herself neck-and-neck with the riderless mare, then grabbed a handful of mane and, hesitating only a second, leapt onto her back.

Only then did Sam sweat. The wild mare bucked and reared and pawed the air, doing everything she could to rid herself of the unaccustomed weight on her back.

Fascinated despite his sudden fear for Louisa, Sam wondered where she had learned to ride this well. She was half-Comanche. The reminder brought with it uneasy memories of other Indians—and the reason he'd been so torn apart about looking up Louisa in the first place. If she knew . . .

Louisa seemed to be glued on the wild mare as she neared the spot where Sam stood. Then she caught sight of him. Her eyes widened and her mouth went slack. The surprise was nearly enough to unseat her. The mare's next buck did.

Louisa slipped to the side, only her quickness in wrapping her legs around the animal's middle saving her from what could have been a deadly fall.

Sam's heart leapt to his throat. "Louisa, for God's sake, hold on!" he yelled, starting to clamber over the fence to save her.

Two men grabbed hold of his arms and pulled him back, and before he could free himself of their insistent grip, Louisa was righting herself.

The crowd cheered.

And Sam dragged a deep breath into pain-filled lungs.

As the wild mare calmed, her bucks becoming half-hearted, Louisa threw a small loop over the animal's head, tightened it, then deftly wound two half hitches around her nose. Exhausted, the mare settled down and her rider was able to take them along the arena's walls to near-deafening applause and whistles.

Sam felt his racing heart begin to steady.

"Look how steady she is after almost falling to her death," Tezco said, admiring the woman in man's clothing.

"Almost as good a rider as I am." Xosi sounded miffed. "I wouldn't have lost my seat in the first place."

The woman *charro* was competition for Xosi and she knew it. Perhaps he would find her later, at the *fandango*. . . .

"When will we set out for the ruins?" Xosi asked.

"Morning's soon enough. We should be well-rested."

We being his band, for he had handpicked his own men to stay with them. That was safest for all. *El catorce.* The fourteen—they'd learned to watch each other's backs.

Her "What about the captives?" surprised him, for he'd managed to forget the odious command.

"I will not help Montgomery sacrifice anyone." Tezco remembered the madness burning in the man's eyes. "We're thieves, not murderers."

"But we must pretend to cooperate," Xosi said.

Tezco knew she was correct. He didn't want to alert the madman to their plans. "We will bring back the necessary number of captives, then. But we will find a way to keep them from Montgomery until we have the treasure, then set them free."

In the meantime, they would pick up some extra money and have themselves some fun.

"Thieves are loose among us!" Luz said indignantly.

Frances, Chaco and Don Armando had gathered near the outdoor dance floor between several large cottonwoods. Having just finished a veritable feast of spicy New Mexican dishes, they all had been relaxed until Luz sprang the news on them.

"You are certain of this?" Don Armando asked.

Though Chaco's elderly parent was dependent on a wheelchair to assist his failing body, Frances knew his mind was as clear as on the day she'd met him.

Hands on hips—at least Frances thought that's where the very pregnant woman settled them—Luz reminded them all, "I was raised in a village of thieves. I know my own kind. I stopped a man from lifting Sarah Gordon's purse and told him to get off the property or feel the blade of my knife between his ribs."

"And he took you seriously?" Frances stared at Luz's stomach.

The Mexican woman's expression grew stormy. "Bearing a child doesn't make me a weakling."

"No, of course not." Frances hadn't meant to question her friend's hot-tempered ferocity—or her ability to wield the knife she always concealed beneath her skirts.

"He very politely agreed to go without a fuss. But thieves rarely work alone."

"Then we'll have to keep an eye out," Chaco said. "Have you told Adolfo?"

Luz nodded. "And he's spreading the word among the men."

"That's about all we can do, then," Frances said. "So many strangers."

The hardworking people of the territory didn't have much to look forward to in the way of recreation, so they took open invitations to fiestas seriously. Normally that didn't present a problem.

"There's my husband now," Luz said as the music started up. She left the others to join him.

"I refuse to allow my birthday celebration to be ruined," Don Armando announced against the sounds of trumpets and guitars playing a Spanish piece. His shock of white hair practically bristled. "A man is eighty only once. Where are my grandchildren?"

"With Marta." The daughter of their housekeeper often took charge of both Frances's and Luz's children.

"Then I shall find them and tell them more stories of *Nuevo Mexico* before it became a territory of the United States." He waved to the servant who waited nearby.

As the doting grandfather was wheeled off through

the crowd, Chaco put an arm around Frances's waist. "Hey, pretty lady, what say you and I have a dance before anyone else comes up with a problem for us to solve?"

Frances gladly swung into her husband's arms. After six years, she still thrilled to his touch. She was very much a woman in love.

A woman in love.

Craning her neck to see through the couples surrounding them, she asked Chaco, "Have you seen Louisa?"

"I want to dance with you, not her."

"Sam Strong is here."

Chaco's arm tightened across her back. "He give you any trouble?"

"No, of course not. It's just that . . ." Frances felt a frisson of fear slide down her spine as Chaco's eyes went all spooky on her. "What?"

"Don't rightly know. I've had this feeling that something was real wrong all afternoon, and Louisa kept coming to mind."

Heart pounding, she calmly asked, "Why didn't you say something?"

One quarter Apache himself, Chaco had the makings of a *di-yin,* or medicine man. His intuitions weren't of the everyday variety. He often had full-blown visions that were enough to scare the dickens out of her. She'd seen some come true in the past.

"Didn't want to upset you, Frankie," Chaco said, softly kissing her forehead. "It was only a bad feeling, and pretty vague. When Louisa almost fell off the mare, I figured that was it. And maybe it was."

Frances didn't for a moment believe it. She continued to move her feet to the music, but she had trouble concentrating. Chaco had spooked her good and her own intuition was telling her Louisa wasn't safe yet.

Could Sam Strong mean Louisa harm?

"You dance like an angel," Javier was saying as he swung Louisa around the hard-packed sand dance floor.

"'Cause I have a wonderful partner."

The pretty words spilled from her lips without difficulty. Javier was a good dancer and good for her spirits. So why was she searching the crowd for Sam? And what did he want with her anyway?

Her gaze met that of a lean, handsome, proud-looking man wearing a *faena* suit. His dark hair hung loose to his shoulders, and he seemed to be awfully interested in her. Javier whipped her out of the stranger's line of sight and into the midst of the dancers.

Both men and women had dug out their finest outfits for the fiesta. Some of the Anglo ranch hands wore fancy Stetsons and white buckskin vests. And she'd seen more than a watch chain or two—some were fine braids, made from their sweethearts' hair. The Spaniards stuck to their flat-crowned hats and short jackets and *calzoneras,* fitted trousers whose bottoms flared out when unbuttoned. Most of the women wore dresses adorned with bows and lace ruffles or collars, and many had matching lace shawls and carried fans.

Louisa had given into convention only enough to replace the *charro* pants with a silver-decorated suede skirt that was calf-length, short enough to show off her new hand-tooled boots. Giving into pride, however, she'd freed her hair so the heavy tresses that were her best feature hung loose almost to her waist, and she'd worn a pair of silver-and-stone earrings whose dangly tips brushed her shoulders.

As the music ended, Javier prettily asked, "Once more?"

"Pardon?" She was already moving toward the refreshment table and her gaze was wandering again. "Oh, I don't think so." She'd fulfilled all her obligations with the ranch hands and was growing impatient for the expected confrontation with their unexpected guest. "Actually, I'm thirsty," she lied so as not to hurt Javier's feelings.

"Then let me get you some lemonade," offered the man she'd been looking for.

Her breath grew shallow as Louisa whipped around to face Sam Strong at last.

"Louisa?" Javier crowded her. "Shall I get rid of this man for you?"

"No. Thank you for the dance, Javier. I'll see you later."

"But—"

"Please."

She sensed rather than saw the ranch hand leave, for she couldn't take her eyes off Sam. Still not the pretty tin soldier she once knew, he was a sight better groomed than the man she'd punched out. His golden hair gleamed and curled over his collar. He was clean shaven and neatly dressed in a spotless uniform trimmed in gold. That was impressive, but she found it even more thrilling that his breath smelled of nothing stronger than jalapeño peppers. He was still the handsomest man she'd ever seen, the scar giving him a dashing maturity.

"What are you doing here?" she demanded.

"Open invitation."

"I mean in the Santa Fe area."

"Looking for something I lost."

Her? "Or threw away."

"I never meant to." He stepped forward, his very closeness smothering her. And before she knew what he was about, he had her in his arms and back on the dance floor where the band played, "A Bird in a Gilded Cage."

"Sometimes circumstances interfere with a man's intentions," he said.

Unsuccessfully trying to ignore the familiar physical sensations speeding through her as they waltzed together, she asked, "What were your intentions, Sam?"

"To come back for you someday."

"Hah!" Too bad he'd given her no reason to believe him. "You didn't even write." And she was pleased when he shifted guiltily and gripped her waist more tightly. "Someday is here, and I don't want you," she told him, caught somewhere between the truth and a lie.

"I already showed you otherwise."

"An aberration, nothing more."

"Shall I prove differently?"

Furious at the reminder of the way he'd kissed her—and of the way she'd responded—she gave him fair warning. "You do and I'll have you drawn and quartered!"

"Ah, the Comanche blood in you getting all stirred up?" Louisa felt the color start to drain from her face until he added, "That's what I always loved about you—your wild nature."

Then warmth and a confusion she didn't want to feel threatened to consume her. "You never loved me."

Ignoring her protest, he went on heatedly. "But aren't you going a little far these days to prove how brave you are? What the hell did you think you were doing riding in that *paseo de la muerte,* anyway?"

Her anger that she'd almost made a fool of herself over him of all people renewed, she asked, "You mean when you made me lose my seat?"

"I mean your participation in such a damn fool stunt in the first place."

Louisa stared at him openmouthed and stopped moving her feet to the music. How dare he think he could walk into her life after six years and tell her what to do?

When she could find her voice, she nearly shouted, "You don't give me orders!"

Glowering over her, Sam yelled back, "Looks like someone should!"

"You've been in the military too long!"

"Maybe I have, but that's about to change."

"You're quitting?" That gave her pause. What did he intend to do with the rest of his life? And where did he intend to spend it?

In Santa Fe?

Little thrills shot through her.

"I'm turning in my uniform after I execute one last assignment," Sam was saying. "I'm riding to West Texas to meet with a man named Ryerson. We're going after a madman who's been killing people."

Her stomach knotted at the thought of Sam putting himself in such danger—as if he hadn't survived every danger fate had thrown his way for seven years. Not that he'd survived them well, she thought, remembering how she'd hardly recognized him all liquored up.

Something truly horrible must have happened to make him want to resign his commission.

Hardly realizing that she was dancing whether she would or no, she muttered, "A murderer."

"Served as an officer with the Confederacy, but he cracked on the battlefield. He was locked up tight in an asylum until recently. Seems he's been gathering followers, an army of sorts. It's my job to stop Beaufort Montgomery before he gives us a real problem."

"Beaufort Montgomery," she echoed.

Louisa was sidetracked from other questions when a sun-bronzed hand clamped down on Sam's shoulder, once more stopping them from dancing.

A deep, smooth voice, lightly accented, said, "I would like to dance with the lady."

Louisa was startled. It was the stranger in the *faena* suit who'd been watching her so intently. He had to be a Mexican, yet he was taller than most and, though lean, obviously very strong. He resembled an ancient warrior, Louisa thought. His amber eyes glittered as he stared down his hawk nose at Sam.

"Sorry, mister." Sam's unfriendly tone belied the pretty apology. "She's already spoken for."

"I can speak for myself, thank you so much," Louisa groused as she tried one last time to wrench herself free from his persistent grip.

She was about to accept the handsome stranger's invitation if for no better reason than to aggravate her current partner, but her intentions were foiled when Sam twirled her back into his arms and strutted to the music, out-of-sync with the waltz until he'd put some distance between them and the dark-haired man, who stared after him with an unnerving expression. Then Sam smoothly glided back into the proper rhythm.

Realizing he'd forced her to continue partnering him despite her wish to do otherwise, Louisa demanded, "How dare you!"

"I would dare anything for you."

And damn the thrill that shot through her at his statement, which sounded so sincere. She laughed harshly. "I guess that's why you left."

"I had no choice. My commanding officer had me transferred."

She glared into the blue-green eyes that were too beautiful to belong to a man. "Was it his fault you stayed away for six years?"

"I was doing my duty."

"By not contacting me?"

"In defending my country."

"By dragging Indians off the land that has been theirs to roam for centuries, herding them onto reservations, then shooting them if they dared to leave without permission of the commanding Bluecoat?"

With each word, Sam withdrew further and further, not only physically, but emotionally as well. That haunted look wasn't always confined to his eyes, Louisa learned. Now it seemed to engulf every fiber of his being. He let go of her and gave her a polite bow.

"Sorry to have troubled you," he said stiffly, then spun on his heel and stalked off.

Leaving Louisa outraged, not to mention frustrated. How dare he leave her in the middle of the dance floor so people could gawk at her?

How dare he not finish this fight?

How dare he not tell her about what made him appear burdened with a guilt greater than any one man should have to shoulder alone?

And how could she be so stupid as to even care?

Determined to do something about that, she made her way back through the crowd, to where the stranger still stood, arms crossed in front of his broad chest.

His expression shifted subtly when she approached him. He looked hungry. And not for food.

Too late to change her mind, Louisa said, "Sorry my partner was so rude—to both of us." She glanced back but couldn't see hide nor hair of Sam Strong. Giving the stranger a winsome smile, she asked, "Have you got a name?"

"Tezco."

"Well, Tezco, if you're still looking for a partner, I accept. Name's Louisa Janks." She took the hand he offered her, then furtively scanned the crowd for Sam.

Wherever he'd disappeared to, she hoped he had a good view of the dance floor.

Back in the shadows beyond the festivities, Sam looked down at the dancers and saw Louisa smiling up into the stranger's face as they began a traditional Spanish number, a slow decorous dance in which the men carried lit candles.

At least the usurper couldn't get both hands on Louisa, Sam thought, even as his mood darkened further.

His gut tore at him, and he could hardly keep himself from doing something about it. Rushing down there and telling Louisa he still loved her. Still wanted her. Wanted her for his wife.

But he couldn't.

He shouldn't.

Her crude stabs at his official duties of the past years had been too close to the truth. In ten seconds, she had reminded him of why he never should have stirred up old feelings in the first place. Louisa Janks was a half-breed, and while she lived the life of the White Eyes, the Comanche remained strong in her heart.

Therefore, he never could be.

He couldn't imagine detailing for her the horrors he'd witnessed during the last couple of years. Certainly not those in which he'd participated. She thought she knew. She was an innocent. Had no idea of the reality . . .

Had no way of knowing what he had done.

If he wanted to be with Louisa, Sam knew he would have to be honest with her. Impossible, for the hatred and condemnation he would see in her beautiful dark eyes would surely kill him.

6

"*I could kill* Sam Strong with my bare hands!" Louisa ranted to Frances a few days later. "I could absolutely wring his neck like I would a chicken's!"

Actually, she'd rarely harmed a living creature in her life—not even a chicken—but Frances was kind enough to refrain from pointing that out.

Louisa felt all wound up. She went on, "He's the most conceited, aggravating . . . sad man I've ever met in my life."

Frances raised her brows. "Sad?"

Louisa nodded morosely and fell into a nearby chair. "Something terrible has happened to change him. He was always a little stiff and full of spit and polish. His West Point training, I suppose. Now, he seems . . . tormented. I can't think of a better way of putting it."

They were about to take tea in Frances's dayroom, a chamber that was filled with perfect golden light and sturdy furniture made from the soft, easily worked pines of the region. The house's interior appeared to be

more Spanish and Indian than Anglo, complementing
the local architecture. Unlike the heavy, dark pieces
imported from the East, the Joneses' furniture was
carved with gracious Spanish designs and brightened
with bold mineral paints introduced by the Indians.

"You sound like you care," Frances stated.

"Just making an observation."

"Liar." She hesitated only a moment before volun-
teering her real opinion. "I think Sam Strong still
loves you, too, or he wouldn't have come back."

Despite her morose mood, Louisa felt her pulse pick
up. "He told me you two talked after our—adventure
in the desert. And I never said I loved him."

"You didn't have to. And yes, we talked. He was concerned about you."

"You mean he was afraid I might be pregnant."

Frances took some linen napkins from a *trastero,* a
massive painted pine cupboard that could be used to
store everything from jewelry to clothing to dishes
depending on where it had been placed. "That Sam
was concerned at all should tell you how he felt about
you, Louisa."

"Or how seriously he took his duties."

"I don't think you were a duty to him then. And you
certainly aren't one now."

Louisa thought her friend was acting like she'd
talked to the man recently. "Did you run into Sam at
the fiesta?"

"We had a few words."

Louisa flushed. "Why didn't you tell me?"

"I've been waiting for you to cool down."

"What did he say?"

"That returning to Santa Fe wasn't only official. He
came for you, Louisa."

But Frances wanted everyone she cared about to be as happy as she was. Louisa wasn't sure she could trust that her friend was telling the whole truth.

"I think you should give him another chance," Frances continued. "Unless you're more interested in that stranger I saw you dancing with."

"Tezco? He is attractive. Some would even say sensual," Louisa admitted. "But I didn't pay him much mind. I was . . . distracted."

By thoughts of Sam, whether she liked it or not. She watched Frances place the napkins on the small round table set in front of the windows.

"Louisa, promise me you'll be careful. Since before the fiesta, Chaco's been having a strong foreboding of something being wrong, and it involves you."

Louisa started, then tried to cover. Chaco's intuition was nothing to ignore. "Maybe he's picking up on my anger with Sam."

"Maybe." Though Frances didn't look like she believed that any more than Louisa did.

Balancing a tray holding a porcelain service from the East that Frances treasured, the housekeeper's daughter arrived. "Señora Jones, your tea."

"Put it on the table." When she noticed Marta's concerned frown, Frances asked, "Is something wrong?"

"I did not want to upset you, but Phillip is not feeling well. His forehead is warm. I made him go to his room to rest."

Tea forgotten, Frances rushed to the door. "I'll be right back, Louisa."

"Don't be silly. I'm coming with you."

Frances became terribly anxious each time one of the children got sick. Doctors were scarce in this part of the country, and the medicines used back East were scarcer. Everyone relied on local native remedies. If necessary, Chaco could even summon an Apache medicine man.

Frances entered Phillip's bedroom with Louisa close behind her, and sat on the bed next to him. The boy was flushed and when he coughed, the sound was deep and harsh.

"He could use some *Yerba Mansa* root," Louisa said.

"Good idea." Frances turned to Marta, who waited in the doorway. "Would you fetch some, along with a rag and a bowl of cool water?"

The anxious young woman ducked her head and darted down the hall. Then Frances focused her entire attention on her son.

"Phillip, how are you feeling, baby?" she asked, putting a gentle hand on his forehead. "Oh, dear. You're so hot."

"Not a baby!" He tried sitting up to prove it, but the movement only provoked another coughing fit. "Gotta go . . . take care of Spangles . . ."

"Spangles will miss you," Louisa assured him from the foot of the bed, "but I promise I'll take good care of him for you until you're feeling better, and I'll tell him you'll be well soon."

Frances gave her a grateful smile. Phillip needed to rest, not to worry about responsibilities that were too much for a sick five-year-old.

Marta returned a few moments later with a portion of the wild plant. "I am sorry, Señora Jones. This is all that is left. And we are low on silktassel, also."

While the *Yerba Mansa* root was good for coughs, the bark and leaves of the silktassel bush were brewed and the ensuing liquid used for the relief of fever.

"Here, Phillip, chew on this."

He made a face and avoided the root in his mother's hand. "Don't like it."

"But it'll make you feel better," Frances coaxed.

"Sure will," Louisa added. "I don't like the taste either." The root was peppery and astringent. "But I take it when I have to. It works."

She was relieved when, after grimacing, Phillip took the root and chewed without making a fuss, something he was wont to do more now that he thought of himself as "grown-up." A series of illnesses around the ranch the past few weeks—no doubt the way Phillip had come by this one—was the reason their supply of native medicines was depleted, though she hadn't realized to what extent.

Frances murmured, "I'll have to send one of the servants to get more herbs and such."

"I can do it," Louisa volunteered. "I was going into town to visit Ma anyway. I wouldn't mind stopping to see Magdalena out at the pueblo."

Formerly one of Belle's girls at The Gentlemen's Club, Magdalena had bragged about being a *bruja,* or white witch. And much to the satisfaction of Frances, who'd taken it upon herself to find new jobs for all the girls, Magdalena had chosen to turn her talents to healing and had moved back to her native pueblo. For several years she'd been teaching both Louisa and Frances about native healing methods and supplying them with the necessary herbs and roots.

"You'll be back by nightfall?"

Louisa nodded. "Is that too late?"

"It sounds fine. Thank you."

"Hey, I love your kids almost as much as you do."

Even if she might never have any of her own, Louisa thought sadly, heading for the door. Damn Sam anyhow. His sudden appearance just made her feel worse about the situation.

She continued to brood about him all the way out to the pueblo. Only after she'd arrived, dismounted and gone inside Magdalena's home did she manage to push the man out of her mind.

"You look worried," Louisa said, noting the *bruja* seemed disturbed about something.

Sorting through her remedies, which she kept in an interior room of her quarters, Magdalena chose the herbs and roots that Frances would need and stuffed them into small leather pouches. Part Spanish but mostly Pueblo Indian, she was a small woman in her mid-thirties, attractive despite her rather flat face. Huge silver-and-turquoise earrings were prominent against the coarse black hair she always wore braided and pinned to her head.

"Some people are missing," she finally said, hands hovering over her supplies.

"Missing?" Louisa echoed uneasily. "How many? When?"

"Two men. They've been gone since the day following the big fiesta on the *estancia.*"

"Could they be in Santa Fe for some reason? Or visiting another pueblo?" she asked, thinking of the other Indian towns with a concentration of attached living quarters gathered around a central plaza not unlike, if smaller than, the city of Santa Fe.

"Their wives say not. They were to be home the night they disappeared. . . ."

A chill shot up Louisa's spine. She remembered the last time men started mysteriously disappearing, only to turn up dead with their throats torn out. A *diablera,* or evil witch, had been responsible then. Louisa had been blamed by some and had almost paid for those lives with her own. The *diablera* was long dead and could hurt no one, she reminded herself.

But Chaco was having premonitions of some kind and they had to do with her. Now this.

Could there be a connection?

"Is there reason to believe the men are dead?" she asked, a catch in her breath.

Placing the remaining leather pouches in the saddlebags, Magdalena shook her head. "This I did not see."

"You have searched for answers then." Louisa meant as a wise woman. She had great respect for the mysticism that was an integral part of Indian life.

The Pueblo tilted her head back and closed her eyes. "I looked into a bowl of water stirred with an eagle feather."

"And?"

"I saw a snarling face with lightning and snakes shooting from the head."

Louisa hugged her arms tightly around her middle. "What's it mean?"

Magdalena's eyes opened and her troubled gaze met Louisa's. "I am uncertain." She secured the leather straps on the full saddlebags and handed them to Louisa. "Perhaps I saw an angry god."

"One of your gods?"

"One with whom I am unfamiliar."

Magdalena led the way into the outer room, simply furnished with clay pots, baskets, sleeping blankets and a grinding stone, where she cooked, slept and took shelter on inclement days. Built of stone and adobe, the thick walls of the pueblo buildings absorbed heat during the day and released it slowly, keeping the rooms warm even during cold winter nights.

"But I sensed his power," the *bruja* stated.

"Can't you learn more?"

"Perhaps. In time. Now it is you who are troubled, Louisa."

"Chaco . . . He told Frances he sensed something was wrong. And that I'm somehow involved." She hesitated only a second before putting her apprehension into words. "You didn't see me in your bowl, did you?"

"No. But to be safe, I could make you a charm."

Louisa's hand went to her shirt, below which she wore the bear claw. "I still have the token that was my father's."

"As you wish."

Niches around the room were decorated both with statues of the Virgin Mary and Catholic saints as well as kachinas, representations of ancient Pueblo gods. The combination of religions was nothing new. Indians were a superstitious people who believed in being prepared and were fairly open-minded when it came to espousing and mixing various beliefs. Perhaps she shouldn't have demurred at Magdalena's offer so readily. What would it hurt, after all, to have as many magic tokens as possible to protect her?

Before she could make up her mind to say something about it, however, Magdalena was already outside. Louisa joined her on the second-story terrace where a woman was baking bread in an *horno*, or beehive-shaped oven, and another was stringing vegetables out to dry.

Below them, the ground floors had no external doors or windows, and entry to the pueblo was through a series of ladders that took the occupants to its various levels and could be removed when enemies approached. Beyond the plaza, Louisa saw a man lower himself into an opening in the earth—the entrance to a kiva, the sacred connection between the underworld and the daily world above. The kiva was the spiritual heart of every pueblo.

"Tell Frances I hope her little one recovers soon," Magdalena said. "And that she should send a messenger if she needs me."

"I'll tell her." Louisa backed down the ladder to street level. "Take care."

Magdalena's gaze remained on her as she secured the saddlebags, freed Defiant from the hitching post and mounted him. Louisa couldn't help wondering what the *bruja* was thinking. If she had an opinion about Chaco's weird feelings, she hadn't been forthcoming. Deciding not to worry about what she couldn't control, she headed her gelding toward Santa Fe, a half hour's easy ride almost straight south.

Even so, she found it impossible to put away all disquieting thoughts. Surmises about the form of danger she might be in, added to the disappearance of the two men, danced around and around in her mind.

But she'd never been a person to let fear rule her life. Setting her jaw, telling herself she had more than enough courage, she fingered the bear-claw necklace and wondered if she shouldn't perhaps start carrying a shotgun or a rifle. After all, if trouble came looking for her, she wanted to be more than ready for it.

The Sierra Madre, Mexico

Quetzalcoatl was once again ready to assume his place in the cosmos.

Having taken leave of his followers and the herds of

animals they'd brought along to feed everyone, Beaufort Montgomery climbed up the side of a rugged mountain until he found an unobstructed view of the west—the direction of the hidden pyramid. With a serpent wrapped about his neck, he stood still and raised his arms skyward to let the power of the elements surge through him, to let the god possess him from the inside out.

And he allowed other gods to pay homage. The fire of the setting sun, Tonatiuh, warmed his face. The wind caressed him, bringing the smell of rain from the storm set brewing by Huitzilopochtli, the god of the south. Soon a moon would rise in the east to flood him with silver light, to illuminate the shadows creeping in from the north.

Shadows, the kingdom of Tezcatlipoca. But Quetzalcoatl did not fear the handsome god who had once been his rival, nor did he fear the shadows. He did not cower before any of this great continent's deities, all of whom would soon be bowing before him, bowing before even the lesser gods of the Mexica.

The Mexica had been there before the Europeans arrived. They had been savage and strong, had conquered any other Native gods. And they would be strong again.

They would rule.

He would rule.

He would be lord of death and master of life.

Beaufort smiled at the thought, especially when he heard the sound of thunder. He glanced to the south and said some words in Nahuatl. "Hail, storms, you are my brothers!"

A vicious zigzag of fire split the clouds in answer. He closed his eyes, imagining lightning issuing from his own head. He felt a fierce heat suffuse him and the serpent hissed, suddenly jerking into death spasms and slipping from his neck.

He glanced at the dead snake, smoke rising from its scorched flesh. His power was growing! Someday, he would be able to kill with a glance.

Meantime, there were the more usual forms of sacrifice. "Hail, all ye gods, we shall soon be fed blood!"

Streams, rivers, oceans of blood.

And fierce, brave hearts.

He had only a little longer to wait for the ultimate ceremonies. And after twenty-two years of imprisonment, he could surely wait with grace. Still, Quetzalcoatl couldn't help trembling with eagerness.

Northern New Mexico

Eager to reach Santa Fe, Louisa concentrated on the road and keeping Defiant at a steady pace.

And so, halfway to town, she was not prepared to be ambushed.

A blur of chestnut whipped out from behind a stand of juniper-dotted rock accompanied by a voice declaring, "Now that's a familiar nag."

Heart speeding up, Louisa slowed Defiant and faced Sam, who still sat his chestnut like he was born in the saddle—the very thing she had initially admired about him.

"He should be familiar since he once belonged to you," she returned smartly.

The day she'd bought Defiant at Fort Marcy had been the first time she'd set eyes on her pretty tin soldier. She remembered it as if the event had taken place yesterday. A brash new lieutenant straight out of West Point, Sam hadn't wanted to sell her the gelding or believed that she—a young woman—could control a horse who had thrown him.

"Not that you were able to ride Defiant without tasting the dust," she reminded him before moving the horse forward.

Sam pulled his chestnut alongside her. "That was a long time ago."

Admiring his arrogant expression—far more attractive and exciting than the sad one that had been haunting him lately—she said, "You were riding a different horse back then. Whatever happened to him?"

"He was shot out from under me in a skirmish." Sam's voice tightened. "I had to finish him off myself."

Louisa swallowed hard. "How horrible." She could hear his heartfelt regret; they had their love for horses in common. But worse: "You could have taken the bullet instead of your horse."

"A lot of men are killed in the line of duty."

He said that so easily, almost as if it were expected. "And you think that's all right?" she asked.

"I think it's unavoidable."

"Of course it's avoidable. You didn't have to join the military in the first place."

He seemed astonished by the concept. "I come from a whole family of military men," he explained. "My father and uncles were cavalry officers in the Civil War. My grandfather served in the military and his father before him. Strongs fought in the American Revolution to free this country from England's shackles." He practically vibrated with the intensity of his convictions. "The men in my family have always been proud to defend our country."

But his sense of duty and history obviously wasn't enough to keep him in the military for much longer, Louisa thought. Why? She remembered Sam saying he'd seen and done terrible things.

Before she could probe in that direction, he changed the subject back to her favorite. "So how many horses do you have now?"

"A few. The sorrel I rode the other night. Another couple of mares I'm training for *charreada* riding. And then I have the most incredible new black stallion. *El Tigre* is still half-wild."

"Like you."

A quick glance at Sam told Louisa he admired that in her. "But I'm getting him settled down."

"I'd like to meet this *El Tigre* sometime. Maybe ride him myself if you'd let me."

"Hah! You can't even ride Defiant," she reminded him. Though she'd never seen him take a fall off the gelding, she'd heard about it.

"Are you sure about that?" Sam taunted. "I might have learned a thing or two about ornery personalities in the past six years."

The way he was staring at her made Louisa think he meant her as well as the horse he had once owned. She found herself in an equally challenging mood, undoubtedly because she was still angry with him.

Maybe she always would be.

"Are you suggesting you could ride Defiant now?" she asked.

"I'm betting I could."

"What? Did you hide a deck of cards in that vest?"

Today Sam was wearing civilian clothes—blue shirt, denim pants, soft brown leather vest—and looking every bit as good as he had the night of the fiesta. The night he had so rudely left her on the dance floor without things being settled between them, she reminded herself.

"I warn you," she said, her desire to wring his neck renewed, "I'm a practiced cheat."

Maybe she could get even in a more subtle way than using out-and-out violence.

"I was thinking in terms of a horse race."

Though she'd been counting on that being his intention all along, Louisa felt her heart jog at another memory. She had forced Sam into a horse race with her and won, but he'd claimed the prize—their first kiss.

"The prize being a ride on Defiant?" she asked, hoping she didn't sound as breathless as she felt.

"The prize being Defiant himself."

"Or your chestnut," she added pointedly.

"Irish?"

She forced a frown to counter the amusement in his blue-green eyes. "Hmm, I don't know. I wouldn't want to make you walk back to town."

"Who said I was going to let you win this time?"

As if he'd let her win the last.

"Aren't you going to a lot of trouble to prove you can ride Defiant? All you gotta do is ask and I'll be happy to let you try."

"Challenging you for the privilege is more fun. What do you say?" Sam urged, the question vibrant with possibilities. "I dare you."

Never one to turn down a challenge, Louisa found herself mentally laying out a course along the road, ending at a distant rock formation. "All right."

No sooner had they agreed on the finish line than Sam stuffed his Stetson down to his ears, gathered his horse under him and yelled, "Ready . . . set . . ."

"Hi-yah!" Louisa finished.

Both horses surged together. Laughing with delight, she lifted her bottom out of the saddle, moved low over Defiant's neck and steadied her weight. A glance at Sam told her that he was in a similar position. He had learned something about racing since their last outing, she noted.

Together they thundered along the crude dirt road that wound up and down and around hillocks. Defiant would pull a nose or so ahead only to lose the advantage to Irish a few seconds later. The horses seemed to be perfectly matched, especially along the straightaways.

Or maybe it was the riders who were perfectly matched. . . .

Then the chestnut brushed a clump of cedar, frightening a bird that fluttered up and away with a frantic beating of wings. With a startled snort, Irish danced to the side and nearly clipped Defiant. Louisa took the advantage, urged her mount to greater speed and was the first to reach the finish line, if only by the length of a neck.

They slowed their horses together, gradually bringing them down to a walk that would cool them out.

Louisa couldn't contain her grin. "Well?"

"You win again," Sam said ruefully.

"You really gotta stop underestimating me."

His expression was contemplative and sobering. Wondering what he was thinking was driving Louisa crazy. For she sensed his mind was already past the race and onto something far more important.

Before she could probe, Sam said, "That's a long walk ahead of me." He stroked the chestnut's neck as if saying good-bye. "Guess I should get started."

Since she'd only meant to teach him a lesson in

humility, not deprive him of a horse he so obviously loved, Louisa told him, "I wasn't serious about the bet."

"Well, I was." He dismounted and kept walking briskly, his horse in tow behind him. "You won Irish fair and square." He tried to hand her the reins.

Which she refused. "I'm not gonna take him, so forget it!"

"I can't forget it." Head high, features composed, he said, "It's a point of honor. A man pays his gambling debts."

"What?" He was being ridiculous, and Louisa could feel her temper slipping. "Another of your stupid duties?"

"You could say that."

"And I *could* say this slavish devotion to duty is plain stupid. I'm sick of hearing about a man's duties!" Sensing her agitation, Defiant danced under her. She calmed herself for the horse's sake. But duty had taken Sam from her six years ago. Duty—if she had been pregnant—would have brought him back. And duty would once more take him away, perhaps to be killed by a madman. "You love that horse! He's yours."

"Not anymore."

Again, Sam tried handing her the reins, which Louisa stubbornly continued to refuse. Reluctant to let him drift off with nothing settled between them yet again, she jumped off Defiant and kept pace with Sam's long-legged stride.

"You can at least get him back into Santa Fe for me. I'm visiting Ma," she explained, as if that made her require his help.

He gave her a long, thoughtful look. "I thought you'd enjoy seeing me on foot and suffering."

"I've never reveled in another person's misery."

The statement made Louisa think again about whatever might be bothering Sam. Whatever had made him turn his back on this precious *duty* of his. "Not even yours," she admitted with a sigh, knowing she would share his burden if he would let her.

"Though I guess I wouldn't blame you if you did."

She gave him a hard look. "Sounds like you're carrying around a load of guilt."

"There are some things a man finds hard to live with."

"Making love to me was hard to live with?" she asked, though she sensed his disquiet went far deeper.

"Not the way you figure."

"How, then?"

"I don't regret making love to you, Louisa. I regret using up your innocence."

"Virginity is overrated," she stated frankly. It wasn't like he'd turned her into a harlot. She hadn't joined Ma's girls in servicing men.

"But you were only sixteen . . . as I had to learn from Frances rather than from you. I was twenty-three. I felt terrible about what I'd allowed to happen. Why did you lie to me about your age?"

While trying not to be touched by the truths he shared with her, Louisa was equally honest. "I didn't want you to treat me like a child."

"Maybe it would have been better if I had—"

"So which part don't you regret?"

"—for your sake," he finished.

They walked along in an uneasy silence for a moment before Louisa said, "I haven't turned out too badly."

"I expected you would have had a family by now, but here you are, still a spinster." Sam shook his head and looked her squarely in the eyes. "I'm not right for you, Louisa. If I ever was."

Irritated, she stopped on the spot and demanded, "So who asked you? Do you have some stupid notion that I've been waiting all this time for you?"

He stopped, too, turning Irish so the horses faced each other. "Whether or not you want to admit it, we have feelings for each other."

At the moment hating him for stirring her all up again, Louisa finally demanded to know, "Then why the hell did you abandon me?"

7

Here it came. Sam had known Louisa would get around to demanding the truth. That time was now and still he wasn't ready. Maybe he never would be.

"I had no say about the transfer—"

"You could have sent me a message explaining what happened!" she interrupted. "You could have made it back to Santa Fe before this. For God's sake, you could have written!"

"I needed time to get a perspective on us," he said truthfully. "Everything was going too fast . . ." Although they had made love, they hardly knew each other in the conventional sense. ". . . and then it was too late."

"Why?"

"Because of circumstances that were out of my control."

Her frustration with him obvious, Louisa asked, "What exactly was out of your control?"

"You being half-Indian, for one."

"That's certainly honest enough," she admitted wryly. "Foolish me, I really believed you were the one man at that time who wasn't bothered that I was a breed."

"It didn't bother me, not for a minute!" He hated the stricken expression he glimpsed before she covered it. "I was afraid you would care."

"About what?" She didn't try to hide her amazement. "That you're not part Comanche?"

"You don't know all the facts." Uneasy, he dropped his gaze. "You've got a big heart. You're brave and loyal. And I've killed people in the line of duty."

"People . . ." Louisa echoed. Frowning, she grew silent for a moment. Then comprehension dawned. "By 'people' you mean Indians. I hate the thought of anyone's dying through violence, period. But why did you think I would find your killing Indians any worse than your possibly killing whites?" She reminded him, "I am half-white." Sighing, she placed a gentle hand on his arm. "I'm sure you only did what you had to, Sam—that you were following orders. That you were doing your 'duty,' as you call it."

Though she didn't look happy, she seemed sincere enough about understanding.

And Sam was sincere when he finally admitted, "Problem is, sometimes orders aren't a good-enough reason to slaughter the innocent."

"You slaughtered innocent people?"

Louisa's dark eyes widened and filled with disbelief. Sam knew she couldn't quite comprehend the scope of his culpability yet, or she would be blazing with hatred instead. Having avoided the issue long enough, he acknowledged a reckless attitude that made him want to share his burden with the only woman he'd ever loved.

Even if that meant losing her forever.

"There was nothing fair or noble about the Apache Wars," he said. "We conquered band after band, then pitted one against the other."

"Tell me."

She had to know, but Sam couldn't help putting off detailing his confession for a while longer. Buying time—a few more minutes in which he could pretend that nothing stood between them—he said, "Maybe we should take a breather, give the horses a rest."

They'd walked quite a ways and had come to a creek that ran just outside of town. Sam led Irish to the sandy bank, Louisa following with Defiant directly behind him. After watering their horses, they retired to a shady slope, a small, cool spot sheltered by a cottonwood, where they tied up the animals before making themselves comfortable, Louisa sitting cross-legged, Sam reclining on one arm.

Sam gazed at Louisa longingly. With her lightly bronzed skin, big dark eyes and black hair plaited over one shoulder, she was an incomparable beauty. Her face might have been lovingly chiseled by a sculptor's tool: high cheekbones, bold but feminine nose, stubborn jaw, full soft lips.

Eyes glued to that provocative mouth he would give anything to taste, Sam said, "I would give everything I have to start over, Louisa. Here. Now. In an ideal world where people live at peace."

"Where a man's only duty is to his own heart and his loved ones," she added. "Unfortunately, we don't live in an ideal world, but so what? There are good things, too, and we have to make the best of the cards that life deals us."

She wanted to understand. To accept. Sam heard it

in her voice, saw it in her softened features. At that moment, he loved her more than he ever had. At that moment, hope sparked his soul.

Filled with a surfeit of emotion, he reached out to touch her cheek and found himself cradling her silky skin against his cupped hand.

"Oh, Sam."

His name whispered through her lips. Regret? A plea? He knew not which. His only surety was that he wanted her as he'd never wanted another woman, that he longed to feel her body pressed up against his own.

As if reading his mind . . . as if longing for the same . . . she uncurled her body and reclined also.

Taking that as an invitation, Sam couldn't help himself. He kissed her. Savored the sweet taste of the mouth he'd never forgotten. Louisa arched against him, her soft curves prompting an immediate response. He was hard and throbbing in an instant. Groaning, he adjusted his body, his hips moving against hers in an imitation of a more intimate act.

He trailed his hand down her neck to the rise of one breast hidden beneath the vest. Even through the cotton of her shirt and the garment below, her nipple responded to his slightest touch. The sensitive flesh pebbled and lengthened and she moaned, the sound a small explosion.

Sam plunged his tongue boldly into her mouth and was met with equal fervor on her part. Shyly, Louisa explored him as he did her. Fingers trailed down his chest to his stomach and below. She traced his length, which grew at her light touch.

Oh, how he wanted Louisa . . . but he couldn't take what she was obviously willing to give, not when he still straddled the truth.

When he drew away, she looked confused for a moment, then focused on his face and again demanded, "Tell me, Sam. Let me share whatever is tormenting you."

And Sam recalled one of the worst episodes in his memory, the bloody one-sided siege that had made him question his own integrity and worth as a human being for his participation. He let go of Louisa and rolled away, knowing he could put off telling her no longer.

"A couple of years back, we were searching for an Apache base and refuge in an Arizona canyon with some White Mountain Apache," he began.

"They acted as scouts?"

He nodded. The Apache were notorious for turning against their own kind—each band being separate and competitive, sometimes enemies—if the rewards were great enough. Staring at him attentively, Louisa continued to sit so close it was all Sam could do to keep his hands off her. When he was done, she might never want him to touch her again.

"The canyon was twelve hundred feet deep and the band was holed up in a cave reachable only from above."

He could see the setting as if the incident had happened mere days ago rather than years. Stark. Arid. Hotter than hell. Awesome that human beings could survive in such an environment.

"A natural parapet of stone at the cave's mouth made the interior nearly impregnable."

"Then how did you get in?" she asked.

"We never did . . . until after . . ." Though sunlight dappled the ground around them where it sneaked through the leaves of the cottonwood, in his mind, Sam was once more bathed in an eerie moonlight.

"We wore moccasins stuffed with hay to reach the chasm's edge without being heard. We waited from midnight until dawn, when we fired on the unwary Chiricahua. A few of their warriors fell dead, but the others refused to surrender."

Others being mostly women and children and old people. At the time, he'd tried to tell himself that their warring on any but the braves wasn't dishonorable, that the Apache were their enemy—that there were no innocents, that any one of the band would carve him up if given the chance.

But even then he'd known better.

"By 'we,' do you mean you personally?"

"Did I pull a trigger? No, not this time. As an officer, I gave commands. . . ."

"What did you do next?" Louisa asked, her voice soft, even sympathetic, rather than harsh and accusing as he might have expected. "Starve them out?"

"We kept shooting. The roof sloped downward toward the rear of the cave, so lead ricocheted from wall-to-wall, wounding more Apaches."

"But they still refused to surrender," Louisa guessed.

He nodded. Now to the hard part.

"On the mesa directly above, the ground was strewn with boulders as big as cannonballs. Soldiers maneuvered them to the edge and, on signal at daybreak, tipped them over into the opening. A mass of stone rolled down into the cave, setting up a cloud of dust big enough to choke us all."

"My God, how horrible!"

She didn't know the half of it. She hadn't heard the high-pitched shrieks of the women, the pitiful mewling cries of children.

Sam's gut churned with the memory.

"When the dust cleared, we entered the cave unresisted. There were bodies everywhere . . . most crushed beyond recognition. Even tiny bodies." His eyes burned and he steeled himself not to let Louisa see his weakness. "Babies." He almost choked on the word. "Dozens of people were killed and only a handful of wounded taken captive so they could be marched onto a reservation where their spirits would die while their bodies continued to go on."

Sam chanced a glance at Louisa. Her face was as pale as he'd ever seen it. Her eyes were filled with disbelief and pain. Not the same pain he felt on the telling of the story, certainly, for she hadn't been there. But the pain of being part of a people who were hunted down and confined like wild animals to small pieces of mostly useless land because they didn't live as the white man did.

Because they had what the white man and his government wanted.

"I-I didn't know . . ."

Realizing Louisa was as well and truly horrified as he'd feared she would be, Sam took his cue and jumped to his feet, glad to have an excuse to avoid telling her the rest. To avoid the worst of his nightmares. She sat staring at the ground as if in shock while he approached Irish. Not a word passed her lips. Not a murmur of forbearance. Sick at heart, but realistic if nothing else, Sam patted the chestnut's neck one last time before removing the saddlebags and a canteen.

"So now you know exactly who I am—"

Her eyes—strangely distant—met his as she interrupted. "Do I?"

"—and why I'm not the man for you."

With that, he turned and strode toward town, ignoring her cry of "Sam, wait!"

If he waited, he would be obliged to tell her the rest, and what good would it do? She was already revolted, and she hadn't heard the worst of his secrets. Besides, the blood would remain on his hands always.

Even the forgiveness he hoped for from Louisa wouldn't cleanse him of his self-imposed guilt.

Feeling guilty that she hadn't given Sam what he needed after practically forcing a confession from him, Louisa warred with herself over whether or not to follow. With him on foot and her on horseback, she could catch up to him quickly enough. But she figured he needed time alone after spilling his guts and sharing his terrible memories.

Or sharing some of his memories, for Louisa sensed there had been something more, something so monstrous he'd feared it would devastate her.

She was devastated now.

Devastated that human beings could be so inhumane to others because they were different. Devastated that a good man like Sam had gotten caught up in something so horrible he could barely speak of it, an act that had gone against the very grain of his basic nature. Devastated that he had followed orders out of some stupid sense of duty.

Or rather had given them, passing on killing orders from his superiors.

For he'd been an officer. Hadn't fired his weapon. Not then, he'd said. So when had he? And what did it matter, anyway? When wasn't important. Whether or not he'd actually pulled the trigger or pushed a rock onto unsuspecting victims was of little consequence. He'd participated in a heinous act.

For that, guilt shadowed him and wrapped around his lonely heart.

He'd wanted her understanding. Her forgiveness. Still appalled by the images he'd conjured for her, Louisa wasn't certain she could give it.

Her own heart heavy, she collected the horses and started back for town, riding Defiant and leading Irish.

Violence was common in the West—she'd come to accept that at a tender age. But deep down, in the inner reaches of her soul, she didn't understand why any more than she understood certain people hating her because her skin was a shade too bronzed, exposing the liaison between her parents that prejudice forbade.

The past had given her reason to be sensitive about the issue, and Sam knew that.

Approaching the edge of town, Louisa decided to check the house instead of going to the Blue Sky, even though she was running so late her mother might have given up on her and gone to oversee the business. Between her stop at the pueblo and her tryst with Sam, she'd lost nearly two hours. It was well past time for the noon meal she and Ma had planned to share.

The neat little house built partially of weathered logs and partially of adobe hadn't changed much since she'd moved out of her attic quarters and onto the de Arguello spread. The cottonwoods had gotten a bit bigger and the fenced-in meadow was empty now but for the two grays that pulled Ma's buggy, but the rest was comfortingly the same.

As was Ma herself.

No sooner had Louisa dismounted than Belle Janks stepped through the front door, a vision in satin turquoise that set off her bright red ringlets. "There you are, honey. I was beginning to think you weren't coming."

"I said I'd be here, didn't I?" Louisa asked, knowing she sounded defensive, but not meaning to. She began to tie up the horses at a hitching rail a few yards from the front steps. "When did I ever break a promise?"

Her mother's brows shot up and her rouged lips puckered. "Oh, I can remember a time or two."

Certain Ma meant her having given her word to behave in the various big-city schools she'd been sent to, Louisa groaned. "Years ago, and only because I didn't want to leave you in the first place." Finished with the horses, she bounded up the front steps.

"That's it, butter me up." Belle enveloped her daughter in a big, loving hug, her habitual, liberally applied flowery scent nearly overpowering Louisa. "So, how come you got two horses—and both saddled? You didn't think I'd be wanting to ride, I hope."

"Nah, don't worry, Ma, I know better than to try to change you." Belle thought the only acquaintance ladies should have with horses was from the distant end of buggy reins. Realizing her mother was continuing to give her a curious look, she said, "It's a long story."

"I got lotsa time."

"Later. Maybe."

Belle shrugged and led the way inside where Elena was just putting food on the scarred pine table fancied up with colorful flowers.

"You waited for me."

"'Course I did. How often do I get a chance to have a meal with my girl?"

Eating the housekeeper's home cooking made Louisa feel a bit better inside, maybe because it brought back memories of her childhood when Ma and Elena both had been overprotective and responsible for all the worrying. Of course, now she was a grown-up, too. The black bean soup and chicken-and-cheese enchiladas were gone all too soon, leaving Ma staring at her with a familiar concern.

"So tell me about the chestnut," she demanded. "I assume you didn't rob no one to get it."

Resigned that her mother meant to get the story out of her one way or the other, Louisa said, "I won it. From a man named Sam Strong."

Belle sighed. "Damn! Shoulda known. I heard he was back in town."

From Frances, no doubt. "I wasn't sure you ever knew who he was."

"Not know the no-account bastard who broke my baby's heart?"

"He didn't break my heart!" Louisa nearly shouted, then, facing her mother's knowing expression, backed down. "So he crushed it a little, but I survived."

"Barely."

"What's that mean?"

"Something in you changed after he left town, Louisa, honey. You treat men like you don't want to care nothing for 'em. And you take too many chances, like you don't want to care nothing for yourself, either. You had me worried for longer'n I can remember."

Refusing to take offense, Louisa insisted, "You like to worry, Ma. It's part of your nature."

"I'm a mother. You wait until you have little ones. If you ever do . . ."

Louisa knew that was an invitation, that her mother hoped she would open up and reveal the secrets of her heart. For once, she considered doing so. She was

tired of hiding her emotions, pretending that everything was all right when it wasn't. Her mother had
gone through some terrible times herself and might
have some answers.

"Sam says he loves me, Ma, that he always meant to
come back for me."

"Then what stopped him?"

"The army. Or his supposed duty to it."

"Duty's a powerful notion. Some men don't feel like
nothing without it."

"And men can be corrupted by it, too."

"Sounds serious."

Louisa took a deep breath and said, "Sam was involved in some terrible things . . . having to do with
the Indian wars. With innocent people—women and
children—dying."

"And that bothers you?"

"You have to ask? Wouldn't it you?"

Belle sighed. "I've seen too much of the world to be
shocked, Louisa. And I've been too protective of you.
War is a way of life and always has been through the
centuries, across all continents."

"But there are usually better reasons for war than—"

"No matter what noble notions a government declares
about its going to war," her ma interrupted, "the reality always comes back to one thing—greed of some
kind. That don't mean most young men don't believe
they're fighting for some higher purpose. They gotta
believe that to live with themselves. During the Civil
War, I met brothers who fought against brothers.
And fathers who fought against their sons. I can't
rightly think of anything worse'n that."

"But the massacre Sam described was so awful."

"Death is a terrible thing, Louisa, but it ain't ever

gonna go away. The reasons'll be different, but the call to duty'll be the same. Sounds like your Sam's not too happy about what happened."

"He's not my Sam. And I don't think he can rid himself of their ghosts."

"Then he has a conscience. And a heart. Can't hardly ask more than that of a man."

Thinking about the way he'd deserted her—fearing that he might desert her again at the first sign of trouble—Louisa stated firmly, "I can demand a lot more."

"And you can be alone for the rest of your life, too."

"Are you saying—"

"I'm saying you shouldn't ruin your life 'cause you can't find it in your heart to forgive human weakness or a man following his call to duty. It's up to you, Louisa, but I hope you try to see his side of things. And I hope you don't put nothing special on those people who died just because your pa was Comanche. Don't find a way to cheat yourself of happiness any more than you have."

"That's not what I'm doing."

"Do you love him?"

"Six years ago, I thought—"

"Now. Do you love him now?"

Louisa sighed and faced the truth. "Yes, Ma, I do love him." She hadn't wanted to admit it, not even to herself, but she was more in love with him now than she had been six years before.

"Then why are you here with me instead of going after him?"

"I can't do that!"

"Why not? He came after you, didn't he? Why else did he come back to Santa Fe?"

Louisa couldn't argue with her mother. And she was glad they had talked. Though it still didn't sit well with her, she had a somewhat different, more practical perspective on what Sam had told her. Ma was right that she shouldn't identify with those people merely because they'd been Apache. Hadn't she told Sam she wouldn't be more bothered by his killing Indians than his killing whites?

It was the killing itself that bothered her, the idea of an ever-present war somewhere, a useless loss of lives.

According to Ma, that would never end.

Louisa feared in that, too, Belle Janks was correct.

West Texas

While barely a week before, Monte Ryerson had been plagued by worry about the lost lives of half a dozen men he didn't know, now the possibility of lost cattle hit even closer to home and commanded his full attention.

"Old Man Hinkley said he came up short more'n two dozen head," his son Stephen was telling him as Monte finished patching up a cow who'd gotten herself tangled in some sawtooth barbed wire.

"How long ago?"

"Wasn't sure. Tracks were old. He figures a week, maybe more." Stephen made a disgusted sound. "What was strange, though, was that the rustlers killed a bull right on the spot. Cut the animal's heart clean out."

"The heart?"

Distracted, Monte let the cow jerk away, leaving the rope he'd tied her up with dangling in his hand. Protesting, she scampered toward a few of the herd grazing on a nearby hill.

"Want me to take some men out on the range and do a head count, Pa?" fifteen-year-old Stephen asked.

Not knowing when this Sam Strong was going to show his face, Monte figured he'd better send his foreman out with some trusted hands.

"Ginny and Cassie prepared a special supper for you," he said of the thirteen-year-old twins. "You wouldn't want to go and break their hearts by not having time to enjoy it properly." He slapped Stephen on the shoulder, the only sign of affection the boy welcomed from his father these days. "Kiss the girls for me, tell Carmen I'll be late and save me some supper!"

"Sure, Pa."

With a wide grin, Stephen stuffed the Stetson back on his head, mounted his pinto in one smooth movement and took off for home like he was chasing a bunch of coyotes. And Monte watched with pride until the dust cloud left by the fast-moving hooves enveloped horse and rider.

Then he sobered.

Cattle being rustled might not be as serious as men having their hearts cut out, though it was something Monte was always prepared to face.

But the mutilated bull . . .

Mounting his horse, he set off to find Jake O'Brian, his foreman.

As he rode, he tried to ignore the uneasy feeling that he was even closer to Beaufort Montgomery than he'd figured.

8

New Mexico Territory

    Sam rode uneasily onto the de Arguello spread after having risen from his bed in the dead of night. He was still putting off carrying out his final assignment for the army. Trouble was, he didn't want to think of never seeing Louisa again. When he'd gotten her message, asking him to ride out before daybreak so she could introduce him to *El Tigre*, he was elated.

Had she really thought she needed to use the wild stallion to lure him out to see her? Didn't she know that all she had to do was say she wasn't through with him?

At least he hoped she wasn't.

Surely she hadn't tricked him into coming merely so she could give him her final good riddance face-to-face. He didn't remember her having a cruel streak.

When she hadn't been able to say anything comforting after he told her the story that day, when she
hadn't come after him, only called to him once to
wait, he'd been certain she never wanted to see him
again. She'd been shocked and he didn't blame her.
So had something happened to change her mind? He
hoped so. With Louisa's support, perhaps he could
find some peace within himself.

He didn't want to think about what he hadn't told
her.

Worrying about Louisa's true motives in getting
him away from Santa Fe, Sam was distracted and
therefore hadn't gotten within a hundred yards of the
outbuildings when he was ambushed. Louisa galloped
Defiant seemingly straight out of hell at him, only to
stop directly in front of his roan, who whinnied and
tried to rear. Sam easily kept the mild-mannered,
good-natured horse under control.

"Morning."

The single word did not make Louisa's intentions
clear, Sam decided. A full moon sunken close to the
horizon cast a silver-blue glow over her lovely features, which seemed to be at peace. Had she accepted
what he'd told her, then?

In case not, Sam put on a bit of bravado. "You certainly were confident that I'd show."

"I knew you wouldn't want to miss this opportunity
. . . to ride a half-wild stallion."

That wasn't why he'd shown and they both knew it.

He wanted to ask her how she felt about what he'd
done . . . whether or not she'd forgiven him. Instead,
he said nothing, merely followed her lead, loping
through the night and into the dawn. The first whisper of daylight accompanied their arrival at mountain

foothills and a rocky formation whose entrance was blocked by a series of split logs. A dark blur on the other side caught his eye.

"That him?"

Louisa nodded. "*El Tigre* watches for me every morning."

Sure enough, by the time she dismounted and approached the makeshift gate, the blur had focused into a stallion, but one who warily watched the human activity from a safe distance back in the canyon.

"He doesn't know you or he'd be right here, making up to me before I could get inside," Louisa maintained.

"You have that effect on the male species."

She avoided looking at him and Sam would swear he'd embarrassed her with the truth even if he'd issued the words in good-hearted jest. He had some effect on her, too, then.

Good.

Indicating he should wait, Louisa stepped into the canyon alone, bridle in hand. A few yards from the opening, she stopped and calmly waited. Nervously eyeing Sam, the stallion lumbered over to her and nosed her shoulder as he passed. He made a tight circle, eyes rolling at Sam, then pranced in front of Louisa until she caught hold of his mane and made much over him for a minute, talking to him in a low, soothing tone while running her free hand along his neck and down his nose.

She was so obviously entranced with the magnificent horse that Sam found himself tensing until Louisa laughed and drew back and deftly put on the hackamore, a bitless bridle that worked by placing pressure on the horse's nose, thereby regulating his air intake.

"You going to ride him bareback?" Sam called.

"I could, but a saddle's safer with this guy. I've been keeping an old one out here." She led the stallion to a nearby rocky shelter where Sam could see the leather tucked in a roofed crevice, no doubt for protection against inclement weather. "Easier than hauling it back and forth."

Again, as she tacked the stallion, Louisa made a fuss over him. Her love of horses was one of the things Sam had always admired about her, but seeing her focusing so much attention on *El Tigre*—and ignoring himself, perhaps?—made him shift restlessly. Disliking what he was feeling, Sam froze.

Surely he couldn't be jealous of a horse.

That's exactly what he was, Sam realized as Louisa tightened the cinch, then pulled on one of the stallion's ears so he would cock his head toward her face. She whispered something and the horse whinnied softly in response.

Sam called himself a damn fool for caring.

But how could he help it when he longed for Louisa to whisper sweet words for him alone, when he longed for her to stroke him exactly as she did the stallion. Well, not exactly, perhaps, he decided, now growing amused by the idea.

As she mounted *El Tigre* and warmed him up, first walking, then jogging and finally loping around the confined canyon, Sam speculated on whether or not Louisa had ever stroked any man but him. Chances were she hadn't if that dance-hall girl Nina were to be believed.

Growing impatient watching, he called, "Can I come in?"

"I'll bring him out."

"Sure it's safe?"

"I've had him out before, and now that he's gotten rid of some steam, I don't see why not. Mount up."

But rather than riding his roan, Sam chose Defiant. He still had a score to settle with the old gelding who'd thrown him more than once before he'd put the horse up for sale. And he still had that same thing to prove to Louisa.

"Feeling daring?" she asked, bringing the black through the opening as he first jogged the gelding in a circle, then took him into an easy lope.

"Give me a chance to warm up." Sam quickly took Defiant through some fancy paces, figure eights where he made the horse change leads several times. "You promised I could ride *El Tigre,* right?"

"Catch me and you can!" she dared, the black stallion shooting off at her invisible command.

Another race. Sam felt as if Louisa liked running him in circles. He didn't even care. He followed, hot on her horse's heels. She was a hellion and a heart-breaker according to the dance-hall girl. And how else had the woman put it? Virgin goddess?

Louisa was a goddess, all right. Sam could almost imagine her riding bareback—and he didn't mean only sans saddle—with that long, heavy black hair streaming around her lightly bronzed, fit body.

The physical distraction that came naturally with thinking about her almost did him in. Not enough to make him lose the race, for once more they were on superbly matched mounts and Sam had quickly caught up to her. But suddenly, the land ahead presented a mirage. . . . He hoped to God he was seeing an illusion of some sort. Did the land really just stop, pitching into nowhere?

"Louisa, what's ahead?" Sam yelled, quickly glancing at her.

Face flushed, eyes bright, lips curving in a smile, she yelled back, "Nothing!"

"Are you crazy?" He was already turning Defiant, but she was going on, as if she meant to leap the chasm. He looked at her again. "Louisa!"

Her cry was one of triumph as, at her secret signal, the horse performed a braking maneuver, crude still, but similar to the one she'd shown off in the *charreada*. The horse's front hooves came to rest mere inches from the drop.

Sam was mad as hell.

He glowered in silence until she backed up *El Tigre* to where he and Defiant waited.

Dismounting, Sam demanded, "Get off!"

"I won."

"The hell you did." Before she knew what he was about, he strong-armed her out of the saddle, and, without giving it another thought, mounted the half-wild stallion, sitting deep in the saddle as the black danced and snorted unhappily at his unaccustomed weight. "Settle down!" he growled to the horse, doubling his command with the vise of his legs. And to Louisa: "Let's go."

Without waiting to see if she did as he dictated, he rode straight back for the little canyon. His displeased mount tried to defy him, but, while kinder to the animal than a halter with a bit, the hackamore was effective. And Sam was determined. Finally giving in to the human's stronger will, the black settled down under him and jogged straight into the enclosure. A glance back assured him Louisa followed on Defiant.

It wasn't until they'd both dismounted and she'd

replaced the split rails that secured the opening that she demanded, "What the hell did you think you were doing?"

"Me? I'm not the one who took a chance with my life."

"Balderdash! People take chances all the time!"

"Not without good cause."

"And what's good cause?" she demanded, her expression one of pure fury. "War? Killing innocent people?"

So she hadn't quite forgiven him. Saddened—not to mention angry that he'd fooled himself into forgetting what lay between them even if for a short while—Sam silently unfastened the stallion's saddle. He was a damn fool, that's all there was to it.

"There's nothing wrong with having courage," Louisa went on as she walked Defiant in a circle to cool him down. "Men who fight useless wars think they have it."

"Some do. Some also think they're doing the right thing by participating in wars. At least they start out that way," he said, meaning himself. "You can't know for sure what's in someone else's heart."

Ignoring that, Louisa said, "Well, he has courage in spades." She indicated the black. "That's why I named him *El Tigre,* the jaguar."

"He might have a big heart and lots of courage, but he's smarter than you," Sam returned. "He wouldn't have chosen to pull that fool stunt on his own. You drove him to the edge of the cliff . . . and if you'd have asked him to do it, he probably would have gone over for you. Is that courage on your part, or sheer stupidity?"

"How dare you?"

"I dare because, whether or not you believe it, I hate seeing lives wasted!" Sam shouted, throwing down the saddle and going for the hackamore, lightly tapping the stallion's nose when he bared his teeth. "Any life. Even that of a horse."

"I would never have hurt him!"

"Not intentionally, perhaps, but what if you had misjudged the distance to that cliff?"

"Well, I didn't."

"But you could have. Then you would both be dead." Freeing the stallion, Sam gave him a light whack on his rump. "Is that what you wanted?" he asked as *El Tigre* shot away to the opposite end of the canyon.

"Of course not—"

Thinking about wasted lives, Sam couldn't contain his fury. He stalked Louisa. "A hellion and a heartbreaker. That's what someone called you. I sure have no argument with the hellion part!"

Dropping Defiant's reins—the horse stilled the moment the leathers touched the ground—Louisa met Sam head on, balled fists at her hips. "I'm not the heartbreaker here."

Sam wrapped a hand around the back of her neck and jerked her to him. Her hands flailed, one coming to rest on his arm. Her eyes were wide, filled with anger and something less definable and infinitely more exciting.

"You're wrong, Louisa Janks," Sam said softly. "If you had gone and killed yourself out there, my heart never would have recovered."

He could feel her heart pounding against his chest. Her breath came in spurts, as did his own. She was angry. And excited.

And when he devoured that excitement with a smothering kiss, attacking her as a starving man would food, she gave him more. All thoughts, all worries, all the heartache and uncertainty standing between them receded in that moment of pure physical and emotional connection. They were two people, simply a man and a woman alone without the world's influences, needy and caring of one another.

Sam knew he would rather die than let go of Louisa now.

Louisa felt as if she might die of bliss as Sam's free hand found her breast and worried the nipple until tingles of excitement shot down her flesh, over her belly and on to the secret place between her thighs. Against all reason, she was in Sam Strong's arms where she belonged. Ma had told her to go after him, and go she had, though she hadn't counted on this happening, at least not yet—not until she could believe not only in Sam's love but in his constancy, fearful as she was of being abandoned by him a second time.

For as certain as she was of anything, Louisa knew she was about to make love with Sam Strong.

She only hoped she remembered how.

Pulling free of the wonderfully smothering kiss, she gasped, "This is going so fast."

"Not fast enough."

His body taut with urgency, Sam swept her to a spot under a cottonwood, where sparse grass blanketed the dusty earth. She didn't think of resisting, nearly giddy with exhilaration at what they were about to do. In one smooth movement, he had her on her back on the earth and was resting on his side, his front pressed up against her.

His blue-green eyes connecting with hers, he vowed, "I feel as if I've waited forever."

She knew she had. No man had ravished her but for a pleasant meeting of the lips since Sam had used up her innocence, as he called it. Not that she would tell him—he would think her foolish. Maybe she was a fool for listening to her heart, for waiting six long years to assuage her loneliness, but at the moment, Louisa didn't think so. She hadn't waited consciously for him but for what was right.

It was providence that the two turned out to be one and the same.

"This feels so perfect," she whispered as he unbuttoned her shirt.

Her hand smoothed the planes of his handsome face, her fingers lightly tracing the scar. He caught her wrist and kissed her palm, as if to distract her from the unpleasant memory the scar conjured.

"You may not be a pretty tin soldier anymore, but you're still the handsomest man I've ever known."

"And you're the most stunning woman . . ."

Sam's words died off as his mouth found her breast, covered only by a light camisole. He suckled her through the material even as he slipped the strap over her shoulder and continued tugging until the breast was freed. She arched her back, pressed herself into his mouth and gasped at the sensations spiraling through her as his teeth met tender flesh.

She realized his hands were tugging at her pants, and she helped him slide them halfway down her hips, somehow without breaking the intimate connection. Then she was working on his belt and buttons and he was busy kissing her neck and her face while she freed him. She could see his tempting male flesh in her mind but wanted to do so in reality. Her insides curled as she stroked his length, which grew hotter and harder with each pass of her hand.

Remembering a love technique she'd overheard Ma's

girls talking about years ago—something meant to drive the customers wild and to guarantee they'd come back for more—Louisa had the irresistible urge to pleasure Sam in this most unusual way. She shoved at him, and, when he lifted his head from where it had once more settled at her breast, his expression was a combination of surprise and wary disappointment. She pushed again, more insistently this time, until he was on his back and she was draped half over him.

A cool breeze swept over the flesh of her exposed buttocks, reminding her of where they were. A quick glance told her both horses had their backs to the couple, giving them as much privacy as was possible under the circumstances.

Grinning, Louisa dipped her head and, using her mouth, did to Sam some of the things he'd done to her breast. When he realized what she was about, he murmured, "Louisa," and dug his fingers into her hair.

She'd never been so excited. He tasted salty . . . and maybe a little forbidden. And he was making low, exciting sounds at the back of his throat. That she had such control over a man who was used to being in command gave her a sense of great power and daring. She reveled in the odd, smooth texture of his flesh. Sam's reaction was to lift his hips and grasp her hair even tighter.

As if he couldn't help himself, he began moving, his rocking rhythm as natural as the one she remembered from their night in the cave. Her own body responded instantly. She used her lips and tongue to add to the sensations he must be feeling while her own breasts throbbed and the tender flesh secreted between her thighs burned for him.

As if he understood that, he rasped out, "Louisa . . .

now!" and pulled on her hair until she freed him and let him guide her up over his body.

Her pants were twisted around her hips and thighs, and Sam struggled with them a moment before he was able to drag the garment below her knees. Her boots stopped the pants from going any further. Not that Louisa cared. Desire sang through her, stroked her very being. She adapted, both to the soft binding around her calves . . . and to the man who so eagerly waited to fill her.

With a sense of destiny, she settled over him—knees spread around his thighs, ankles bound together inside his calves—sighing when his flesh parted hers, melded in ecstasy and made them one.

This was as it should be.

"I've waited so long for this," Sam whispered with a groan.

Louisa merely smiled, rapture—and Sam—filling her.

She felt as she did when seated on a wild horse. Reckless. Daring. Happy. She rode Sam as she would the stallion, her hips moving to an inner rhythm, her thighs tightening around his hips. He moved, too, and stroked her in every place he could reach, one hand finally settling on a breast, the other at their joining. He found and stroked her creamy hidden flesh, quickly creating a most pleasurable pressure.

Louisa moved faster, panting, trying to satisfy the urgency he created and built in her. Her gaze settled on his face, at once hard and achingly vulnerable. When his body stiffened and his features convulsed, she convulsed as well, a ripple effect starting from her center where they were joined and spreading to every inch of her being.

His fingers never stopped stroking her until she gasped

and cried out, "No more, please!" for the pleasure had become too intense.

Then, while she was in this weakened state, Sam rolled her over onto her back, somehow maintaining the coupling while taking command. He was kissing her neck, her face, her lips, murmuring her name over and over.

Louisa closed her eyes, satiated and yet not. How could she ever get enough of the man she loved?

They lay there, locked together for what seemed like forever but must have been only a few minutes before Sam started moving in her again. Louisa's eyes flashed open in surprise to meet his arrogant grin.

"Something wrong?"

Breath already coming in quick spurts, she shook her head and joined the foray, moving as much as she could while digging her nails into Sam's back and buttocks, urging him to bliss yet again.

"Uh-uh," he whispered. "This is one time when I want you to cross the finish line first."

To that end, he traced a fiery trail from her neck to her breasts with a very clever tongue. While his teeth worried her nipple, which instantly hardened, his clever fingers found their way back between their bodies so he could stroke her with the seed he had spilled in her. Louisa burned and her body filled with pressure even faster than before. Her back arched of its own volition. And before she could stop herself, she cried out loudly as he brought her to a shuddering climax more intense than the first.

Only when he seemed content that he'd brought her the ultimate satisfaction did he speed up his own movements, at the same time kissing her deeply. Once more Louisa found herself digging her nails into his buttocks to urge him on. Within seconds, his breath exploded into her mouth as his body first went taut, then collapsed on top of her.

They lay together, bodies slicked with sweat despite the cool mountain morning. Gradually, little things intruded on the focus Louisa maintained on Sam. A scrabbling in the nearby brush. An unhappy neigh coming from across the canyon—*El Tigre*—an answering snort from Defiant who still stood nearby, his back discreetly to them.

With a burst of renewed energy, Sam rolled onto his back. He laughed, the sound pleasant though tinged with no small irony.

"What's wrong?" Louisa asked, pulling up her camisole.

"Just look at us," he said, as they both straightened their clothing. "We didn't even take time to undress properly. Next time I want you completely naked."

He leaned over and gave her a smacking kiss.

That he assumed there would be a next time eased Louisa's fears a bit. She tried to appear more relaxed than she felt when she said, "Sounds like you plan to stick around a while. What about that assignment? That madman?"

His too casual "I guess I'll have to go soon" didn't exactly satisfy her. "Major Anderson came to see me yesterday and suggested I've had enough rest and recreation." He grinned. "I suppose I have now."

He was ready to go now that he'd bedded her?

Jerking her pants together at the waist, she said tersely, "I'm sure you'll do your *duty,* as always." And no doubt would steal away without telling her he was leaving like he had before.

Seemingly unaware of her growing outrage, Sam

teased, "You really are a hellion and a heartbreaker, just like I heard." He got to his feet and finished buttoning his pants. "Of course, I also heard you were a virgin goddess."

Louisa frowned. "Virgin goddess?" She didn't like his smugness. "Nobody knows exactly what I've done or with who."

He gazed at her for a moment, his voice tightening just a tad. "So you're saying it's not true?"

Louisa narrowed her gaze at him and rose, ignoring his offer to help. "You of all people know the answer!"

"I know what happened six years ago and now," he returned much more soberly, his gaze intent on her face. "What about in between?"

He was asking her about other men? Now that made Louisa furious. "What about it?" His assumption that he hadn't been the first had driven a wedge between them six years ago, and now he was questioning her again.

"You haven't, have you?"

But he didn't sound sure, making Louisa steam. Not wanting him to have the upper hand, especially when she wasn't reassured about his commitment to her—and considering she was certain he hadn't remained celibate—she said, "You don't know what you're talking about."

"I think I do." He sounded like he was trying to convince himself when he said, "You haven't been with another man or you wouldn't have been so wild in my arms just now. Admit it."

Louisa would rather be bitten by a rattler than admit any such thing. "Don't fool yourself, Sam Strong. Even I'm not stupid enough to sit around mooning over a no-account for six years."

"You didn't think I was a no-account then," he said,

suddenly sounding too sure of himself for Louisa's comfort. "You told me you loved me."

"So I was young and stupid. I grew up."

He considered that for a minute, then said, "I don't think so."

"I'm not a child any longer!" She was sick and tired of people treating her as if she were.

"I meant I don't think you've been with other men," he clarified.

"Really. Then where did I learn to pleasure you with my mouth?" she asked, purposely leaning in to taunt him by puckering her lips provocatively. "You didn't teach me that." And she was livid that whatever she might have done in his absence was some sort of issue.

Try as he might, Sam couldn't prevent his expression from tightening. Satisfied that she'd gotten to him, Louisa turned her back on the snake. What did it matter who she had or had not been with, anyhow? She hadn't known he would return for her. And she was with him now, for heaven's sake. He didn't have the right to ask for more than that. Aware of Sam's gaze burning into her, she first returned the saddle she used on the stallion to its shelter, then returned to Defiant and patted his neck affectionately.

"Hey, there, old boy, ready to get back before someone misses us?" she asked as if Sam weren't even present.

Defiant bobbed his head, hitting her in the shoulder. She kissed his velvet nose and, gathering the reins, prepared to mount.

"Louisa, you can't just leave like this."

"Oh, can't I?" she asked coolly, though inside she was seething.

She wanted Sam to rip the reins out of her hands, throw her down to the ground and make love to her yet again, all the while telling her he didn't care how many men she'd been with and promising never to leave her. Waiting a moment, she gave him his chance. When he didn't take it, she swept up onto Defiant's back and glared down at Sam.

"You'll have to leave, too. *El Tigre* doesn't know you and I don't want him upset."

"Damn it all, woman, *I'm* upset!"

Good! Louisa smiled sweetly and indicated the canyon's entrance. Sam took his cue.

Only after he was outside the gate and mounted on the roan did he demand, "You want to tell me what the hell just went on here?"

"Sam, honey, if you don't know, I'm sorely disappointed in you." She wanted him to accept her, want her, need her, never leave her—but saying so would be humiliating, especially if he wasn't willing to or couldn't do all those things. So instead, she got even for some of the hurt she felt by taking a shot at his male pride. "I thought you were more sophisticated than that. We had a great little tryst, but nothing to get in a lather about. It was fun, and I might be interested in trying you again sometime."

She might think Sam's outraged expression funny if the situation weren't so emotional.

"When hell freezes over!" he vowed, cursing under his breath and giving the roan a good kick. Squealing in surprise, his horse took off at a lope.

And Louisa turned her back on him, glad she didn't have to pretend she was sophisticated and uncaring anymore. To her fury, however, twin tears rolled down her cheeks.

Sam Strong had a way of bringing out the worst in her. Too bad she couldn't up and forget him.

9

Aztec, New Mexico Territory

Tezco was finding Louisa Janks to be unforgettable, Xosi realized as they led their band through the ruins of the ancient pueblo named Aztec, because legend had it was built by Indians related to the Aztecs of Mexico. They carefully picked their way around dirt- and scrub-covered mounds that held who-knew-what secrets of a past life. Hard to tell anyone had lived here at all.

"Perhaps I will go back for Louisa," Tezco suddenly announced, making Xosi's heart fall.

"It would be madness to return where we took other captives," she said, reminding him of the two men they'd stolen from one of the pueblos near Santa Fe. Even now their prisoners rode in the middle of the flank, each with his own guard.

"I told you about the golden-haired soldier who is after Montgomery."

Knowing he'd overheard such a conversation on the dance floor, she asked, "What of it?"

"I don't want to fight the man. If I take Louisa, maybe I can use her to keep him away."

More than likely her brother was using this as an excuse to have Louisa for himself. But, realizing that his mind was made up, Xosi didn't try to talk him out of this foolishness.

"There, ahead!" Tezco suddenly said, pointing to a rounded area in the midst of a great, open plazalike space.

Not for the first time, some unnamed fear fluttered through Xosi as they continued riding through this canyon of ghosts with its silent ruins standing sentinel over them. She could almost feel the spirits of the dead rise to watch them as they stopped at what looked like the sealed kiva Montgomery had told them about. The spiritual center of every pueblo, the kiva could only be entered through its roof via a ladder.

Tezco dismounted, giving orders to the others to do the same.

"I wonder if we will be forced to wrest our portion of the disk from the spirits," Xosi murmured, getting a distinct chill.

By early evening, they had managed to unseal the kiva's entrance and had slipped a ladder of tree branches and rope down into its depths, but the two Pueblos refused to join them in entering the sacred space.

"We will not commit such sacrilege!" the first cried.

The second added, "Anyone who dares to rob the sacred kiva of Aztec is cursed!"

Annoyance crossed Tezco's features. "Tie them up

and secure them so they can't go anywhere," he told his men. Then he lit the first of several torches they had made, and descended.

Xosi followed, ignoring her discomfort.

The Aztec kiva was antechambered and multi-leveled. Huge masonry columns supported the heavily beamed, if rotting, ceiling, and built-in benches curved along the walls. The thieves spread out and found hidden niches that yielded beads, necklaces and pottery, but to Xosi's disappointment they found nothing of real worth. In the floor was a round, navel-like notch of the *sipapu,* symbolic of where humans emerged from the earth, which gave spiritual access to still another world deeper below.

Something stopped Xosi from wanting to enter. A draft shot along her spine, making her wary. "Perhaps we should force the captives to go down there and look," she suggested.

"Ghosts can't hurt you," the practical Tezco maintained.

But an apprehensive Xosi wasn't so certain. She waited until Tezco was all the way down, until he gave a shout of triumph, before she joined him. Reluctantly, she descended, forcing her feet to her bidding. Tezco stood at a stepped altar, in the center of which lay a portion of a large golden disk stamped with an ancient design.

"Beaufort Montgomery may be crazy, but he is no liar!"

When he lifted the disk portion and showed it to her, a draft of cold, mold-laden air swept through the underground chamber. Xosi knew she should be awed by the gold. Instead, she was concerned about the spirit tunnel she knew would be secreted behind one of the walls. Stepping back, she looked around fearfully for its entrance, fingering the chain of her necklace, accidentally releasing the clasp.

The little mirror clattered to the hard earthen floor.

"At least it's not broken." Tezco placed the gold piece under one arm and squatted to pick the necklace up. As he rose and handed it to Xosi, his eyes widened.

As did hers. A face that resembled Tezco's stared out at them—a face with Tezco's features but crowned by a strange headdress and flanked by huge round earplugs. The face's ferocious gaze burned.

"Ah-hh!" As if the mirror were on fire, Xosi dropped it again. "What was that?"

"Nothing." Tezco set his jaw stubbornly. "We just thought we saw something. There are shadows down here."

But Xosi recalled Montgomery talking about Tezcatlipoca and sighting what was hidden. "It was more than a shadow."

The mirror had landed shiny side down. Tezco used the toe of a boot to turn it over. "Look, nothing but our reflections."

But Xosi thought he handled the necklace gingerly when he picked it up the second time. Her hand trembled as she took it. Another current of cold air raised her hackles as she slipped the chain about her neck and slid the mirror into the safety of the opening of her shirt.

Xosi only hoped the captives hadn't been correct that stealing from the kiva would place a curse on them all forever. She also hoped the face they had sighted in her mirror hadn't been an angry god.

* * *

Santa Fe, New Mexico Territory

Sam figured he was cursed to be alone for all time and therefore happily renewed his friendship with the liquor bottle after he left Louisa. He'd started before noon and had been drinking half the afternoon. Whiskey made a man feel better, never questioned his intentions and had no way of filling him with a horrible and unreasonable jealousy that sickened him inside.

"Bartender, my glass is empty." He banged it against the surface of the bar for emphasis.

"I thought you were going easy on the hard stuff," Jack Smith said, silver eyebrows raised in what could only be interpreted as admonishment.

Sam glared at the man through bleary eyes. "Aren't you supposed to sell as much of this swill as you can?"

"Belle gives me some discretion in that area. She don't like trouble."

"I'm no trouble. Just need another drink so I can go upstairs to my room and pass out." He'd barely slept the night before, and when he had he'd dreamed of Louisa . . . making love to some faceless cowpuncher.

Muttering under his breath about men who didn't have the good sense to know their own limit, the bartender was about to pour him another when a man spoke up. "He's had more'n enough." Jack Smith immediately pulled the bottle away from the glass and backed off.

Sam turned his glare on Chaco Jones, who stood close enough to punch for his interference . . . and whose intent gray gaze spooked him a little.

"What do you want?" Sam asked, trying not to flinch under what appeared to be an accusing stare.

"A coupla words with you. Someplace a little more

private." Chaco indicated a table toward the back of the bar area, away from the few afternoon patrons sparsely populating the place. "Now."

There was no arguing with the former gunslinger, who looked as dangerous as any man, especially with the Colt strapped to his thigh. Maybe if he were sober. And armed, of course. But not when he was leaning heavily on the bar to support himself after downing enough whiskey to numb him. Chaco could easily humiliate him by forcing him to it. With a sigh, Sam heaved himself toward the table in back, and with difficulty managed to make it there in a semistraight fashion. He threw himself into a chair and Chaco took the one opposite.

"So what is it you want to talk about?" Sam asked, figuring Louisa had something to do with this unforeseen visit—not that he would be the one to bring up her name. "Here to offer me a job?" he taunted.

Chaco's expression hardened. "You and I both know why I'm here."

"Plan to horsewhip me?"

"Maybe I should've done that the first time."

Sam stared at Chaco. "How many men have you roughed up on her behalf?"

"None."

"Then why me?"

"Because she loves you."

Sam laughed. "Me and how many others?"

Chaco wasted no time in lunging out of his seat and grabbing Sam's shirtfront, easily hauling him out of his chair. "You watch your mouth if you want to keep those pretty teeth of yours," the former gunslinger growled. "There are no other men. Never have been."

"But she said—"

"Probably a lot of fool things." Contemptuously, Chaco threw Sam back into his seat. "Louisa's got a mouth on her the size of a canyon. But her heart is even bigger. You broke it once and now it looks like you're aiming to do it again."

"She told you that?"

"She didn't have to."

Caught by Chaco's gray gaze again, Sam remembered the talk about him. That he was *di-yin,* subject to the visions of an Apache medicine man. He was related to Geronimo. The skin at the back of Sam's neck rose. Did Chaco know what part he'd played in capturing his uncle along with the last of the free-roaming Chiricahuas and boarding them on a train headed for the Florida swamps?

If so, Chaco hid his hatred well. His contempt for Sam sat on the surface, however, when he said, "I don't know what Louisa sees in you."

"Not much."

"Like hell."

"Then why did she purposely drive me away?" Sam asked, for the first time realizing exactly what Louisa had done. "She bragged about other men!"

Chaco cursed under his breath and said, "She's afraid."

"Bull. She's the bravest woman I've ever known."

"With her life, yes, but not with what's inside her. Not with her love. Did you say anything about having a future together?"

Sam thought a moment, remembered admitting he didn't know where he wanted to live or what he wanted to do. He hadn't meant without her, but he hadn't exactly put it to her that way. "No, but—"

"Or did you tell her you wanted to be a part of her life?"

"Not in so many words—"

Chaco cut him off again. "A woman needs to hear those things. Did you even tell her you love her?"

"Of course I did." He had, hadn't he? Or had that been six years ago, after which he'd gone off and left her? "I'm not really sure I used those exact words. I was thinking them, though."

"You are a fool, Sam Strong."

Sam couldn't argue. "So what the hell do I do now?"

"Depends on what you want."

"I want Louisa, man," he said without thinking. "I love her. Always have . . ."

Then he remembered what else he hadn't told her. All the life drained out of him and he slumped back against the chair. Silence stretched between them and when Sam finally looked up at Chaco, he was startled by the empathy he saw in the other man's eyes.

"You're not the only man with a secret hell," Chaco told him. "Life isn't always pretty and it sure isn't always fair, but it has a way of balancing things out in the end if you let it."

Sam swallowed hard. Chaco undoubtedly had been referring to his own background as a gunslinger. And if he didn't know better Sam would swear that Chaco had just read his mind, that he knew . . .

"If you really want Louisa, then give her a chance to understand."

"If she'll even speak to me."

"Oh, she will." For the first time since he'd entered the saloon, Chaco lightened up and actually smiled. "You might not like everything you hear, though."

"I'll chance it." He had to. Without Louisa, he had no life. "Are you going back to the ranch soon?"

"Soon as I leave here."

"Then would you give Louisa a message? Ask her to meet me at the canyon in, say, three hours."

"Around six."

Sam nodded. That would give him enough time to sober up and make himself presentable before riding out to meet her. It would give him some time to work up his courage as well, for he had to make certain no more secrets lay between them.

"You do right by Louisa," Chaco warned as he stood and adjusted the brim of his black wide-brimmed hat. "Or you'll answer to me."

"If I don't do right by her, you go ahead and shoot me dead," Sam said fervently. "Because without Louisa, my life won't be worth living."

Watching Chaco leave, Sam knew that if he messed up this time, he would never have another chance.

She would give Sam one more chance and that would be that, Louisa thought, hoping he wouldn't disappoint her yet again. Not that she had much faith. He was a stickler when his duty was involved, but somehow he didn't seem to know how to handle relationships. She'd agreed to the meeting only to please Chaco and Frances, both of whom threatened to drag her to the canyon if she refused to go on her own.

She couldn't believe her friends were worrying over her love life when their own children were sick. Actually, Phillip was on the road to recovery thanks to Magdalena's herbs, but now little Amelia was running a terrible fever and seemed to be much worse than her brother had been.

Louisa put her own worry over the children away for the moment. Having arrived at the canyon a bit early, she decided to work some more with *El Tigre,* even though she figured she wouldn't be alone for long. She had the feeling someone was following her, yet she hadn't been able to spot anyone when she'd tried. Undoubtedly her nerves were getting to her and she "sensed" Sam's imminent arrival.

The feeling wouldn't go away.

Louisa took one last look around for any sign of a rider. Not a cloud of dust in sight. Removing the split rails, she whistled, the piercing sound bouncing off the canyon's walls. The stallion was already on his way toward her as she set foot inside.

As usual, he took her mind off more serious matters and lightened her heart. Acting ferocious, he came straight toward her, then feinted at the last minute.

"You don't scare me, you rascal. Haven't you figured it out yet?" she asked.

Snorting, he circled her, then came to a complete stop within reaching distance. Louisa made a fuss over *El Tigre* for a moment before producing the hackamore from where she'd tucked it under her belt. She bridled him quickly and was in the midst of saddling the stallion when she finally heard another horse's hooves *clip-clop*ping on the sandy earth outside the canyon. She stiffened. Her heartbeat speeded up and her breath came in short spurts, making her angry. More than ever, she wanted to be in control.

And so when she heard soft footfalls some distance behind her, Louisa ignored them. Not wanting to make a fool of herself, she needed a minute to get her emotions in hand—and to that end fussed over the stallion, who threw up his head, rolled his eyes and whinnied nervously as though he'd never met Sam before, much less been ridden by him.

"Calm down," she said soothingly, running a comforting hand up the horse's neck. Sam could just wait until she was good and ready to talk to him.

"He seems pretty wild."

Louisa flew around at the lightly accented voice that did not belong to Sam Strong. Her eyes widened at the self-assured smile she encountered.

"Tezco Baca!" Today the lean and fiercely good-looking man was wearing a cowpuncher's outfit—shirt, vest and chaps over his pants—all covered with red-brown dust, as though he'd been riding long and hard. "What are you doing here?"

"I followed you from the ranch."

So she hadn't been imagining things. "Why?" she asked. "I thought you'd left the area."

"I came back . . . for you."

"What?" She laughed. "You're gonna get a job on one of the local ranches so you can court me?"

He laughed and shook his head. "My band is riding for central Mexico and I'm taking you with us."

A small part of Louisa was flattered—she wasn't blind to the man's spectacular looks—but a bigger part was wary. He seemed serious, as though he'd made up his mind and she had nothing to say about it.

Taking a step closer to *El Tigre* in case she needed a fast getaway, she said, "I don't think so."

"Then think again," he said, his soft words in contrast with the striking hard planes of his face. "You dazzle me, Louisa Janks. Not only your beauty, but your inner fire." He moved closer, making the stallion dance nervously. "When I saw you ride in the *charreada,* I recognized a kindred spirit. I knew you were the woman for me. And when you asked me to dance, I was certain you knew it also."

Stroking the stallion's neck to keep him calmer than she herself was feeling, Louisa forced herself to relax. She'd been warned her flirting was going to get her into trouble someday. Well, trouble had arrived. But she was used to dealing with infatuated ranch hands. Though handling this man might be a bit more difficult—he was in truth a real man rather than the boys who normally courted her—surely she could manage it.

"I'm flattered, I really am. But I love New Mexico—"

"You can learn to love old Mexico as well," he said, deftly cutting off her argument. "The differences are not so great as you may think. And after I finish a particular job I must do—one that will give us great wealth," he added, as if the lure of money would have the power to persuade her, "perhaps you can convince me to return here."

His sheer stubbornness and his determined expression made her edgy. "That won't be necessary since I'm not leaving."

"I would prefer you come of your own free will."

Thinking on the alternatives made Louisa's mouth go dry. "I'm spoken for," she stated, wondering if she truly was . . . and wondering where in the hell Sam had gotten himself to. It must be past six now.

Tezco went on as if she hadn't spoken. "But you will come with me if I have to tie you up to make you."

That's all she needed to hear. Louisa made her move, placing a foot in a stirrup. Tezco moved as well. And *El Tigre* shied, thwarting her. She ducked Tezco and put the horse between them.

"He'll make a fine addition to our stock," Tezco said, reaching for the stallion's bridle.

Instinctively protective of the wild horse, Louisa

lashed out at his rump, giving him a good swat as she yelled, "Hi-yah!"

The stallion shot straight for the unimpeded opening to the canyon, and Louisa was directly on his hooves. But Tezco was faster. A running tackle had them both on the ground, rolling, Louisa eating dust.

"I see I shall have to keep more than an eye on you until you give me your trust," Tezco murmured, his lips too close to her ear for comfort.

He hauled Louisa to her feet. Then she kicked at him and struck him over and over, but her furious struggle was for naught. Like the ancient warrior she had imagined him to be at the *fandango,* Tezco was incredibly strong and fit. It didn't seem to cross his mind that she might get away from him. Not that she stopped trying, not even when he dragged her to Defiant, where he produced leather thongs.

"Damn it! You can't do this! You're gonna have a couple of gunslingers on your tail!" If nothing else.

"Gunslingers? Well, they will not catch me. I have been pursued by the best of Diaz's army, yet got away."

Which didn't lift Louisa's spirits a bit. She aimed another vicious kick at Tezco before he tied her hands behind her and lifted her to the gelding's back.

"It would be better not to tire yourself out," he told her, deftly avoiding yet another blow, this from her booted toe. "We have a long journey ahead of us."

Not if she could help it. Using her legs, Louisa signaled Defiant to move off, away from the bastard. The gelding responded immediately, but so did Tezco. He grabbed Defiant's reins and soothed him in Spanish, then mounted his own horse. The look he gave her was not exactly amicable. He tacked a notice of some kind to the post.

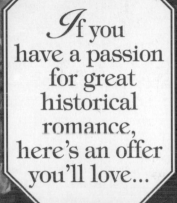

*I*f you
have a passion
for great
historical
romance,
here's an offer
you'll love...

4 FREE NOVELS

Reader Service.

Yes! I want to join the Timeless Romance Reader Service. Please
send me my 4 FREE HarperMonogram historical romances. Then
each month send me 4 new historical romances to preview without
obligation for 10 days. I'll pay the low subscription price of $4.00 for
every book I choose to keep--a total savings of at least $2.00 each
month--and home delivery is free! I understand that I may return any
title within 10 days and receive a full credit. I may cancel this subscription at any time without obligation by simply writing "Canceled"
on any invoice and mailing it to Timeless Romance. There is no
minimum number of books to purchase.

NAME

ADDRESS

CITY   STATE   ZIP

TELEPHONE

SIGNATURE

(If under 18, parent or guardian must sign. Program, price, terms, and conditions subject to cancellation and change. Orders subject to acceptance by HarperMonogram.)

AFFIX
STAMP
HERE

Before she could ask about it, he warned her, "And it will also be better if you do not try anything so foolish again. I will do whatever is necessary to keep you safe."

Thinking that sounded like a threat, Louisa furiously decided she would do whatever was necessary to get away at the smallest opening. She could only hope the stallion would run true to form and go after his mares. Someone on the ranch was sure to sight him running free. His being all tacked up would alert them that she was in trouble of some sort.

Then Chaco and Adolfo would be sure to come after her.

Looking ahead, she saw several other riders in the distance. Waiting for them? Her heart sank. Tezco had said something about a band of men. How many? She counted four, but there could be others. If Chaco and Adolfo rode out after her, they were already outnumbered. If one of the men she cared about was killed because of her . . .

No, because of Sam! she amended.

Where the hell was he? This was his fault, she decided. He'd asked her to meet him and then didn't even show up on time. As they drew closer to the waiting horseman, she cursed the day she'd met him.

If it weren't for Sam Strong, she wouldn't be in this predicament.

Sam found himself in an honest-to-God predicament when he spotted the black stallion running hell-bent-for-leather away from the canyon. It had taken him longer than he'd figured on to get sober and cleaned up. He was nearly half an hour late and Louisa was probably doing a slow burn waiting for him. On the other hand, if she knew he spotted her runaway horse and let him go, she would be madder than a hornet.

And when he realized the horse was fully tacked . . .

Heart in his throat, praying Louisa hadn't done something so foolish that she'd finally gotten herself thrown and hurt bad, he went after the horse, crossing directly in its path in an attempt to cut him off. The roan was no match for *El Tigre* in sheer speed, but Sam was counting on the stallion knowing him and feeling some irresistible urge to obey.

The black slowed but ducked his head and tried to go around Sam, who uttered a soothing, "Whoa, boy."

Although the roan wasn't the fastest horse running flat out, he'd make a good cowpuncher's mount. He could twist and turn with the best of them. Sam was able to play with the stallion, thwarting his attempts to continue in his preferred direction, finally getting close enough to the wild beast to reach out and grab the trailing reins.

Furious, *El Tigre* spun on him, shrieked and started to rear. A good, hard tug on the reins changed his mind. The stallion settled, snorting, sucking in air through his nose the second Sam let up the pressure. Though he sure as hell didn't look happy, he seemed resigned.

"That's better," Sam said, pulling alongside the stallion and maneuvering the roan next to him. Before *El Tigre* knew what he was about, Sam heaved himself onto his back. The stallion danced and Sam sat deep in the saddle, murmuring, "Steady, boy, steady." He even patted the lathered neck in an effort to calm him. Riding Louisa's horse would be the fastest way to her, and Sam's gut told him he needed to be as fast as he possibly could.

He kept his eyes on the horizon, hoping against hope to see Louisa coming toward him on Defiant in pursuit of the stallion. No such luck.

El Tigre had come directly from the canyon without veering off anywhere if his tracks could be trusted. Sam followed them to the canyon's mouth where he was in for another start.

No Defiant. No Louisa. If she'd gone after the stallion, why hadn't they crossed paths?

Sam dismounted and tied up the horses, then took a good look at the ground. His stomach clenched at the signs of a struggle—someone with larger, deeper footprints dragging someone smaller.

A large man had forced Louisa to mount Defiant, then had ridden hard in the direction opposite the ranch.

Then he noticed the wind-tattered paper stuck to the post. Stalking the several yards to get to it, Sam felt his stomach knot. He quickly read the missive.

Do not come after Montgomery if you value Louisa's life

Louisa had been kidnapped.

And by someone who was connected to Beaufort Montgomery!

Rage pushed aside his shock that one of Montgomery's followers had come as far north as Santa Fe. All Sam could think was that he'd asked Louisa to meet him out here where she had been vulnerable to attack. And he was furious that he'd been too late to prevent it. He mounted *El Tigre,* figuring the stallion could outrun anything with four legs. But he hadn't gotten far before two sets of hoofprints became half a dozen. The man who'd taken Louisa hadn't been alone.

Sam stopped and stared off into the distance, horrified. Louisa the prisoner of a handful of men who were taking her to Beaufort Montgomery, a madman who sacrificed his victims by cutting out their hearts. The implications were too morbid to contemplate.

He had to save Louisa, that was clear.

Also clear was the knowledge that he couldn't deal with Montgomery alone, after all, not to mention his followers. From the look of their tracks, these men were bandits mounted on good horses, not peasants on burros. Sam could take on one such man, maybe two or three with surprise on his side. But half a dozen? If tracking became difficult, he'd lose them for sure.

Hating to abandon the woman he loved even for a short while, Sam turned *El Tigre* back toward the canyon where he would pick up the roan before going on to the ranch for reinforcements.

Somehow, they would get Louisa back from the bastards who'd stolen her before they reached Montgomery, and if she would let him, Sam would spend the rest of his life making this up to her.

10

"*I'll get Louisa back* if it's the last thing I ever do," Sam told Chaco the next morning as the crew they'd managed to gather overnight got ready to leave the de Arguello spread. Guilt sluiced through him. "If I hadn't been late, this wouldn't have happened."

The ex-gunslinger shook his head. "There's no use placing blame, or we're all in trouble—my wife and I told her to go meet you. And Louisa was out at that corral every day as it was. Somebody with bad intentions could've happened along at any time."

But Sam refused to excuse himself.

Or the kidnappers. He was going to make the bastards pay.

He brooded and Chaco remained silent as they packed the last boxes of ammunition. The older man looked dead tired and Sam knew the fatigue was twofold. Not only had Chaco spent the night gathering supplies and rounding up pack animals and men, he'd also had to deal with his little daughter's life-and-death illness. The three-year-old was running a fever so high that a doctor was on his way from Santa Fe. A Pueblo woman skilled with medicinal herbs was attending to the girl now, while Frances Jones hovered at her child's bedside, totally distraught.

"I'd be coming along myself, if it wasn't for Amelia," Chaco said.

"I know."

And Luz was in labor, or the tough little Mexican Adolfo would be saddling up as well.

"But Javier and Ben are good men. They can ride and shoot with the best of 'em."

As well as fight over Louisa. Though happy to enlist anyone he could find at such short notice, Sam had been doubtful when Chaco had told him the two youths wanted to head out on the rescue mission. He'd prefer the handpicked soldiers Major Anderson had offered but had been told he'd have to wait for them for at least a day or two.

With Louisa involved, Sam didn't want to wait one hour.

"Javier and Ben will behave," Chaco assured him. "Or else you can send them home or shoot them where they stand. I told them I gave you my permission for either."

Sam had already informed his small posse that they'd have to take orders from an army captain or they could stay behind. Both Javier and Ben had soberly agreed. Eager to start, they sat their horses as Sam finished tying a diamond hitch on one of the pack mules he was borrowing from Chaco. Both Irish and his roan had made the long journey from Arizona to New Mexico, and Sam wasn't sure they were up to another so soon. Though he had a few reservations about *El*

Tigre's temperament, he'd decided the mustang would be a tough, surefooted mount.

He would need a tough mount if they were forced to track the kidnappers down into the Mexican mountains, where he figured bandits would flee, followers of Montgomery or not.

"Wanta cup of kick-mule coffee before you start?" Chaco asked, seemingly aware of Sam's own fatigue.

"Not a bad idea."

He'd been up most of the night himself trying to find a good tracker. He'd settled for a Jicarilla Apache who worked for the army. At least Major Anderson had been able to come up with that. Sam told himself he'd probably do better without a crew of uniforms anyway. Some people who could help them might be scared off. Anderson had been surprised he'd wanted to head out so fast, but Sam had insisted he had a direct and vital lead. He'd shied away from admitting his personal interest.

Chaco led him into the kitchen of the adobe ranch house and poured them both mugs of steaming liquid from the coffeepot. "Could even fill up a canteen for you to take along if you want."

"Sounds good. When it's empty, we can use the canteen for water." In dry desert country, one could never have too many. "I hope the tracker will be able to locate springs when we need them." Such as when they were too far from a town or a ranch's wells.

"That map I gave you will help."

It was a crude chart on which Chaco had marked water holes he remembered from the past. As a gunfighter, he'd worked for clients as far south as Texas and northern Mexico.

Sam observed the other man closely. Though he was

trying to keep his face emotionless, Chaco's tight mouth and sad eyes revealed his worry for Louisa.

"You have to take care of your little girl," Sam told him. "And your wife. I understand. Louisa will understand, too."

Chaco stared down into his mug. "I know what life can hold for a breed. She's been like a younger sister to me. If Amelia gets better in a few days, if Adolfo is available, we could set out after you."

"Do as you think best. In a few days, I plan to have found them."

And unless the madman were with the bandits, to hell with the scheme of dealing with Montgomery. If Sam found Louisa, he'd bring her back safe and sound. To hell with the army.

He'd rescue Louisa if he had to die for her.

Which would be ironic, since, after so many years, Louisa Janks was the reason he finally wanted to live.

The Sierra Madre, Mexico

"The gods will live!" shouted Beaufort Montgomery to his crowd of followers. "They will make their full presence known in the world again! Tonight we shall feast to that!"

A cheer went up in the steep-sided barranca, a canyon where they'd found the hidden pyramid just as Beaufort had predicted. Surrounded by the isolation of dry, rugged mountains, most of the structure had been buried, appearing as a huge mound covered with soil, rocks and scrubby desert plants. It had taken more than thirty of his fifty-some disciples to unearth an upper tier of the stone building.

But unearth it they had, and if there had been any doubters before, there were none now. He blessed the day so long ago when he'd purchased the ancient Aztec codex, then found the medallion, deciphered its inscription and invoked its powers. He'd known he'd been touched by divinity then, that divine presence had begun to possess him. It had helped him shed his attachment to his base human life by showing him the true glory of death and pain. At least the Civil War's battles had served some purpose.

His followers scurried about, building fires, carrying water from spring-fed wells near the pyramid, choosing a steer from the herd they'd brought across the desert plateau between the east and west ranges of the Sierra Madre. Of course, the animal would be killed in the correct sacrificial manner before they roasted its flesh.

But first the ground needed to be consecrated with human blood.

Realizing the peasants were not aware that they needed further personal commitment, Beaufort climbed to the top of the pyramid and shouted for attention. A hush fell over the assemblage.

"Respect for the gods! Fall to your knees!" And as they did so, he went on, "Those of you who have knives, prick your skin, let the blood fall onto the earth. Then pass the knives on to the next person!"

Some looked frightened.

To reassure them, he took out a narrow, sharp blade of his own. "Do not shame yourselves by fearing a tiny wound. See what Quetzalcoatl will do for you!"

Holding the knife aloft, he muttered a blessing in Nahuatl and plunged it into his chest. Blood splattered his robe and an *ah-h-h* came from the audience.

But he felt no pain, not even as he slid the knife out again. He had no fear, knowing the wound would quickly heal. He would not die, being a god.

"Blood for Quetzalcoatl! He is willing to shed his for you! Give your blood to him!"

Already his disciples were following his command, pricking their arms or hands, sometimes their faces. Like him, the truly devout would find that their wounds healed quickly. As for those with less faith, they would take their chances with infection. Beaufort wasn't concerned—if such people died so ignobly, they simply weren't brave enough to live.

West Texas

Louisa questioned her own bravery when the Mexicans holding her hostage emerged from a dry riverbed and surprised several cowboys working with some cattle. She wasn't sure who shot first, but her mouth was dry with fear as Tezco dragged her off Defiant and shoved her back down the riverbank.

She crawled up again to peek through the tall, weedy grasses just in time to see one cowboy riding off hell-bent-for-leather and a second shot right out of his saddle. Horses milled and bullets continued to fly from the guns of the Mexicans and two cowboys who'd been left behind on foot. A yelp sent a chill through her. Someone had been shot. Vastly outnumbered, the last man raised his hands and surrendered his gun.

Louisa climbed on up the bank as the band swarmed around their newest captive. They tied his hands and lifted the other cowboy to his feet. The man had been shot in the shoulder. One of the Mexicans had been wounded as well; he'd taken a bullet in the thigh. But Tezco, the band's leader, seemed more unhappy over the stranger who'd fallen from his saddle.

After squatting to examine the body, the handsome Mexican shouted, "He is dead!" His face flushed with anger. "We are thieves, not murderers!"

One of his men shrugged. "They shot first."

"There was no choice in the matter, brother." Voice cold, Xosi approached Tezco. "And better them than us."

Louisa had learned that Xosi was female and Tezco's sister on the very first night they'd ridden away from *El Tigre*'s corral. The striking woman was temperamental and obviously disliked her. Every evening before the band retired, Xosi sat near the campfire, smoking one *cigarillo* after another and glaring daggers at Louisa. Once she had even expressed outright hatred when Tezco wasn't looking. Louisa tried to stay out of her way.

Which wasn't easy, considering they were all traveling and camping together. Sometimes Louisa daydreamed about hanging Xosi and Tezco from tall trees . . . after she'd first strung up Sam Strong, of course.

At least the gun battle had made Louisa forget about her angry, obsessive musings. Real death lay on the plains; glancing back at the fallen cowboy as they rode away, she swallowed the big lump in her throat.

They rode onward at a fast pace, despite carrying the wounded and driving a steer. Tezco spurred his own mount, leading Defiant and grumbling about the Texas Rangers he feared would now be on their trail.

Louisa only wished the Texas Rangers would find them. From the beginning, she'd hoped someone would come after her, that Sam would remedy the situation he had created. But after days of travel, she hadn't sighted a soul. Today, in West Texas, a figure on horseback would be easy to spot. The never-ending, dry brown prairie rolled to the horizon beneath a sky that seemed even larger than New Mexico's.

Louisa spent most of her waking hours fighting fatigue and discomfort as the sun blazed down on them. They rarely stopped to rest, choosing to chew on jerky and stale tortillas instead of taking noonday meals. To keep her mind off heat and sore muscles, she played mental games, visualizing every sort of escape. When she had run out of ideas, she conjured schemes of revenge, with torturing Sam Strong her favorite. Such anger stopped her from recalling any lovemaking, any tender moments they'd shared.

She didn't want to feel sorrow, which would weaken her. She wanted cold fury and keen craftiness as her saddlemates.

But today, Louisa nearly drifted off in the hot afternoon sun. Only some lusty shouts from the bandits awakened her in time to keep her from falling off her mount. With her dislodged hat hanging from her neck by its string, she gaped at the mountain range rising straight ahead, the gray-brown peaks like iron fists punching up through the prairie into the sky.

Tezco turned in his saddle. "We will be camping early tonight, near a spring. There will be fresh water and grass for the horses."

Good. Poor Defiant. Though he had been traveling pretty well, thanks to the good care she'd always given him, the aging gelding had lost weight. She prayed he wouldn't grow sick or unsound—if the bandits forced her to abandon him in some desert, she knew she'd fall into a mad rage, what Mexicans called "having the *coraje,*" and would fight her captors tooth and nail until they had to kill her.

The weary party made their way up a faint trail leading into the foothills. Reaching the higher elevation, they zigzagged through piles of rocks, skirted the edge of a sheer drop, and entered a long, stony passageway that finally opened into a narrow canyon. There the vegetation grew thick and green, in contrast to the sparse pickings they'd passed so far.

As the band halted, Louisa heard a sweet musical sound—water rippling—and saw a thin spray trickling down a tiered wall of rock perhaps three hundred feet high. At the bottom was a dark pool about a hundred feet in diameter, draining into a creek that flowed for only a few dozen yards before it was swallowed up by the thirsty soil. Spring fed, the place was an oasis that would keep some plants green all year round.

Again there were whoops from the bandits, who slid off their horses to fill their sombreros with water. Tezco dismounted and helped Louisa down so Defiant could join the other horses for a long drink. Then the animals began munching the long grass that sprouted everywhere, even between rocks.

Louisa held out her hands for Tezco to undo the leather cords binding her wrists, a luxury granted for a few hours once the band stopped for the night.

"You may wander freely this evening," he told her. "You cannot escape. This canyon has only two entrances and I am posting a guard at each. Tomorrow we shall make our way along a mountain trail leading down to the Rio Grande."

The Rio Grande. Once they entered the wilds of Mexico, Louisa would have an even more difficult time getting away. She refused to let her hopes sink, though, refused to believe she was doomed to be a bandit's plaything.

Distressed, she walked away, indicating she had personal needs to take care of. Tezco let her go, as usual treating her with more deference than she'd expected. He hadn't tried to rape her, at least not yet. Thinking on that, she put a few yards between herself and the camping area, gazing closely at her surroundings. Sumac bushes and masses of cockleburs grew among grasses and low-growing oaks. Some of the plants poked their heads out of deep crevices. Perhaps there would be smaller canyon offshoots along tomorrow's trail. If she were lucky and could find a hiding place, she might be able to disappear.

At the moment, though, hunger would soon beckon her back to camp. Having butchered the steer and started a fire, the bandits were roasting beef for the evening meal. Meanwhile, a man was tending to the wounded, including the cowboy they'd captured. Now they had four male captives. Louisa had long ago noticed the two Pueblos being held by the band—the missing men Magdalena had spoken of. She could understand Tezco carrying off a woman, but why would bandits want captives?

Puzzling on that, she cringed when one of the wounded men screamed. No wonder—she knew the bullets were being dug out with a heated knife. Cauterization might help the wounds to heal but certain herbs would be better. Glancing back at the cockleburs, Louisa remembered Magdalena showing her how the plant's prickly pods could be opened and the seeds within crushed as a treatment for abrasions and wounds.

Well, much as she thought she'd like to hang a few people, she hated letting anyone suffer terrible pain.

When Tezco approached, no doubt to see what she was up to, she asked, "Do you have a pair of gloves I can borrow?"

He raised his brows. "Gloves?"

"I want to pick some cockleburs—the seeds inside can be used to treat the men's wounds."

"Are you a *bruja*?"

Would it frighten him to think she was? She hoped so. "I know something about medicinal plants."

To her disappointment, he didn't seem concerned. "Wait here." He returned to the campfire area and came back with a piece of soft leather and a small wooden bowl. "I will help you with these plants."

"I don't need any help."

But he shadowed her anyway, following her even further from the camp, standing far too close and watching as she pulled several barbed, sticky burrs off their dried stalks to deposit them in the bowl.

"Is it the captured *vaquero* you wish to treat or my man?"

Removing one burr from its two-foot stalk, she noticed a stand of smelly neighboring plants known as jimson or locoweed. Her pulse picked up. "I intend to treat both."

Tezco laughed softly. "You are so kind? So selfless?"

"Not everyone is a kidnapper and a thief."

Though she wondered if she should try her luck as a poisoner. If she managed to pluck some prickly fruit from the jimsonweed, then somehow mix a little of its juice into the spicy beans they ate every day, the bandits could get very sick.

"Not every thief is evil," Tezco told her.

"Oh, sure, I bet you're a regular Mexican Robin Hood."

"Who is this Robin Hood?" Tezco came up behind her, plucking the bowl from her fingers and tossing it to one side. Then he pressed her against him. "If you are kind to some man, *querida,* I want him to be me."

Surprised and uncomfortable, she pushed against his chest and gazed longingly at the jimsonweed. "Let go."

"Must I anchor your arms against your sides?" he asked, struggling with her and looking annoyed as he did so.

His muscles were like bands of steel. Louisa caught her breath as he angled his head to kiss her. She tried to turn her face away. "Leave me alone!" As angry as she was with Sam, he was the only man she would ever kiss willingly again.

"*Querida,* lovely one," Tezco said reprovingly, "do not fight me so. You will like it."

His lips covered hers with practiced mastery. One strong hand holding her wrists, he slid the other up and down her spine so that her back curved and her breasts flattened against his chest. Murmuring endearments, he rocked his hips so that she'd feel the hard proof of his desire.

Now he's going to rape me, Louisa thought with despair. Desperate, barely thinking, she panicked, poked a leg between his and shoved her knee hard into his groin.

Tezco grunted and bent over double.

Giving her a chance to run.

Her heart pounded as she flew along. She hadn't the slightest idea of where she was going, except that it was away from Tezco and the camp. Burrs tore at her trousers. A weed-shrouded rock tripped her. She went down hard.

As she struggled to her feet again, her path was blocked.

Eyes narrowed, a glittering knife in her hand, Xosi sneered. "At last, I shall carve you up like a chicken. You will not be pretty anymore when I finish with you, *puta*. . . . Whore! You should have been grateful that my brother deigned to so much as look at you!"

When she lunged, Louisa feinted, knowing the jealous woman truly intended to kill her. She dropped into a defensive crouch, watching Xosi's knife hand, knowing she had to be quick enough to grab the other woman's wrist.

If she failed . . .

Louisa's biggest regret was that she would never see Sam Strong again, much less get even with him.

11

"I will make you pay for the problems you have caused!" Xosi shouted, and launched herself at Louisa.

Eyes on the knife, Louisa caught hold of the other woman's wrist as they hit the ground together. Xosi screamed with rage and rolled, taking Louisa with her, fighting to free her knife hand. The Mexican woman was strong but Louisa somehow managed to hold on.

A crowd of bandits gathered, whistling and shouting encouragement.

One man even laughed as he called out, "Scratch and bite, *gatas! Ai-ee!*"

Not amused, Louisa kicked at Xosi, finally knocking the woman away from her. The knife flew out of the Mexican's hand. Louisa jumped for the weapon, but Xosi was quicker. Rolling to her feet, Tezco's sister once again attacked, the vicious blade aimed at

Louisa's middle. Louisa feinted, whipped around and slammed Xosi in the back with closed fist. Screeching, Xosi stumbled and nearly fell.

Louisa went for a rock, only to have Xosi charge, knocking her to the ground a second time. Forced to concentrate once again on avoiding the knife blade, Louisa held on to the woman's wrist and gritted her teeth as Xosi tried to bite, kick and pull her hair. Blind with rage, she shoved Xosi backward and punched her in the face.

Blood streamed from the Mexican woman's nose as she scrambled to her feet. Before Louisa could rise as well, Xosi threw a handful of sandy dirt in her face. Temporarily blinded, Louisa desperately tried to clear her eyes . . . only to see the knife plunging down toward her. . . .

"Stop! Now!"

The knife hovered in midair, inches from its target, then withdrew as a recovered Tezco pulled the kicking, swearing Xosi away. Holding his sister firmly around the middle, he tore the knife from her grasp and let her screech to high heaven.

Then he yelled at the gathered bandits, "Go back to the campfire! This is not a spectacle for your amusement!"

Grumbling, the men moved away and Xosi finally settled down. But as her brother released her, she glared at Louisa. "How can you protect this—this *puta!*"

"She is not your worry," Tezco said firmly.

"But she should be yours—there will be hell to pay because of her. She is nothing but trouble!"

Tezco remained silent and Xosi stomped away.

Louisa struggled to her feet and dusted some of the grime off her clothing, keeping her gaze lowered.

From the frying pan into the fire. Who knew what the man would do to punish her for hurting him?

No matter that she'd only been trying to protect herself.

But he now acted as if nothing had happened and suggested they walk back to the camp. Passing the spot where he'd tossed the wooden bowl, he stooped to gather up the scattered burrs.

"You need to make the medicine, yes?"

Was he really going to forget about everything? She took a deep breath. "I could use a few more cockleburs." And a chance at the jimsonweed.

"I will gather them for you." He kept one eye on her as he plucked more burrs, a few minutes later asking, "Is this enough?"

She'd forget the jimsonweed, at least for the moment. "That's plenty." She'd try to sneak out of camp after dark. "I'll need a knife to open the burrs."

"I will do that for you as well."

Because, she was certain, he thought she'd try to carve him up. He didn't trust her, with good reason. Not that she would ever again try to disable him unless she was forced to do so. He seemed to be the only person with any power over Xosi, who wanted to kill her. Temper blunted by the knife fight, Louisa knew she was going to have to keep her emotions in check, play the cards that had been dealt her and wait for the right time and place to make a move.

She memorized the exact location of the clump of jimsonweed as they ambled back to the camp.

After Tezco opened the cocklebur pods, Louisa squeezed out the seeds and used a bent spoon to crush them into a pulp. Then she added water to spread the substance more easily. Using strips of cloth as bandages, she smeared the medication on them and applied them to the men's wounds. Tezco's man flinched with pain. The cowboy named Roberto tried to smile as Louisa placed the bandage on his shoulder. He was of Mexican heritage, if not birth, and he thanked Louisa in both Spanish and English.

In the latter tongue, he also asked, "Why are we being held prisoner?"

"I don't know." She gave him a sympathetic look. "I'm a captive myself. I don't even know where we're going, except that it's somewhere in Mexico."

She knew Tezco overheard but he didn't offer any explanations. He allowed her to wash her hands and the utensils in the pool of water, then walked her toward the fire so she could get some supper. Her middle felt hollow. Eagerly taking a tin plate piled high with meat, she added beans and several crude cornmeal tortillas.

Tezco took a plate for himself and sat down beside her. After wolfing down several bites of food, he asked, "Who is this Robin Hood?"

Frances had told her about the children's book she'd sent away for several years ago. "Robin Hood is a legend from old England. He was a thief who robbed from the rich and gave to the poor."

"Ah, I see." Tezco wiped up some beef juice with a tortilla. "Perhaps I am like such a man."

"Robin Hood didn't carry off women."

"I give to the poor . . . some of the silver I steal," he argued.

"Oh?"

"My bandits are merely thieves, most of us forced into such a life." He sounded earnest. "My father was an honest man, a rancher who didn't agree with

Porfirio Diaz's methods. The *rurales* shot my parents in their bed one night, and Diaz helped himself to their land."

Something in his tone and expression made her think he was telling the truth. "When you were a child?"

"A very young man. I had to take care of my little sister from then on. She has had a very hard life."

Louisa couldn't help adding, "And now she has a very hard attitude."

"She is jealous of you. But she will learn to accept you."

Louisa hoped she wouldn't be around long enough to receive so much as a crooked smile from the vicious Xosi.

He added, "You will also learn to accept me."

Louisa's blood chilled, and she silently called out to Sam to find her. But no, she couldn't count on him, a man who'd run out on her once before. Knowing she could only count on herself, she waited until Tezco took her plate back to the band's cook, then rose and sneaked away from camp.

A full moon had risen and flooded the landscape with pale light. She glanced at the horses, tethered and grazing, and stared in the direction of the canyon's mouth. She was certain the lookout Tezco had posted was sitting there with a rifle across his knees. Insects twittered loudly and a breeze rustled through the leaves. Still, Louisa heard the soft footfalls coming up behind her.

Tezco laughed. "Now where are you going, *querida?*"

Stiffening, for he might try something again, she said, "I want to check on my horse."

"He has already been taken care of."

"I still want to see him."

As Tezco ambled along a few feet behind her, she found Defiant in the small herd and spoke softly to him. He nickered and she kissed his nose before checking his back for saddle sores, then running her hands up and down his legs to check for swelling. Finally, she examined his feet for loose stones. Thank goodness, the horse seemed fine.

"You're a good old boy, aren't you?" she whispered, patting his neck. But she thought his big, liquid eyes seemed sad and scared. "Yeah, I know." She wished they were home, too.

"You are very skilled with horses," Tezco remarked.

"I break them, train them. It's the way I make my living."

Despite her trying to harden her heart against him, she envisioned Sam, a picture of fluid grace when he'd raced her on Irish. Her throat tightened. He'd always been nearly as skilled with horses as she. . . .

"Perhaps you work too hard." Tezco's low voice brought her back to the present. "A beautiful woman like you should have a softer life, with servants."

"I like my way of life."

"You would choose such, even if you were wealthy?"

"I don't care about wealth."

Or settling down—no doubt he thought he could tame her. Disgusted, she stared past him at the quiet camp, fires getting lower as the darkness deepened. Most people had stretched out in their blankets, though the night was young.

"I assume you *do* want to be wealthy," she continued, "though I don't see how your trip up to New Mexico Territory did much good. You aren't leading pack mules loaded with gold, and your captives aren't worth anything."

"Not to most people, I agree."

An odd answer, one that puzzled her even more. "What are you going to do with those men?"

She couldn't see his expression but the way he was standing, with arms quietly folded across his chest, made her think he was assessing her.

"You do not need my reasons."

She kept at him. "I don't know why you're being so secretive about your prisoners. It seems crazy."

"Believe me, I am not the crazy one."

She nearly stumbled over an indentation in the ground. In the moonlight, it looked like a deep, ancient hoofprint. Having wondered about similar markings she'd seen on the way to this canyon, she said, "I heard some of your men say they'd never been out of Mexico before. But this looks like a trail."

"One that is not ours, though we will follow it to the Rio Grande and pick it up on the other side. Many years ago, the Comanche rode out of Texas every autumn to terrorize the Mexican countryside."

Comanche? Louisa felt a little thrill.

"*Ranchos* and villages could count on the Indians arriving as soon as the harvest was over. There were so many, they came so often, their horses' hooves cut trails that remain even today. Now the peasants thank *Dios* the Comanche ride no more. They stole horses, burned, killed, even attacked by moonlight."

Louisa thought of painted, easy-riding warriors. She thought of her father, whom she'd never known. "I'm half-Comanche."

"Ah, no wonder you are so brave and fierce."

"And no wonder I don't choose a soft life."

Even in the dim moonlight, she could see his smile. "I will always allow you to do as you like, *querida,* if that is what is worrying you. I do not want your spirit broken. I only ask that you be true to me."

Untouched by his reassurances, she gritted her teeth. If she did what she liked, she'd be riding out of here. "You kidnapped me. We're not having a love affair."

"Not yet."

Not ever. Sam was the only man she wanted to share a bed with. But best not to challenge him openly, not when he had her so completely in his power. Intent on tying her wrists for the night, Tezco slipped a couple of leather cords from his belt and indicated she hold her hands together in front of her.

"Why are you doing this? You posted guards. I have no place to go."

"You may remain free as long as I can watch over you. But when I need to sleep, you must be bound. You might try something foolish and hurt yourself."

How nice that he worried about her. But she held out her wrists. Thank God, he simply tied them, making no attempt to so much as kiss her, much less drag her into his bedroll. Her action this afternoon might have made him realize she wasn't thrilled by the idea. Maybe he would back off. Perhaps he really was decent-hearted, though a thief.

Though she still wondered what he was doing with those captives.

Tezco spread out her blanket, then his own several feet away. Wishing her good night, he lay down and wrapped the blanket tightly around him. Night at a higher elevation was sure to be on the chilly side.

Louisa pulled her blanket up to her chin. The moon floated in the sky high above. She stared at the glowing orb, huge and white-faced. Thousands of stars winked and clustered on either side as if paying it homage. She could hardly believe the same beautiful sky was at this very moment shining down on the people she loved so far away—Ma, Frances, Chaco, Adolfo and Luz, the children . . . Sam.

No, she didn't want to include Sam, she thought, appalled when she realized a tear had seeped out of one eye. She swiped at it angrily. Where the hell had Sam been the night she'd been kidnapped? Where the hell was he now? As usual, she couldn't trust him. He'd probably turned his back and taken off, the same way he left her in Santa Fe six years before.

Louisa sighed, still gazing at the moon, and mused on moonlight raids. If she squinted her eyes, she could imagine Comanche warriors riding through the night's shadows. She could also imagine herself with them, her hair loose and twined with feathers. She'd be ready to screech war calls, shoot arrows, steal horses, go after the White Eyes soldiers.

Like Sam.

His too familiar face haunted her inner visions. No matter how she tried to forget about him, memories of Sam always returned. In disgust, she closed her eyes and told her imagination to quit playing tricks on her. Like her body, it obviously needed rest.

West Texas

Monte Ryerson stood frozen in the moonlight, for a moment thinking his imagination played tricks on him. A figure on horseback galloped past the barn straight toward him, leading another horse with what appeared to be a dead body stretched across the saddle.

Jake O'Brian spotted his employer and pulled his

foaming mount up in a flurry of dust. "They killed Tobias! God only knows what they did with Roberto and Shorty!"

"Who? Where?" Monte struggled to keep his composure. He grabbed the reins of the horse that carried the dead man, recognizing him even in the semidarkness. Grief twisted his gut—he'd known Tobias for almost twenty years. "What happened, man?"

"It was all so fast, I ain't rightly sure." But as Jake dismounted, the words spilled out. "The far west range—we was counting cattle, rounding up some stray steers. Then they hit us, rode up out of a dry riverbed. Musta been at least fifteen or twenty of 'em."

"Rustlers?"

"Guess so. They was armed to the teeth and looked to be heading for Mexico. A pack of bandits, if you ask me."

Monte noticed lantern lights flickering from the direction of the bunkhouse. The other ranch hands had heard the galloping hooves and were coming to investigate.

Jake went on, "Tobias and me, we rode off when bullets started flying. I was some ways away before I realized he'd been shot off his horse. And the other two hadn't got the chance to mount and follow either." He heaved a sigh. "Guess they was pinned down by gunfire. I shoulda stayed and fought for them."

"And then you'd be dead, too."

"Or would've disappeared along with 'em," the man admitted. "When I rode back to get Tobias, there was nary a trace of Roberto or Shorty. Nothing but a hat on the ground and all those hoofprints heading south."

Which was strange. Only Indians took prisoners and there were no more free-ranging bands around.

As soon as the hands found out what was going on,

Monte ordered one of them to take care of the horses and a couple of others to carry poor Tobias to the barn and wrap him in a blanket. Either they'd have to bury him on the ranch or send his body to the undertaker in El Paso tomorrow morning.

He escorted Jake into the ranch house and tried to get him to eat, but all the man wanted was a stiff drink. His grizzled, mustached face was pale, his eyes haunted.

Angry, Monte made a decision. "We're going after them."

Jake merely raised one bushy brow. "Don't want to notify the sheriff or the Rangers?"

"It'd take too long and I don't know as they'll want to cross the Rio Grande. We need to pick up those tracks while they're fresh." Though Monte could probably follow the bandits anywhere as long as rain didn't wash out their prints; tracking was something he'd learned from his Comanche father. "Maybe there's some way we can get Roberto and Shorty back alive."

"I'm with you."

"Then you'll need to get a good night's sleep. Meantime, I'll ask someone to line up some fresh horses and supplies for the morning. Maybe a couple of the other men will be willing to come along, too."

Even if chasing bandits weren't part of their jobs. Even though Monte himself had ranch duties and was awaiting the arrival of Captain Sam Strong. Roberto had a family—he couldn't face them if he didn't try to get the man back.

"Where are you going tomorrow, Pa?"

Monte turned at the sound of his son's voice. Stephen propped his rangy frame against the door lintel. He was the only parent his kids had, Monte thought guiltily.

But he also felt a responsibility for the people who worked for him.

"Jake and I are gonna be gone for a couple of days. There's been some trouble." Might as well be honest. "Tobias is dead. Roberto and Shorty are missing."

Stephen reacted immediately, straightening, his expression shocked. Raised on a ranch, the boy had dealt with death before, if not the violence of a random shooting. And he'd liked Tobias. "What happened? The rustlers?"

"Probably. A band of Mexicans headed for the border."

"I'll get my stuff together—"

"No!" Monte watched his son's jaw harden in that stubborn way that made him resemble his mother. "Your sisters need someone to take care of them. I want you to stay here."

Still, the boy objected. "Pa—"

"You'll be in charge, son, the man of the family and the owner of this ranch."

Stephen's expression changed as he suddenly realized the implications and started to worry. "Are you saying you might not make it back?"

"There's always that possibility." Monte rose to pat Stephen on the shoulder. "But I'm too tough to go down easy. And I don't think there's many Mexicans who want to start another war." Not after Texas and the U.S. defeated them in 1848. "All I'm asking is the return of my men."

He would use threats and persuasion first, the promise of gold and cattle second. Bullets would be a final resort.

The thought of doing battle yet again was a real nightmare.

*   *   *

Plagued by nightmares, Tezco had resorted to rising in the middle of the night and taking long walks around the camp. That seemed to halt the bad dreams and made him tired enough to sleep soundly until the sun came up.

He wished he and Xosi had made amends; he wished he could talk to her. She was the only one to whom he might admit such troubles. He was being haunted by the mysterious, fierce face they had both seen in her mirror that night at Aztec. The strange entity appeared at the start of each of his nightmares, snarling some garbled language before taking off on the night wind. Then he himself became the entity, gazing down at a shadowy pattern of mountains and canyons revealed by pale moonlight.

A practical, not particularly religious man, Tezco had no idea as to what was causing this vision to haunt him. But if the dreams didn't go away, he was seriously considering seeking out a priest or a *bruja*.

Xosi would be surprised, he thought, glancing toward her sleeping form as he stirred the embers of the fire. Once more wishing he had her counsel, he sat down and stared into the leaping flames. When he started to get sleepy, Tezco finally rose and returned to his sleeping place. Thinking he had caught a sudden movement from Louisa's bedroll, he stood still for a moment, waiting. But she remained quiet; she had probably only turned over in her sleep.

He sighed, wishing he could wake her, assure her that everything would be all right. The captives she was so concerned for would be set free as soon as he gained access to Beaufort Montgomery's *tesorería*.

Though she claimed wealth meant nothing, she would surely be impressed with all the horses she could buy with Aztec gold.

Imagining Louisa's pleasure, Tezco could almost taste her sweet, soft kisses, feel her taut body pressed against his own. If only they were that close now. A little lovemaking would make him forget about the nightmares. But so far Louisa seemed unaffected by him. Not that he planned to give up, nor to take the young woman against her will. He had been truthful when he said he did not want to break her spirit.

Because he desired her love.

Tezco realized that with surprise. He was *in love* for the first time in his life—the reason he risked his sister's wrath. And that was why he would stubbornly wait for both women to come around.

Now if only he could dream of Louisa instead of snarling faces, his sleeping problems would be of a much more pleasant ilk.

12

West Texas

Sam often dreamed of Louisa. The first night his search party camped in Texas, he awakened out of a dead sleep, fully expecting her to be lying in his arms. His heart nearly broke when he realized she wasn't there, would never be there unless he could get her back from the kidnappers they'd been chasing for days.

With a sense of urgency, he rose. Light barely glimmered in the east, announcing the arrival of dawn. He went to the campfire, stoked it and added a few more branches of dried brush. Then he started cooking breakfast with the last ration of bacon. They'd have to make do with jerky, hardtack, coffee and beans from now on.

The smell of frying meat awakened Ben and then Javier. They got up, yawned and started packing up their bedrolls.

"Where's the Apache?" Ben asked, running a hand through his tousled sandy hair.

Sam shrugged. "Don't know. Around here somewhere." He never could figure out where or when the Indian slept, but the man didn't make his bed near the campfire.

"Prints still headed south?" Sam asked when the tracker put in an appearance in time for mess call.

The man grunted. "They ride for Mexico. Now there's more, maybe nineteen or twenty mounted men."

"More?" Javier raised a dark brow.

They'd all been discouraged when they got some miles from Chaco's place and realized they were up against more than a dozen men. Not that Ben or Javier had expressed any more desire to turn back than had Sam.

"Was a fight over that way." The Apache gestured to the plains beyond the dry riverbed. "Saw some rifle shells, blood, a flat place where somebody fell. The Mexicans maybe killed a man and took two others."

"Took them?" said Sam. "Captives?"

The Apache's expression didn't change. "There's prints from two more horses now . . . and a steer."

"*Dios,*" Javier muttered. "I can understand the steer. I can even understand someone wanting to steal Louisa. But captives? What are these men about?"

Sam had some idea—more victims for Montgomery. Not that he'd gotten around to telling the others about the whole situation. Maybe he shouldn't.

"We'd better get going, don't you think?" asked Ben. "Those bandits are still traveling fast."

Faster than Sam had thought they would. That had also been discouraging. He gazed around at the Texas prairie, suddenly seized by an idea.

"I'm not sure about exactly where we are. I need to

look at a map before we set out." Sam dumped the
dregs of his coffee on the ground, then riffled through
his saddlebags. When he found what he was looking
for, he unfolded the piece of paper and raised his
brows at the markings Major Anderson had made on
it. As luck would have it . . . "We might be able to
come up with some reinforcements, more supplies."

If the riverbed was where he thought it was, Monte
Ryerson's spread was only a few miles away. They
could be camped on the man's land right now.

"Reinforcements?" repeated Javier, frowning.

Which was the extent of the objections the others
made before setting out. A short distance later, they
rode through a big gate with the name RYERSON
swinging on a plaque overhead. The ranch was fairly
large, with three or four barns, a sprawling house and
at least half a dozen corrals.

A knot of men were gathered near the house and
Sam motioned for his band to stay behind him as they
approached. Though Ryerson was said to be willing
to comply with the army's inquiries, he was still a former
Reb, some of whom remained hostile toward anything
that had to do with the U.S. government, even after
twenty years.

Sam let *El Tigre* prance forward, keeping one hand
near the rifle boot attached to his lightweight, army-
issue McClellan saddle.

A tall figure detached itself from the group near the
ranch house and came to meet the visitors. An arrest-
ing, powerful-looking man with wide shoulders, a
strong bronze profile and short blue-black hair, he
appeared to be a breed if not a full-blooded Indian.

"I'm looking for Monte Ryerson," Sam announced.

"You found him. What do you want?"

Sam introduced himself. "Captain Strong."

"U.S. Army. Been expecting you." Ryerson slid his unflinching black gaze over Sam's tan cotton shirt and the blue pants with gold stripes down the legs. "This the new officer's uniform?"

"I figured identifying myself as an active army captain might scare off some help we could use."

Ryerson nodded toward the three riders behind Sam. "We, as in you and your men? Don't count on me right now, as far as Beaufort Montgomery is concerned. Got my own problems. Bandits murdered one of my men, took off with two others. We're riding for Mexico."

"Fate seems to be dealing some kind of hand," Sam mused. "Those bandits are some of Montgomery's followers. They kidnapped my woman to keep me off Montgomery's back. I got the message in writing."

Ryerson shifted, looking thoughtful. "Seems like fate sure is playing games here. I was about to take off with my foreman and a couple of others." Again, his glance took in Sam, the Apache scout and the two younger men. "Eight is a hell of a lot better odds than four against twenty. Guess we should join up."

Sam agreed. "Time's wasting." He added, "Think we could pick up a few extra supplies from you?"

Ryerson was amenable and the eight riders left in less than half an hour. The rancher and his party had already been hitching up their own horses. Jake, the rancher's foreman, was an older man with a weathered face and a big mustache. He said little, riding off to one side with Ryerson's other men, a redheaded Anglo and a Mexican cowboy.

Ryerson himself rode abreast with Sam, who surreptitiously eyed the other man, hoping he hadn't made a mistake. From Ryerson's subtle return inspection, he assumed the rancher was thinking the same thing. They'd been of a mind on tracking down Montgomery and stopping him, but they were strangers, after all.

Strangers from two different sides of a war, though Sam himself had been too young to serve.

By the time they'd come in sight of a mountain range some miles south and stopped for a short rest, however, everyone knew everyone else's name. Sam realized he could be wrong, but he thought Monte Ryerson and his crew were good men who would be of real help in a tough situation.

And the more he observed Ryerson and spent time in his company, the more Sam felt certain he had a lot of Indian blood.

Because of that, Sam felt some discomfort discussing military tactics of the Apache campaign, a subject that came up with Ryerson's probing and one that Sam had managed to forget about due to his concern for Louisa.

But who knew what tribe Ryerson was related to? And various groups of Indians had been fighting each other long before the white man came.

The rancher was a very intelligent man, mentioning political events and territorial problems he'd read about in newspapers. Sharp-eyed, he noticed the case of heliograph equipment on the pack mule. Though he hadn't been sure how he'd use it, Sam explained what it was—tripods with sighting rods that could adjust mirrors to flash in Morse code.

"Morse code?" said Ryerson. "That'd work real well in mountainous areas. I'm familiar with it—taught myself to read it, if that's any help."

It was. "Might be safer to split up when we get the chance, then."

Ryerson nodded. "On the other side of the Rio Grande. The fastest way through that range up ahead is a chain of narrow canyons—each one snakes right into the next. The bandits are following an old Comanche trail."

Comanche. Which brought Louisa to mind once again. Envisioning her, Sam suddenly noted the bear claw Ryerson wore strung on a cord around his neck. The way the claw was mounted, small feathers and beads on either side, reminded him of Louisa's necklace. She said it had belonged to her father. Was Monte Ryerson also part Comanche?

But Sam wasn't sure how to ask about such a thing. And before he got the chance to try, they were mounted and riding hard down the trail again, spurred on by the promise of a spring-fed arroyo where they could rest this afternoon and replenish their water supplies, maybe even set up camp early and stay the night.

Not that the latter particularly appealed to Sam. Not when he was so worried about Louisa, he just about counted every minute and every hour of every single day.

The Sierra Madre, Mexico

Louisa had nearly given up counting the passing days as the bandits carried her farther into Mexico. The Rio Grande was at low ebb this time of year, and they'd been able to cross the great river at a point where the shallow water roiled among gravel bars.

Afterward, they'd picked up the Comanche trail again, following it through the hills on the other side of the river, then across a high desert plateau barren except for cactus, creosote bushes and other sturdy plants that needed little moisture to grow. At least the band seemed to know where to find water themselves, stopping at springs or *tinajas,* deep holes that held rainwater.

One night a storm had come up, and Louisa used the distraction of slashing rain and lightning to try an escape on horseback, hoping she was headed back for Texas. But Tezco had caught her, wrestled with her and returned her to camp covered with mud. She'd had to dress in some of Tezco's clothing until they could wash her clothes and let them dry.

Tezco had shouted at her for the first time after that escapade, then seemed to withdraw grimly into himself. But Louisa would swear that his personality had been changing in subtle ways since they first set foot in his home country. She'd noticed an odd, inflamed mark on his arm when he took off his muddy shirt and realized with surprise that the winged serpent was a brand that had been burned into his flesh.

Who would brand someone?

But Louisa soon forgot about it as the days passed. Tezco shadowed her, watched her, but spoke little. Kept separate from the other captives most of the time, she felt starved for conversation.

Usually not one to brood and tired of daydreaming about revenge on Sam, Louisa found herself reviewing her life—the shame of being a madam's child, the difficulties she'd had fitting into "proper" schools, the problems she'd faced as a half-breed.

Already passionate and rambunctious, she'd flaunted her differences and become a rebel. She'd made her own niche in life, though her mother disapproved along with society. Louisa had defied everyone. After

Sam rejected her, she'd become more embittered, twice as rebellious, tried to count coup on death itself.

No wonder Ma and Frances had been so concerned about her. Maybe her challenging, belligerent attitude had even driven Sam away and attracted Tezco, and brought about her abduction and imprisonment.

Now Louisa felt truly caged, though surrounded by the wild, wide-open spaces and towering mountains of the Sierra Madre.

Today, when the bandits stopped to spend the night in a desolate canyon, she sat on a rock and watched the sun slide behind a barren, rugged western peak. The horses chewed on tough desert grasses, while the men dug a water hole in a muddy spot of the dry riverbed that meandered through the canyon. Louisa would have helped build fires and work at other tasks if Tezco would allow it.

But he rarely tolerated the other men speaking to her, much less approaching her. That was to be his prerogative and his only. Happy he was somewhere else at the moment and that her hands were untied, she soon rose to take a leisurely stroll, heading for the river. Mesquite trees and other heavy brush lined its banks, but she found an open spot and made her way through to look down on the now deserted water hole.

The recent rain must have caused a flash flood, since dead branches, pebbles and other debris lay strewn near the rocky edges of the dry water course. In the center, green grass and weeds were trying to sprout in the sandy soil. Thinking Defiant would appreciate a treat, Louisa jumped off the bank and knelt to pluck some stalks. She paid little attention to her surroundings until she heard a subtle noise.

She glanced up . . . meeting the golden gaze of a

huge spotted cat that had come to the water hole to drink.

Only a few yards away, the jaguar stared, its powerful muscles tensed, its tail twitching. Knowing eye contact could be taken as a threat by the wild creature, Louisa remained still, continued kneeling and slid her gaze to the ground. She was more awed than afraid. *El tigre,* as the Spanish called the jaguar, was a magnificent big cat with a fierce and fearless heart, but, like most predators, it had no reason to attack a human unless cornered.

Smiling for the first time since being dragged from her home, she listened to the soft lapping of its tongue against the water.

Crack, crack, crack . . .

Bullets suddenly whined past, one careening off the edge of a rock. With a snarl, the jaguar jumped straight up in the air, a blossom of red blooming across its chest. The big cat tried to run, even as more bullets ripped through its flesh.

"No!" Louisa screamed, rising.

The animal made several desperate leaps, then wobbled, twitched and rolled to the ground in a bloody heap.

Rifles in hand, Tezco and another man hurtled down the banks. "You should have stayed down!" he yelled at Louisa. "We could have shot you!"

Stiff with grief and fury, she couldn't speak. But when Tezco approached her, she stepped back and finally found her voice. "Stay away!"

He frowned, his amber eyes cool. For a moment, they reminded her of the jaguar, but she knew they reflected an intelligence that was far more lethal than that of the spotted predator.

"How could you kill such a beautiful creature?" she

raged. "You can't stand seeing anything living free and wild. You'd rather it was caged—or dead." She patted her chest, offering her own heart as a target. "Why don't you shoot me? Go ahead!"

Tezco's frown deepened. *"Querida . . ."*

"Don't call me darling! I'm not your darling; I never will be! And I'm going to be free again . . . or else I'll be dead!"

She wouldn't cry. She refused to weep in front of Tezco or any of his followers. Bolting away, she scrambled up the riverbank and ran as fast as she could toward the camp. Her legs pumped, her heart pounded, the wind whistled past her ears. The pain in her lungs felt good as she fought for breath. She ran right past some startled men tethering a horse, past the cluster of captives at the edge of camp, only stopped when she had to, finally falling to her hands and knees, panting. For a couple of minutes, she could do nothing but let her heart slow, trying to catch her breath.

"What is wrong, Señorita?"

Recognizing Roberto's voice, she looked up. The captive had managed to haul himself to his feet and follow her. A soft-spoken man, he was recovering from his gunshot wound, thanks to her, and had gone out of his way to show his gratefulness.

"I heard the shots," he explained, his expression concerned.

She rose, her knees shaky. "They killed a jaguar."

"El tigre?" He looked thoughtful. "Ah, well, it could bother the horses."

Louisa didn't think so. "It didn't seem to be starving. And there are plenty of rabbits around here, even deer." Not to mention that the campfires would keep wild creatures at bay. "It was a beautiful animal."

"Yes, they are beautiful," Roberto agreed, his expression registering sympathy for her obvious grief. "I am sorry you feel bad."

Another captive approached—Roberto's friend, Shorty. "Did I hear you say they killed a jaguar? Damn, I thought those shots meant we was being rescued, what with all the talk about flashing mirrors and such."

Rescue. Louisa's pulse suddenly picked up. "What about flashing mirrors?"

Roberto explained, "I heard Tezco and another man say they had seen flashes of light on the mountainsides today, as if someone were signaling with mirrors."

"I hope it's the Texas Rangers," Shorty said.

"Or anyone who wants to free us," added Roberto. "Though they should be careful. The bandits are on the lookout. Tezco is talking about climbing the mountainsides to find these men."

The death of the jaguar pushed aside, if not forgotten, Louisa gazed up at the surrounding peaks. Was there someone out there, someone who wanted to free them?

If it was Chaco and Adolfo—even Sam—she prayed they'd brought a lot of help or else would be smart enough to hide until they got the chance to sneak up on the camp.

Rescue. She fingered the small packet she'd carefully carried inside her trouser pocket since Texas. If push came to shove, she might even get the chance to wage war from the inside out.

The mere thought of being free sent adrenaline zinging through her veins, made her heart want to fly with the wind.

*   *   *

Gazing through his army-issue monocular, Sam caught sight of Louisa and felt his heart speed up. From this distance up on the mountainside, he couldn't make out every feature but he recognized her walk, her bearing, and saw that she seemed to be unhurt. Thank God! He adjusted the small telescope more carefully, wishing he could gallop his horse down into the canyon and take her in his arms.

But he would have to contain his excitement, be careful and patient, take one thing at a time. First, he had to communicate with Ryerson and make plans. Since it was now dusk, they couldn't use the mirrors. They would have to wait until dawn.

Sam was glad the man had joined up with them for other reasons than his knowledge of the Morse code. The rancher had been serving as tracker since they entered Mexico. Complaining about demons with snakes growing out of their heads and evil lurking in the west, the Apache had started acting strangely as soon as they crossed the Rio Grande. Sam had been only half surprised when the Indian didn't show up for breakfast one morning.

But they hadn't needed a tracker to follow the bandits' trail today. They'd caught sight of the party around noon; they exchanged signals from opposite sides of a pass and stayed close ever since.

Before the light died completely, Sam took one last look through the monocular, disappointed that he could no longer spot Louisa. She was so invitingly close. And in spite of knowing that he should be careful and wait, he felt tempted to sneak down into the canyon this very night. Perhaps he could even get a chance to steal back the woman he loved.

As soon as Ben and Javier appeared, he made his plans. "I'm going down to check on the lay of the camp. I'll keep to the brush beside the riverbed."

Ben nodded in agreement. "We'll back you up."

Danger for himself was one thing; danger for others another. "You need to stay up here. Keep me covered if I come running."

"And what if they catch you?" asked Javier.

"Then find Monte Ryerson and figure out where and when to best set up an ambush. I'll keep Louisa safe when the bullets start flying."

He couldn't tell whether the young men were pleased with the idea, but since they'd agreed to follow his orders, they made no objection.

Sam took *El Tigre* down a narrow arroyo cut into the mountainside and left the horse in a sheltered area near the riverbed. Then he faded into the brush, skulking along, finally falling to his belly when he got close enough to hear the rise and fall of voices from the camp. When he thought he also heard a soft shuffle behind him, he swung his head around nervously, then decided he must be imagining things. If someone were on his tail, he wouldn't be able to see them anyway. The waning moon had risen, but its pale light barely relieved the evening's blackness.

He crawled forward, attempting to get a closer look at the camp. He saw tethered horses and men moving around by firelight, but no Louisa. He scanned the area carefully, tried to pick out faces . . .

And heard the distinct snap of a twig. There *was* someone in the brush behind him. Nervous, he drew his Colt to train it on the darkness. He had his finger on the trigger when he recognized the moving shadows coming toward him.

"Ben! Javier!" he whispered harshly, angry that they'd disobeyed his orders. "I told you to stay back."

Both young men dropped down beside him.

"We saw some hombres heading this direction," Ben explained. "We couldn't leave you here on your own, no matter that you said you didn't want backup."

Sam tensed. "Someone's coming this way?"

"Yeah, and on horseback."

Sam didn't like the sound of that. "Let's get out of here."

Taking the lead, he crawled backward several feet and stood up . . . only to have the brush suddenly explode around them. Yelling, mounted men charged forward, swinging rifles like clubs. Trying to run, Sam was knocked flat by a horse, falling so hard he dropped the Colt and saw stars. Bedlam reigned with shouting and the sharp *crack* of gunfire.

"They go that way!" someone cried in Spanish as hooves thudded away.

"*Dios,* Pablo is shot!" someone else yelled, and swore a blue streak.

Feeling around, Sam located his gun and got to his feet again . . . only to come face-to-face with the end of a shotgun. He could feel the hard barrel pressed against his forehead.

"Throw your weapon down, Señor," said the cold, smooth voice of the rider who'd come up on him, "if you want to live."

Seeing no choice at the moment, Sam did so.

"We will round up your friends and bring you all back to camp together."

Sam looked around. He couldn't tell if Ben and Javier had been caught. The brushy area still echoed with the noise of snorting horses and the cries of the bandits.

Nearby, a man knelt beside a fallen body. "Pablo is dead, Tezco."

The rider heaved a deep sigh. "Put him on a horse and bring him back to camp. But first pick up this man's gun." Then Tezco motioned with the shotgun. "You will go to the camp on foot, Señor."

Sam marched forward, coming out of the brush and heading for the firelight up ahead. More bandits joined them, one rider leading *El Tigre*. They'd obviously found the horse where Sam had left him, reins weighted down by a rock. Still no sign of Javier and Ben.

As if he knew what Sam was thinking, the man named Tezco asked a burly, squat companion, "Where are this one's *compadres?*"

"They got away."

Thank God.

"You let them escape?"

"We couldn't see, Tezco. We wounded one, I think."

If so, Sam hoped the bullet hadn't found a life-threatening target. He was angry again that Ben and Javier had taken it upon themselves to follow him.

"They got away?" Tezco swore angrily. "They will come back tomorrow and kill the rest of us!"

"Perhaps not," said the burly bandit. "There were not so many—only two or three."

Tezco brought his horse up closer to Sam. "Do you have two friends, Señor Gringo? Three? Or more?"

"Two."

Then Sam stumbled, teeth rattling, as Tezco slammed him in the back with the butt of the shotgun. Pain shot across his shoulder blades, but he didn't cry out.

"You had better not be lying, Señor."

"I'm not lying." Unless one counted leaving out Monte Ryerson.

"Your friends killed Pablo."

And now the bandits were going to return the favor? Having faced death before, Sam remained calm. "What else did you expect them to do? You attacked us."

"You were following us. Didn't I warn you not to come after us, after Montgomery, if you wanted to keep Louisa safe?"

"You *have* kept her safe," Sam said warningly, though he was in no position to do so. He'd seen her with his own eyes, but he had no idea of how they'd treated her.

"She's no longer your concern." Tezco stared at him. "There were only three of you. Bah, against *el catorce,* you didn't have a chance, no matter how much you talked with mirrors."

So the bandits had seen the heliograph. Perhaps Ryerson or Sam himself hadn't been careful enough, or maybe the Mexicans were simply keen-eyed. Not to mention that they wouldn't be as superstitious about flashing lights as the Apache.

Sam glanced up, thinking about Ryerson perched somewhere on the opposite side of the canyon. Surely the rancher had heard the gunshots and would be lying low. Surely Ben and Javier would be able to join up with him.

Tezco remained in a foul mood as they walked into the bandits' camp. A man rose from beside a fire where he'd been scraping some kind of spotted animal skin. Everyone else was already standing, guns in their hands, eyes on Sam. The band was alert and armed; they had obviously been expecting trouble.

Tezco gestured to Sam, then at the body. "Look, see what has happened because of the killing in Texas? Now Pablo is dead." He pushed at Sam again, though not so hard this time. "And this fool has come chasing us . . . following a trail of blood."

There was murmuring and narrowed glances. A couple of men approached the horse that carried Pablo facedown. They lifted off the body.

Someone spoke with anger. "Let us kill this gringo."

"Kill him?" A smaller figure pushed through the crowd.

Sam recognized a woman, despite the trousers. But, with disappointment, he saw she wasn't Louisa.

The woman stared at Sam speculatively. "He is a soldier."

Sam was glad he was fluent in Spanish. Otherwise, he wouldn't have known half of what was going on.

"Of course, he is a soldier," growled Tezco. "I told you about him in Santa Fe."

"I do not care if he is a cook or a shepherd. How shall we kill him?" asked the tallest bandit. "Shall we stake him out to lie naked in the sun?"

"Slit his throat," offered someone else.

"We will not kill him," stated Tezco, dismounting. He faced the group, some of whom made disappointed noises. "There has been enough death. We ride before dawn."

He went on to explain the existence of two more men. The woman, whose name was Xosi, suggested they use Sam as a hostage, threaten to torture him until the other "snakes come out of their holes" the following day.

She wasn't a bad-looking—if tough—woman, Sam thought. She was also Tezco's sister, he realized as the bandits made plans. They would pack up most of the camp tonight and keep a careful watch.

That was all he heard before they tied his hands

and led him away. His escorts took him to the other side of the camp—the captives' area. With surprise, he noticed a couple of Pueblo men but had no time to wonder about them as he was searched for hidden weapons and pushed to the ground.

"Oh, no!"

The muted cry got Sam's attention. Turning, he saw Louisa staring directly at him, her posture stiff, her eyes wide. Sam caught his breath and drank in the sight of her.

She turned her back on him. One of the men who'd brought him walked off, while the other moved some distance away to smoke a *cigarillo* and keep watch.

Sam slid his gaze back to Louisa, noting that she appeared thinner. She folded her arms and turned slightly, also glancing at him. Her expression seemed different, more somber and guarded than proud and wild the way he remembered. Sam wondered if the bandits had hurt her. He felt anger burning in his gut.

He wished they could talk.

The chance came when the man with the *cigarillo* moved farther away to talk and laugh with one of his companions.

Acting casual, Louisa ambled over to Sam. "What are you doing here?" she whispered.

He longed to touch her. "What do you think? I came for you."

"That was a crazy thing to do." Her voice throbbed with emotion.

"Maybe."

"What a fool you are, Sam Strong!" And, looming over him, she kissed him hard on the mouth.

He was a fool all right. A fool for Louisa.

He inhaled her scent and savored the softness of her lips. He would have done anything, traveled anywhere, faced any danger to experience this one moment in time. Nothing could have stopped him.

"Think Sam and his men stopped some bullets?" Jake O'Brian asked Monte after they heard gunfire down in the canyon.

"Maybe the Mexicans were just shooting at some game." Though hunting after dark didn't make any sense. "It's important that we keep close watch, no matter what happened." Monte was worried, but there was nothing he could do until daylight.

"Want me to take the first turn?" the foreman asked.

The older man looked exhausted. "Why don't you eat and rest awhile?" Monte said. "I can watch for a few hours."

Then he'd wake Jake or one of the other two cowboys back in the cave. They'd been lucky to find such a good shelter, with several branching tunnels and more than one entrance. Exploring, they'd found an opening that wasn't visible from the bandits' camp and were even able to build a small fire.

Jake left and Monte walked to the edge of the sheer drop that lay in front of the cave. He stared down at the fires glowing like small red eyes in the darkness and wished he could see the bandits, figure out what was going on. But even if he had Sam's telescope device, he wouldn't be able to see much in the dim light of the waning moon.

13

The surface of the tiny mirror seemed to emit a dim glow as Xosi gazed at herself by firelight. She was tired of traveling and could barely remember when she had last taken a bath. She could not remember when she had last been concerned with her looks.

But the handsome blond gringo Tezco had captured today had at least reminded her she was a woman. She frowned at her reflection, pursing her lips at how dirty and disheveled she appeared, and then moved the little mirror higher to get a better look. . . .

Which was when she saw a man in the oval of the mirror instead of her own image.

"Ah-h-h!" She dropped the mirror so it swung on its chain, the terrible vision she and Tezco had had at the pueblo coming back to haunt her.

Chills crawled up her spine.

Her brother had insisted they had only imagined

things that day, but he had obviously been wrong. Xosi's hands shook as she peered into the mirror one more time, ready to pull off the necklace and throw it away.

She paused only when she realized that this was not the vision she had had with Tezco—a fierce face that had glared directly out at them with burning eyes. This man in the mirror seemed ordinary, even good-looking, and merely gazed into the distance. It was Xosi who seemed to be observing him like a *bruja*.

Fascinated, Xosi brought the mirror a little closer, admiring the man's powerful build and his strong blade of a nose. His dark eyes did not burn. Instead, they seemed wise. His firm, wide mouth looked sensual.

Mesmerized, Xosi examined the mirror carefully as if she were admiring a little picture—the light was dim, but she could tell the man stood before the mouth of a cave and above the edge of a sheer drop. Far below him glowed tiny flickering lights that resembled fires.

Campfires?

With surprise, Xosi suddenly knew the man was staring down at their camp. She even knew exactly where he stood; she'd seen the sheer cliff face on the mountain above them. She narrowed her eyes—yes, the position of the fires also indicated the stranger's location.

Xosi had heard about *brujas* reading the future or the truth of the present by gazing into the reflective surface of a bowl of water. Why would a mirror not do as well?

Not that she'd ever had any magical abilities. Or wanted them.

Nevertheless, Xosi was certain the mirror had shown her the truth, something that should be shared with

Tezco. She remained resentful toward him, but he needed to know about the stranger, most certainly an enemy, on the mountainside, handsome though the man might be, handsomer even than the blond gringo. Xosi preferred dark men. She widened her eyes then as she watched the man in the mirror put down the rifle he carried and open his shirt. He had hard, flexing muscles. Well, she could watch a little while longer, she supposed, before going to find her brother.

"You came to find me," Louisa murmured, deeply touched, and she kissed Sam yet again.

Though his hands were bound, he managed to caress her cheek. "I want to take you in my arms."

"That'd be a bit difficult at the moment."

Especially when a guard might be observing them. Glancing behind her, Louisa noticed the burning arc of a *cigarillo* as a bandit threw it to the ground. She had no idea what the Mexican had seen but decided it was best to limit her gestures of affection. She scooted over, leaving a few inches between herself and Sam. But that didn't mean she couldn't gaze at him hungrily. His beard-stubbled, dirty, scarred face looked more beautiful than she ever remembered.

"No more kisses, then?"

She wanted to say yes, to share the flame of her desire. "Not if we want to stay on Tezco's good side."

"Is he the bastard who kidnapped you?"

The edge to Sam's voice brought back her own anger and soured some of the initial sweetness at seeing him. "He followed me out to *El Tigre*'s corral." Then she said accusingly, "What the hell happened to you anyway? You were supposed to be there."

"I was late, getting cleaned up."

At least he'd come after all. "I thought you'd gone off and deserted me again."

"I never deserted—"

She cut him off. "Let's not fight, Sam. Tezco will be suspicious if he sees us arguing. He's got a lot of power as the leader of this band."

"I noticed him ordering the others around."

"I met him the night of the fiesta." She ignored Sam's frown. "You saw him, too. Remember the candle dance?"

"I remember." He added, voice cold, "I'll kill him if he's touched you."

Her reaction to Sam's ferocity was double-edged. On the one hand, she was moved that he wanted to defend her honor. On the other, she couldn't help remembering the way he'd questioned her about other men, and after he'd been gone for so many years.

Though still indignant over that argument, she knew the safest course right now was to be truthful. "Tezco hasn't done any more than try to kiss me, though he wants me to be his woman."

"I'll still kill him—he had no right to carry you off."

"I'd settle for putting him in jail." Gazing at the nearest campfire, where some bandits were preparing to bury the body of the man who'd been shot that night, she shuddered. "I've seen enough death for a while, thank you." Not that she blamed Sam for firing on an attacker.

"Are you all right?"

The emotion in his voice nearly made her cry. She swallowed, refusing to let her voice shake. "I'm okay outside. Inside, well, I've been doing a lot of thinking."

"Thinking about what?"

"My life. I've been riding for a fall."

"I agree you may have taken a few too many chances. But you'd be bored if you played it completely safe. You're an exciting, courageous woman."

She couldn't let herself off that easily. "Except my courage wasn't always of the good sort. Sometimes I did whatever I wanted, come hell or high water, not caring in the least what happened to me." Or how her friends and family felt.

"I know what that's like."

She raised her brows at his sympathetic tone. "You took too many chances in the army?"

"At times. But the worst problem came afterward—I've been a down-and-out drunk."

She hadn't thought of his use of alcohol in quite that way. "Maybe we both want to die. Ma and Frances told me I did, but I wouldn't believe it—until this happened, until a bandit stole me away from my home, kept me prisoner, treated me like some kind of possession."

"You're blaming yourself?"

"I flirted with Tezco at the dance. I went out to the corral by myself and didn't even check to see if anyone was following me—"

Sam interrupted with a growl of anger. "I'm going to kill him for sure, as soon as I get loose!" Then he added fiercely, "You have a right to be wherever you want, Louisa, whenever you want to be there. It's against the laws of God and man to steal anything, doubly so a human being." He went on, "I can't stand seeing you like this. This man is trying to destroy your spirit."

Tezco claimed otherwise, but the situation he'd put her in had taken its toll. Thank God Sam was helping her regain her perspective. A weight seemed to lift from her heart.

"I cherish your pride and your wildness, even your fearlessness," Sam told her. "I always have."

He cherished her. Wasn't that the same thing as saying he loved her? Still, Louisa longed to hear the exact words. Feeling needy and lost, something she'd rarely admitted to in her life, she wanted to hear about the deep, crazy emotions that had made Sam come after her all on his own.

She leaned forward. "So when you went to the corral to meet me and saw that I was gone, you just took off after me?"

"I waited until the next morning. I had to gather supplies and round up some men. This Tezco character left a note telling me not to go after Montgomery if I wanted you safe. He works for the madman."

Louisa started. *Had* he come after her, then, or was he merely fulfilling his duty, attending to that last assignment to get that madman, Beaufort Montgomery?

"There were four of us to begin with," he was saying, "me, Javier, Ben and an Apache tracker. Of course, that was before the Apache disappeared."

So Sam hadn't come alone, but he hadn't brought army men. Maybe he *had* come just for her. "The bandits saw your flashing mirrors."

"The heliograph. I was wondering about that."

She stared into the darkness. "Ben and Javier are out there?"

"I hope so. They scattered when the bandits attacked tonight, but one of them might have been wounded and neither can track."

Louisa digested this information, also hoping the young men were safe.

"They should have stayed put where I told them to," Sam complained. "I should have stayed on the mountain myself. I was stupid and crazy to try to sneak up on the camp so soon. I just had to try to get closer to see if I could smuggle you away."

"You were crazy, huh?" *Madly in love?*

"I've been out of my mind for days. I couldn't get over the fact that I should have been at that corral like I said I would be. Then this never would have happened."

She didn't want to hear about guilt; she desperately desired a declaration of love. "Now who's blaming himself? You came for me—that's enough."

"No, it's not enough. It was my duty not only to find you but to free you. Instead, I managed to get captured myself."

Duty? So Sam *had* come after her out of duty.

Already emotional, Louisa felt a jolt of pain as sharp as if she'd been stabbed with a knife. She jumped to her feet. "I can't believe you're spouting off about duty in a situation like this! They could kill us both! Don't you have a heart and feelings?"

Sam looked surprised. "Louisa—"

But she turned her back, stalking off. She didn't realize Tezco was approaching until she met him face-to-face.

He didn't appear happy. "What were you doing with the captives?"

She bit back her temper. "Only talking."

"With the blond soldier."

"So?" She shrugged and started to walk off.

But Tezco caught her by the arm. "I remember him from New Mexico Territory. You were dancing with him, weren't you, *querida?*" He jerked her closer, his grasp like iron. "Is he your lover, perhaps?"

Louisa's hurt and anger faded some more. Tezco claimed to be a thief, not a murderer, but who knew what he'd do to a man he saw as a rival?

"He was only a would-be suitor."

"You are trying to protect him."

She could tell the Mexican was angry and tried calming words. "I don't want to see anyone hurt, not even you." She assured him, "That man was never more than a suitor." Not seeing any other choice, she lied, "I don't want to be with that man. I don't like him."

"But you still do not wish to be with me?"

As put out with Sam as she was, she was going to have to flirt with the bandit to keep him from doing harm. She lowered her eyelashes, trying to smile engagingly.

"You are handsome, Tezco, and brave. What woman would not want you?"

Appearing surprised, he smiled, his teeth flashing white against his tan skin. "And what is this? Do you speak of yourself? You have forgiven me for stealing you away? For the hardships of the trail? For shooting the jaguar?"

"It's not up to me to forgive. I only hope you'll be kinder in the future."

"If you ask prettily, I will be."

Taking hold of her chin, he raised her face for a kiss.

Now what? Louisa thought, panicking, her pulse racing. She'd gone too far.

A strident voice interrupted them. "Tezco!"

Louisa had never been happier to see Xosi.

"I must talk to you . . . alone." The Mexican woman glared at her brother's captive. "It is important. Very important."

Reluctantly letting Louisa go, Tezco nodded. But he assured her, "I will come back."

And what would she do then? she wondered, her mind awhirl. Unless she could figure out a way to keep Tezco at arm's length, Sam's arrival had created a very serious problem.

As Sam watched the scenario being played out before him, he called himself every kind of fool. Even as she'd gotten angry and risen in a huff, he'd realized Louisa had wanted him to tell her he loved her instead of prattling on about duty.

Now he had to sit helplessly and watch her smile and flirt with the bandit leader. Though bound, he was tempted to struggle to his feet and launch himself at the other man.

Not that doing so would help him . . . or Louisa.

Hot with jealousy, especially when Tezco took hold of the woman Sam truly did love, he still was able to rationalize and understand that she was probably doing what she thought she must. Her stiff back and guarded expression surely meant she feared Tezco rather than liked him.

Unless her discomfort came from guilt.

No, he didn't want to doubt Louisa. She'd been telling him the truth about her relationship with Tezco, Sam assured himself.

Cool down.

The only important thing now was a plan of escape. He glanced up at the dark shapes of the surrounding mountains, wondering where Monte Ryerson was and if Javier and Ben would be able to join up with him. In the excitement of seeing Louisa, he hadn't gotten around to telling her about the rancher and his reinforcements; he'd nearly forgotten about Ryerson himself.

His main hope now was that the rancher would be able to engineer some kind of ambush.

"I saw a man in my mirror," Xosi told Tezco in all seriousness. "Perhaps he is planning an ambush. We need to do something about him and as soon as possible."

"The mirror again?" The hair on the back of Tezco's neck rose as he recalled what they'd seen in the ancient pueblo, what he encountered all too frequently in his restless dreams. "What kind of *brujería* is this?"

"I do not know how I am able to see it," Xosi admitted. "But I am certain I do—the man actually exists." She gestured. "He is there, at the mouth of a cave and near the stretch of rock face. He is watching our fires, waiting. We should attack him before he attacks us." When Tezco remained thoughtful and silent, she asked, "Would you like to look in the mirror yourself?"

"No!"

She jumped, startled.

He struggled to speak in a soothing tone. "I believe you." He knew his sister was telling the truth, knew there was something magical about her little mirror. But he simply could not bring himself to look into it at the moment, fearing what he might see. "Perhaps this man is one of the soldier's *compadres* who ran away from us earlier. We should climb the mountain and take him at dawn."

"No, we should go now," said Xosi. "He will not be expecting us and he is, after all, only one man."

"He is the only one you saw."

"Then bring torches. We will sneak up to the cave and light them, smoke the other men out."

Tezco nodded. "I am always respectful of your cunning. An attack at night will not be expected. I will tell the men."

Xosi smiled, looking happier than she had for days. Perhaps they could finally heal the rift between them, Tezco thought.

Meanwhile, he would make sure that he left enough men to guard the prisoners and make the camp look like it was running normally. He would tell them to stoke the fires and prepare another pot of beans. With all the shooting and the death of Pablo, his band had hardly had a chance to eat their evening meal.

Tezco himself was not hungry, at least not for food. Thinking of the way Louisa had flirted with him, he smiled and wished he did not have so many responsibilities and distractions keeping him away from her. But he felt certain there would be pleasures to enjoy with her in the future, just as he had been sure that she would change her mind about him if he gave her enough time.

How much time did she have? Louisa wondered as she watched most of the bandits divide into two groups and slip off into the shadows. She'd heard something about their plans and feared they were on the trail of Javier and Ben. She prayed the Mexicans wouldn't kill them.

Meantime, she had to launch her own attack. Luckily, a pot of beans still simmered on the main campfire and the bandits were always hungry.

Ignoring Sam, who was sitting some feet away from the other prisoners, she'd approached Roberto and Shorty to have a few quiet words with them.

Then she took out the small packet she'd carried in her trouser pocket for days and unwrapped the rag holding several jimsonweed seeds that she'd collected by sneaking out of bed in the moonlight. She used a rock to crush them against a tin plate. The resulting juice was toxic, though she hoped to use only enough to make the bandits sick.

When she was ready, she gave a subtle sign to Roberto.

The cowboy got to his feet. "Help, help! A snake! A rattler!"

As expected, the few men left to guard the captives came running.

"A snake!" yelled Shorty. "There it is—shoot it!"

The bandit in charge of the cooking turned his back to his pot of beans, straining to see what was going on. While he was engrossed in the commotion, Louisa flitted over to the campfire and dribbled the contents of the plate into the pot. Then she stirred the beans, using a big stick lying near the fire.

"There is no snake!" shouted one of the guards. "You are loco!"

"It went under a rock," insisted Roberto.

Swearing under his breath, the cook suddenly turned back to the fire, his eyes widening when he spotted Louisa.

She let go of the stirring stick and tried to smile. "Mm-mm, these smell so good!"

"You are hungry, Señorita? Let me fill your plate."

"*Gracias,*" she said, handing it over, hoping he didn't notice the bits of seed husk sticking to the sides.

When he didn't, she breathed a sigh of relief and ambled off toward the edge of camp. In the darkness, she dumped the beans out onto the earth and started calculating the amount and kind of supplies a group of seven people would need to survive a trek through the dry wildness of this part of the Sierra Madre.

No, make that eight people.

Louisa realized she'd left out Sam. But then, that had to be because she wasn't used to him being around, not even in New Mexico.

Angry again, she wished there was some way to let him eat a few beans, only enough to make him slightly ill. But, of course, she couldn't really do that. She simply wasn't that cruel.

14

"*Drop your gun, hombre,*" ordered the woman bandit who took Monte prisoner. "Then raise your hands to the sky."

Monte didn't see as he had any other choice, since the woman was accompanied by several men as well armed as she. He let his rifle drop, wishing he'd paid closer attention to the subtle noises he'd heard in the dark. But he hadn't expected an attack to come at night or for the Mexicans to know exactly where he and his men were.

"If you value your life, do not move," the woman said, coming closer to lift his handgun from its holster.

With a smile, she ran her hands over his torso, buttocks and legs, searching for hidden weapons. She raised his denim pantlegs to make sure he had no knives in his boots and slid her hands up his inner thighs. "Nothing dangerous there."

Angered and a little embarrassed, he growled, "All depends on the circumstances."

"Xosi, is this man alone? Have you searched the cave?"

A new voice. Monte flicked his gaze to the other side of the cave's entrance. More bandits. His heart sank. If he'd seen any prospect of escaping before, he now thought otherwise.

Xosi poked him in the chest with her gun. "Do you have friends hiding in the cave? How many?"

"Friends?" repeated Monte loudly. If he couldn't get away himself, he could at least warn the others. "There's nobody else in the cave—"

"Quiet!" Xosi snarled, slapping his face so hard it stung. "I know what you are about!" She turned to the leader of the second group of bandits. "Light the torches, Tezco. I will keep watch over this braying donkey."

Alone, Monte hoped, so he'd have the chance to wrestle her gun away. But again he was disappointed when the bandits separated, some accompanying the one called Tezco with torches, the rest staying behind with this Xosi. He thought of Jake and the other two hands rolled up in their blankets, praying they'd heard his voice and had already run out the other entrance.

Gunshots and noise told him they hadn't. Damn! Shoulders stiff, he stared into the dark cave until the torches flared back into sight. Jake stumbled toward him, ahead of several bandits with guns drawn. The foreman's head was bloody, his expression grim.

He came up beside Monte. "The other two got away. I probably would've escaped, too, if I hadn't been so dead asleep."

Nobody dead. Monte let out his breath in relief. "They shot you?"

"Nah, got tangled up in my blanket and hit my head on a rock."

"I ordered you to remain quiet!" said Xosi, stepping closer to slap Monte again.

His temper flared. "If you do that one more time, lady—"

"You'll what?" Placing a hand against his chest, she leaned in close enough to brush her breasts against his body.

To Monte's chagrin, he was relieved when Xosi stepped back.

"So there were two others?" she asked.

"Yeah, two. And so what?" Monte said belligerently. "They hightailed it out of here—you'll never catch them."

At least he hoped not. He breathed another sigh of relief when Tezco and the rest of the bandits showed up, empty-handed and swearing mad. His men had been able to get away and had also taken all four horses.

Of course, that left Monte and Jake on foot.

As well as in the clutches of these criminals.

Worse, the two men who'd fled into the night didn't know how to track. If they lost sight of the Mexicans for even a few hours, they'd never be able to keep up. As he was marched down the mountain, Monte hoped that Sam and his crew were still alive and that his ranch hands would join up with them.

Only when they reached the camp and he spotted Sam did Monte realize the situation was about as bad as it could get.

Louisa had a few qualms about what she had done, but the situation was desperate.

Having heard shots ringing through the canyon, she

feared for the lives of Ben and Javier. Anxious for the bandits' return, she crouched down some feet beyond the firelight, and was surprised when Tezco brought two complete strangers into camp—a mustached fellow with a cut on his head and a tall, dark, muscular man who looked like an Indian in white man's clothes.

His face a hard mask, Tezco ordered that the new prisoners be tied up securely and thrown down with the other captives. Then he paced before the entire group.

"How many men are you?" he demanded. "There were two in the cave, two or three by the riverbed. Were they the same? Who are you and what are you after? You will answer these questions or I will make your lives a misery."

When no one offered any explanations, he confronted Sam. "Are these your friends, soldier?"

Sam merely gave the Mexican a cold look, which made Tezco even angrier. Louisa flinched when he made as if to kick Sam.

"Answer me—tell me the truth!"

"All right, there's a whole regiment of cavalry over the horizon."

"Liar!" Tezco flushed, and his fists balled.

He was going to attack Sam and Louisa could do nothing.

"Wait, brother." Xosi laid a hand on Tezco's shoulder. "There is no reason to lose patience. I will help you question these men." Then she gestured toward the surrounding bandits. "We are strong, we have many guns. No one will dare attack until dawn. We should first post guards and keep watch."

Tezco calmed and nodded, agreeing that they should

organize the camp to begin with, as well as make decisions about heading out the next day.

Louisa watched the pair amble toward the cooking fire and thought nothing could have worked out better for her own plans. Questioning the prisoners would surely keep Tezco busy for a few hours . . . until he got too sick to see straight, much less talk. Jimsonweed caused nausea, dizziness, blurred vision and blinding headaches.

If the weed worked as it was supposed to, all the bandits who ate even a few spoonfuls of beans would be ill. Some had already helped themselves and others came up to do so as Tezco issued orders, positioning guards about the camp. Xosi placed a big helping for herself on a tin plate.

Tezco complained, "We are now short one mount." He told the cook, "Unload a pack horse. We will be low on supplies but the captives need not eat for a day or two."

God must be smiling on her, Louisa thought, having been worried the beans would also be offered to the new captives. To be safe, though, in case Roberto or Shorty didn't get the chance to warn them, she decided to take matters into her own hands. While Tezco remained at the cook fire, she rose quickly and approached the dark, muscular man.

"Don't eat the beans," she whispered.

He stared at her curiously, as well he might. But he said, "You're Louisa. I'm Monte Ryerson. Sam joined up with us—we've been traveling together since Texas."

Sam. Louisa suddenly felt his eyes on her. But she ignored the little thrill running up and down her spine to ask Monte, "Are there really other men waiting out there?"

"Don't count on it."

Louisa tried not to show her disappointment. "Even so, we'll be able to get away." She glanced behind her and saw Tezco turning in her direction. She whispered fiercely, "Don't eat the beans! Poison!"

She flitted away before crouching down again, this time not far away from Sam. She should warn him, too. "I need to tell you—"

"I know. You wanted me to say I love you."

What presumption. Even in the tense situation, he angered her easily. "This is no time for true confessions."

"I wanted you to know, in case anything happens—I do love you, Louisa. I just didn't get the chance to say so before."

"Lie to Tezco, not me," she said bitterly. "You tried to do your duty. You should be satisfied."

"Louisa—"

She cut him off. "I don't want to hear it. You have nothing to gain . . . unless you want to make sure I don't leave you tied up while the rest of us escape."

His eyebrows shot up. "Escape?"

Noticing Tezco approach, she jumped to her feet, saying for effect, "Don't talk to me anymore. Leave me alone!"

If she'd said that to begin with, when Sam had waltzed into her life again after six years, maybe neither one of them would be in these straits.

Louisa kept to the fringes of the camp, though she remained near the captives. Tezco and Xosi questioned Monte Ryerson and the mustached man, who claimed they'd been tracking the bandits to get Roberto and

Shorty back. Monte tried to bargain for everyone's release. But as Louisa expected, Tezco sneered at the offer of money and cattle.

"And how many other men rode with you?" He remained angry that no one would say for sure. "Are they waiting to attack us tomorrow?"

"Don't think you'll have to worry about that," Monte drawled with a shrug, keeping Tezco on edge. "I'm sure they're long gone."

Tezco swore, getting impatient again. And as before, Xosi calmed him with one touch.

"Perhaps you will change your mind about telling the truth when you are hungry," she told Monte Ryerson. She waved a spoonful of beans before his mouth. "Perhaps you will not eat again until you tell us everything we want to know."

Monte looked a bit nervous as she swiped the spoon right across his lips. He turned his head, quickly wiping his mouth on his shoulder.

"You do not like our food?" Xosi asked. "Then go hungry."

Xosi moved away, Tezco following to speak with her.

In spite of her anxiety, Louisa yawned. It was getting late. But she could neither allow herself to sleep nor make plans with the other captives. She remained very aware of Sam, who seemed equally cognizant of her. At least his eyes were focused on her every time she glanced at him . . . until he got hold of Xosi's discarded plate. Having a difficult time attempting to feed himself with his hands tied together, he managed to take an awkward bite.

"No!"

Horrified, guilt-ridden because she hadn't warned him, Louisa bolted to Sam's side, kicking the tin plate over in the dirt and stomping on the beans. Sam appeared as astonished as Tezco and Xosi, who both turned to look. The bandit leader came closer.

Louisa said sheepishly, "You said the captives couldn't have any food for a day or two, right?"

"You are enforcing my commands now, *querida?*"

Shrugging, she turned and walked away, figuring Tezco could puzzle it out. Hopefully, he wouldn't have time to dog her for the truth. In case he thought to anyway, she traveled even farther from camp, avoiding the skin of the jaguar stretched out and weighted down by stones. Even in her strained circumstances, she felt another twinge. The beautiful hide had covered a living creature such a short time ago.

Perhaps she'd soon be dead as well—she'd meant what she said about either gaining her freedom or dying. She only hoped she wouldn't cause someone else's death. She couldn't help worrying a bit about the amount of jimsonweed she'd mixed into the beans. Magdalena had said the plant could be very toxic.

But what other choice had she had?

Shivering in the chilly high desert night, she wrapped her arms about herself and walked out to visit the horses. Defiant nickered a welcome, and she leaned into his warmth, stroking his nose.

"Good boy. I'm going to get you home if it's the last thing I ever do."

She glanced up when another horse snorted nearby— a black one who nearly blended with the darkness. Yet, she could make out the familiar shape. . . .

"*El Tigre!*" She could hardly believe her eyes. "What are you doing here?"

The stallion snorted again and tossed his head.

"*Tigre!*" She hugged his neck, noting that the spirited animal was secured with two ropes, not one. Then she ran her hands along his withers and over his back, the hair on which was matted down from a saddle. "Who's been riding you? Sam?"

Of course. No one else could do so.

The same way no one else could ever possess her heart, no matter how much she wished differently.

Cramped and aching, Sam wished he could stretch out on a nice soft bed. A bed? Slowly coming to on the hard ground, he realized he'd dozed off.

Someone was groaning nearby. A bandit staggered by, dropped his rifle to the ground and vomited. Then the man collapsed in the mess.

What the hell? Sam tried to raise his head and swallowed back a wave of nausea and dizziness. Damn, he didn't feel too good himself. His hands were numb due to his tied wrists, but it was his stomach and his head that were driving him crazy. How could he plan their escape when he felt like this?

The world stopped spinning long enough for him to glance about the camp. Everything seemed quiet. A line of light edged the eastern mountains—dawn. Why weren't the bandits getting ready to ride? He noticed a couple of other Mexicans lying a few yards away.

One of them moaned. "What is the matter with us, amigo?"

"I think I am dying," the other gasped. "Poison."

Poison? *The beans.*

Sam remembered Louisa kicking the plate away from

him. He'd been stunned by the action, wondered if her captivity had finally driven her a little off in the head. But now it was his own mind that was muddled—he could recall very little of what happened the rest of the night. Everything had seemed a little dreamlike. Still did. Like the image of Louisa flickering and wavering above him right now.

"Sam."

Her voice was solid and real and concerned. "Louisa?"

She knelt beside him, slid his head in her lap, stroked his brow with gentle hands. "Oh, my God, why did you have to eat?"

He wished he felt good enough to fully enjoy her ministrations. "I'm dying?"

Her dark eyes filled with tears. "Surely not. You didn't have that much."

Which didn't reassure him a whole lot, though somehow it didn't seem to matter. "Well, at least I can die in your arms."

"Oh, Sam!" She choked back a sob.

His heart swelled. "And at least you care. I've never seen you cry before."

"Of course I care," she said, lips trembling. "I love you, Sam. I always have."

Someone nearby cleared his throat, making Louisa stiffen.

"What kind of poison was in the beans?" Monte Ryerson asked.

For a moment, Sam had forgotten about the other prisoners, forgotten where he was and that he intended to get Louisa out of here, not die in her arms.

Louisa sniffed and straightened her shoulders. "Jimsonweed."

"The leaves?" asked Ryerson.

"A few seeds. I crushed them and mixed the juice in the big cooking pot."

"Only a few seeds shouldn't kill anyone," the rancher said. "Most jimsonweed isn't lethal, especially at this time of the year. It just makes you sick as a dog."

Monte Ryerson didn't sound sick at all. Once again, Sam tried to raise his head, noting that his surroundings didn't rock quite so crazily.

"You'd better get busy and cut us free," Ryerson told Louisa. "I don't know how long the bandits will be down."

She helped Sam sit up, then got to her feet, picking up a knife she'd laid on the ground. "I already cut the Pueblos loose."

"I saw," said Ryerson.

"They took off like the devil hisself was after 'em," added Jake O'Brian.

He and Roberto and Shorty all seemed fully awake and in control of themselves.

"That wasn't very grateful of those Indians," Louisa groused while working at Ryerson's bonds. "After I went to all the trouble of warning everyone last night."

Though his mind worked slowly, Sam started realizing the full import of what she said. Louisa had poisoned the beans in an escape attempt. And she'd obviously warned the other captives, which was why none of them were sick.

Except him.

His soft mood changed as he wondered if she'd been weeping out of guilt, rather than true caring.

"You warned everyone but me?" he asked angrily.

"Sorry, I just didn't get the chance."

The same words he himself had used when he tried to apologize the night before. His stomach clenched again. His head pounded. "Poisoning me is a bit far to go for revenge, don't you think? Because I couldn't say I loved you exactly when you wanted me to?"

Making a disgusted noise, Louisa turned to scowl at him. "Don't flatter yourself. I don't have time to think about revenge for something so petty."

With a savage movement, Ryerson broke the cords Louisa had been sawing at. "Suppose we can wait until we're on the trail back to Texas to finish this lovers' spat?"

Flushing, Louisa threw Sam a filthy look and moved on to Jake O'Brian.

But thinking of how sick with worry he'd been over her since she'd been taken, Sam remained angry, slightly dizzy, not caring that he was making a scene. "How about cutting me loose first? At least you owe me that."

"Go ahead," Ryerson told her as he helped himself to a knife and a pistol from a fallen bandit's belt. "I'll take care of Jake and the others."

Louisa scowled ferociously as she cut Sam's bonds. He scowled back, rubbed his wrists and shook his arms. She backed up and didn't offer to help as he got to his feet. When the world spun again, he stood still, squeezing his eyes shut for a second.

When he opened them again, a man seemed to leap out of nowhere to grab Louisa. Tezco.

She cried out and dropped her knife.

With one hand twisting her long braid of hair, the bandit leader savagely jerked her back against his chest and held a blade to her throat. The feathered bear-claw necklace popped out of the neck of her shirt.

"Throw down your weapons or I will kill her!"

Ryerson stood still, frozen in the process of freeing

the last captive, Shorty. Roberto paused as well, looking stricken.

"I will slit her throat, I swear!"

Knives dropped to the ground and Ryerson threw aside his pistol, while Sam attempted to gauge the distance between himself and Tezco, tried to decide if his wobbly reflexes were fast enough to take the other man. He might be irritated as anything at Louisa, but he still loved her.

As if second-guessing him, Tezco dragged Louisa backward. His unusual knife had an inlaid handle and a very sharp dark blade. He glared at Sam. "Move over there with the rest of them, soldier."

Sam did as ordered, his mind churning. Perhaps he couldn't use force but he could try to reason with the man. "You wouldn't really kill her," he told Tezco. Not when the Mexican was so enamored of Louisa.

But Tezco appeared unmoved. "I do not want to harm her, but you have left me with no choice." He assessed the group, settling on Roberto. "Tie up the big man, then the soldier." When Roberto didn't immediately obey, he shouted, "Now! This woman saved your life. Would you sacrifice hers?"

That threat put the cowboy in motion. Roberto had tied Sam's hands again when Louisa cried out.

Sam went rigid. "You're hurting her!"

"She deserves some pain. My men and my sister are too sick to walk."

Ryerson said, "They'll be better in a coupla hours." Then he asked, "What about you—didn't eat any beans?"

"I wasn't hungry." When Roberto had finished tying up O'Brian, Tezco told the man to throw him the pistol. With a smooth motion, he finally released

Louisa and scooped it up. "Now tie the hands of this wildcat," he told the cowboy, pushing her toward him. "I do not trust her for even one minute."

"You're smart not to," Louisa spat, "because I'd do the very same thing again."

"I have been far too kind to you, *querida*. You do not deserve such treatment."

Meaning the Mexican was going to mistreat her from now on? Sam gritted his teeth, knowing he'd never be able to stand that. He'd either kill Tezco or be killed himself.

"Killing—taking a life—is sacred when it is done to feed the gods," said Beaufort, instructing his followers as usual as he went about his sacred work.

But sacrifice wasn't the most important topic at the moment. Today, this very moment, he finally stood before the great door of the buried *tesorería*. Servants had dug their way down into the deep, dank passageway beneath the pyramid. Signaling for silence, Beaufort closed his eyes, recalling each and every word of the incantation he'd memorized.

When he opened his eyes again, he took a deep breath before speaking loudly and clearly in Nahuatl. "Hear me, Great Entrance, I command you to open. This by the power of Quetzalcoatl!" Then he followed that up with the other gods' names, pronouncing them correctly and in order.

Silence. Fashioned of smooth, featureless stone, the door stood still.

For a moment, Beaufort feared the incantation had failed. He feared that Quetzalcoatl would not possess him after all.

Then there was a shudder, a murmur that seemed to come from the earth itself. Dirt sifted down from the ceiling of the passageway and the followers behind him backed away with little cries.

Beaufort stood, unafraid. He had come too far to leave now.

With a grumble, the earth trembled and the huge door swung open. It was at least eight feet high and twelve inches in width.

He had triumphed! The god breathed through him! "Bring the torches!" he shouted, mesmerized by the glitter of ancient artifacts.

He remained triumphant some hours later as he relaxed in his personal quarters. Some exquisite pieces from the *tesorería* glimmered on a makeshift table beside the three recovered sections of the sacred wheel.

"So beautiful!" breathed the comely female servant Beaufort had brought in to amuse himself today.

Of course, she was probably far more impressed with the gold itself than the true significance of the objects upon which she was gazing.

"But the wheel is broken—will you join it together, O Great God?"

"As soon as the fourth and last piece reaches our new city."

And as soon as Beaufort himself inserted the most important part, the center with its sun-god face and hollow interior meant to hold a still-warm heart. Of course, until it was time for that final ceremony, he'd stored the center with the rest of the treasure in the *tesorería*. In spite of his power, he wanted utter safety.

Now he threw a cloth over the rest of the wheel. "Tezcatlipoca should be arriving any day."

Smoking Mirror would be surprised to see the wonders Beaufort's followers had wrought in the narrow valley. Working day and night, they'd uncovered an entire side of the stone pyramid, excavated the passageway beneath it and dug irrigation ditches, which snaked out from the springs and nourished grassy plants and newly planted crops. They'd caught birds bare-handed, torn off feathers and sewed until their fingers bled to fashion splendid costumes for their god. They'd built a mud-brick house for him and several smaller ones for his highest ranking warriors.

The common people did whatever he bade them; they were filled with rapture if they could but breathe the same air as their exalted leader. They didn't care if they had to live in crumbling shelters fashioned of brush, stones or wood. They lived to serve.

Which was as it should be.

Though the number of his followers had swelled with the addition of entire villages of Indians from isolated villages in the mountains, Beaufort-Quetzalcoatl provided for them all. Though out of season, tomatoes, yams and other delicacies ripened with supernatural briskness in soil that had been blessed by sacrificial blood. Flowers bloomed that were usually not seen beyond spring or summer. In awe, the peasants bowed before him, most flattening themselves completely against the ground.

But the miracles were just beginning.

Courageous hearts had already been cut out on the altar at the top of the pyramid, yet the completed sacred wheel would need the bravest heart of all. Then and only then, when that steaming organ occupied the wheel's center, when the correct incantations were said, would the gods truly live again, breathe in the flesh and bless the Mexica with plenty and splendor.

Beaufort felt himself ready to take on this highest task: to truly become Quetzalcoatl. King of the gods, he would raise the world out of darkness, stop the sun from dying, give his people the strength and courage to dominate the earth.

He had only one niggling doubt . . . and that concerned his holy celibacy.

Even a god sometimes had needs.

Thinking about that now, Beaufort turned to his pretty servant. "Now you will amuse me, sweet one. Take off your clothing."

"Yes, O Great God." She shimmied out of her tunic and skirt, revealing voluptuous brown thighs, rounded hips and high, firm breasts with dark nipples. She presented herself proudly, without a blush. She was certainly no maiden.

Actually, Beaufort suspected the woman had been something of a lightskirt in her own village—which was good, considering his taste as an observer had become increasingly demanding. He hardened beneath his robe.

"Now sit down on the bed and part your legs—I shall call in the young men who are to be your partners."

The men, both Zapotec Indians from the south, were captives slated for the altar. As such, they were to be indulged in any kind of diversion, allowed anything but their freedom. Beaufort stepped discreetly into the shadows but watched intently as his eager servant seduced the young men with her mouth and tongue and hands. She soon had them naked, aroused and panting.

She glanced Beaufort's way, sloe-eyed as she rolled the most excited of the captives onto his back and mounted him. Rocking her hips, riding him, she parted the lips of her sex so that the slippery pumping movement of the man's engorged penis could plainly be seen.

Beaufort nearly lost hold of his senses but caught himself at the very last moment.

Turning away for the first time since he'd begun his little voyeuristic rituals, he assured himself that the captives deserved every joy. Their paltry lives would soon end; their blood would soon seep into the earth; their hearts would be small, barely significant gifts for the gods.

Still, what a price one had to pay for eternity.

15

The Sierra Madre, Mexico

The next couple of days crept by like an eternity for Louisa. She'd come so close to winning freedom for herself and the other captives, so near to escaping the clutches of the bandits. The Mexicans had recovered from the poisoning, of course, and only Tezco's protection had saved her from their angry revenge. After he threatened to harm her, she was surprised when the worst he offered was separation from her fellow prisoners and a cold attitude. But then, however violent his band might be, she'd come to believe Tezco himself was truly no worse than a desperate thief.

Not that the knowledge completely banished her fear of him.

Or made her desire him.

For Louisa wanted only Sam. She agonized over his

ill-timed declaration of love and could dream of nothing else but trying to heal the rift between them. What she would give to talk to him, argue with him, simply lie beside him and exchange sweet words in the night.

But she had no occasion to speak to him at all for some time after the poisoning. She never had a chance to approach him until the afternoon the bandits lined up no more than two abreast to file through a particularly narrow pass. Tezco had left her behind and ridden ahead, an uncharacteristic action, so she slowed Defiant and nudged him into a shallow area off to the side until she spotted Sam on *El Tigre*. The man looked grim and haggard; he had a big bruise on his jaw.

"Are you all right?" she asked, moving Defiant over beside him. She wanted to touch Sam, to tell him she loved him.

"I'm alive."

"You've been eating?" She was worried because Tezco had threatened to let the prisoners go hungry.

Sam gazed at her as if to ask why she should care. "We had food." He added, "And it wasn't even poisoned."

She swallowed guiltily. "I told you I was sorry." Though he'd made her angry at the time, too annoyed and distracted to tell him about the beans. "I wouldn't poison you intentionally, you know that."

And didn't he remember she'd told him that she loved him? But he said nothing now, not that he forgave her, but rode along gazing straight ahead. She sighed.

"Your friend Tezco gave us some hardtack and strips of jerky," Sam finally went on. "He seems to be more threat than deed."

"Tezco isn't my friend."

"Uh-huh. He'd like to be a lot more."

Surely he didn't think she condoned that. "I don't blame you for being jealous."

"He hasn't hurt you?" His mouth tightened as if he wanted to ask, Or touched you?

She said, "Nothing has changed. He's never done more than kiss me, and that was miles and miles ago." She gazed at Sam's bruise, wishing her hands weren't tied so she could stroke it gently. "Who hit you?"

"One of Tezco's men—he didn't like being poisoned."

"But you had nothing to do with that!"

"We were trying to escape. He had to take his wrath out on someone, I guess." He rubbed at the bonds chafing his wrists. "Tezco intervened in that, too. Otherwise, the man would probably have killed me."

"From the first, Tezco insisted he and his band are thieves, not murderers. I'm beginning to believe it's the truth, at least in his case."

Sam gazed at her assessingly. "Was he only joking when he threatened to kill you?"

"I don't think he would have done it."

"Too bad you didn't let Ryerson and me know, then— we would have made a move on him when we had the chance."

"A knife at the throat doesn't make a person feel much like talking," she admitted.

"Well, what's done is done." Again, Sam examined his bonds. "So we're still captives."

Louisa knit her brows. "Why would bandits want captives anyway? I never have been able to figure that out. And where are we going?"

"I don't know." But he had an odd expression on his face, as if he knew something and he wasn't telling her.

He was probably being negative. Whatever happened, wherever they ended up, she didn't want to be separated from him. "We can still try to make an escape."

He merely nodded.

"We *can*." She wanted to see a spark of hope in his eyes. "Even if those men who were with you lost our trail. We still have Monte and Jake, Roberto and Shorty. That's six of us. All we need is the right chance."

"And some guns."

"Which isn't impossible. I have more freedom moving around the camp. I'll see what I can do."

Sam quirked a thoughtful brow, for a moment looking more like himself. But before Louisa could come up with a scheme, the horses in front of them halted, forcing them to rein in. Loud voices echoed up ahead. A pebble rolled down a rocky wall, alerting her to someone walking above. She glanced up, catching sight of a brown man wearing a loincloth and carrying a rifle. He waved the band onward.

She leaned toward Sam. "An Indian."

"Not from any tribe I know. But I've never been this deep into Mexico before."

The long line of bandits started up again, halting only for a moment at what seemed to be the brush-filled end of the pass. Then the brush gaped open, a cleverly constructed gate thrown outward by more armed men. Inside a great crowd waited, the high walls of a canyon their backdrop. The crowd parted as the first mounted bandits rode toward them. Waving reeds and flowers, the people cheered, some playing drums, rattles or little flutes.

Monte came up beside Sam and Louisa. "What the hell is this? Are they welcoming us?"

Sam shook his head.

Spotting the bandit leader up ahead, Louisa noticed even Tezco seemed unnerved. Glancing right and left at the crowd surrounding them, he exchanged quick words with Xosi and checked his nervous horse. All the horses were jittery, Defiant snorting and acting like he wanted to shy. *El Tigre* made low squeals in his throat and rolled his eyes.

A strange odor filled the air.

And further ahead, a great tiered stone pyramid emerged from a mound of earth, an expanse of narrow stone steps on its exposed side leading up to a flat apex where fire glowed. Louisa's eyes widened. The crowd closed in, men taking hold of the prancing horses' bridles.

More flutes. More drums. More cheers.

And then a tall, white-bearded, outlandish figure stepped out on the topmost tier of the pyramid. A hush fell over the assemblage.

"Oh, my God—" murmured Monte.

But Louisa's eyes were drawn to the spectacle before her.

"Welcome!" the man on the pyramid boomed in Spanish, his exotic feathered headdress waving with the projected power of his deep voice. Wearing a bright green cape over a long white skirt, a gold and turquoise neckpiece on his bare chest, waving a staff in one hand, a rattlesnake in the other, he spoke some words in a strange language. Then he addressed the newcomers again. "Welcome, Tezcatlipoca and Xochiquetzal."

Tezco shouted, "I brought the thing you asked for!"

"Your gifts are blessed," boomed the outrageous personage high above. "Please bring forth an honored guest."

A guest? Confused, Louisa looked to Tezco, who was frowning. The bandit leader gestured for his band and the captives to dismount. Louisa did so reluctantly as Tezco made his way toward her, several men in loincloths flanking him on either side.

But they passed right by her, and one of the men pointed at Sam. "*El Rubio.*"

The blond. The dark-haired, brown-skinned crowd had noticed the conspicuous Anglo with the fair hair and scarred face.

"They want you to come with me," Tezco told him.

Sam frowned. "I don't think so."

The bandit leader quirked his lip. "You must meet Quetzalcoatl."

Louisa didn't recognize the name. But she was concerned for Sam and tried to move people aside to follow him as the guards accompanied him toward the pyramid.

The crowd was tightly packed. Only *El Tigre*'s rearing and snorting kept any space at all cleared. Fearing the stallion would get himself into trouble, she struggled toward him, taking his bridle from the strangers who held him. At least the powerful animal's threatening movements kept people from pressing in on her. When she got him under control, she turned to look for Sam, saw that he and Tezco and the guards were climbing the pyramid stairs.

Monte Ryerson came up beside her, his black eyes wide and focused on the scene before them. "I don't like this."

"Don't like what? What's going on?"

He pointed. "See those steps? That's blood."

"Blood?"

She looked more closely and observed the stains

darkening the stairs, as if rusty splashes and rivulets had dribbled down them. Blood. The strange, sour odor. No wonder the horses were spooking.

Louisa shivered, a chill sweeping through her. "Why?"

"Quetzalcoatl's an Aztec god. He requires sacrifices—human sacrifices. They cut the living hearts out of their captives."

The chill Louisa felt turned to cold horror. Somewhere, sometime, she had heard about the ancient bloodthirsty Indians. Frozen in place, she stared, watching the small entourage approach the very top of the pyramid.

"Whose heart are they going to cut out?" she whispered, her own heart in her throat.

"I don't think it'll be Tezco's."

Sam!

For a moment, Louisa's breath actually stopped. Her muscles tensed, became stone. Then heat started to glow, flaring up in the vicinity of her middle, spreading outward slowly, then faster, then as furiously as a brushfire. Her eyes burned. Her body shook. Beside her, Monte was saying something about Beaufort Montgomery, but she wasn't listening. Her lips trembled and finally opened in a great shout. *"No-o-o!"*

Unthinking, oblivious to the crowd, she sprang for *El Tigre*, leapt to his back and slapped the reins as she kicked his sides. The horse plunged forward with a squeal.

Screams. Curses.

Louisa only rode harder, yelling, "Out of my way!"

People fell or were brushed aside. Someone dived for the mustang's bridle. But the man jerked back when Louisa kicked him.

"I said, get out of my way!"

The crowd parted. *El Tigre* broke into an all-out gallop. Heading for the earthen side of the pyramid, Louisa rode the mustang straight up the steep incline. His surefooted hooves dug into the soil.

Lying flat against the stallion's heaving neck, Louisa saw the man she loved struggling with his captors. She screamed to high heaven, calling his name over and over. "Sam! Sam!"

Would the last thing he ever heard be her horrified cry?

Sam was horrified. Not exactly knowing what the crazy, white-bearded man had meant by "guest," he'd ignored the rank odor of blood as Tezco took him to the top of the pyramid where a great altar rested. It was only then he realized what they meant to do to him.

Human sacrifice!

Sam struggled but the surrounding men were too many and too strong. For a moment, staring into their bronzed faces, he felt as if the Indians he'd fought for years were finally getting even with him. They ripped off his shirt, tied his feet and laid his body across the huge stone so his head hung down. Tezco stood only yards away, his own face a mask of horror. Hadn't his captor known what was meant for him, then? Sam wondered.

The leader of the group, the man in the headdress, was a white man like himself. Beaufort Montgomery? He now held a wicked oval-shaped obsidian blade aloft. Sam swallowed bile. He had seen plenty of death, but never like this. The noises of the crowd below the pyramid became a roar. Some people screamed. Sam thought the thudding sound he heard was the pounding of his own heart until he distinguished hoof-beats coming closer.

A furious black horse and a wild-haired, wild-eyed rider suddenly exploded onto the pyramid tier. Dear God, it was . . .

"Louisa! Get the hell out of here! Go!" Sam screamed at her. "Save yourself!"

"Sam!" Louisa beat the reins in the faces of the men who tried to stop her, screaming, "Let him go!"

Sam thought the madman would now kill the woman he loved. Tezco tried to stop her, only to be knocked flat as the black horse wheeled from one side to the other, striking out with sharp hooves.

The costumed white man had backed away, dropped his staff and let go of his rattlesnake. The creature slithered to safety in a dark crevice of stone. But to Sam's amazement, the white-bearded man seemed pleased. A great smile spread across the insane face beneath the feathered headdress.

His blue eyes blazed fire as he commanded, "Do not hurt her! Come away!" He held up a hand, as if he were trying to calm Louisa. "You may have this man if you want him, young woman. Do not despair."

Louisa appeared confused. "Sam, are you all right? They haven't hurt you, have they?"

"I'm fine."

"Thank God." She spoke soft words to the stallion, settling him down despite the hands trying to grab the horse's reins and drag her off.

"Leave her!" the leader told his men. And to Louisa, he said. "Very courageous—both the beast and the woman." Then he began issuing orders. "Free *El Rubio*. Cut his bonds. Prepare one of the houses for them. Take them there, provide them with servants."

But as one of the men came toward her, Louisa shouted, "Stay away from me!"

The madman motioned to his followers. "Let her lead the horse herself." He prodded Sam toward her. "And here is your prize, lovely brave one."

Tezco objected. "What is happening? All this talk of the soldier as a prize, Louisa *having* him. This brave woman is mine, Beaufort Montgomery!"

"Quetzalcoatl. Please use our correct titles, Tezcatlipoca. This woman belongs to all the gods."

Tezco looked as if he wanted to spit on the crazy white man. "I found her, took her, brought her here."

Blood churned through Sam's veins. So he had indeed found Montgomery. He'd give anything to choke the life from the bastard, but any display of hostility on his part would probably get him killed on the spot. Then who would take care of Louisa?

"You were truly clever, Tezcatlipoca," the white-haired madman was saying, "for you have offered us the bravest heart."

The bravest heart? Meaning Louisa herself would be sacrificed? Sam tried not to panic, tried to keep a cool head. He'd need one to get them out of this. For if it was the last thing he ever did—and it might be—he intended to see that Louisa got away safely.

Another pair mounted the flat pinnacle of the pyramid: Xosi with a second captive. She locked eyes with her brother, as if warning him of something. To Sam's dazed eyes, it seemed that only the surrounding armed men kept Tezco from stopping Montgomery as the madman chanted while this newest victim was tied to the great stone. Two of the men casually kept the barrels of their rifles pointed in the direction of Tezco's chest.

"Oh, my God!" cried Louisa, her expression horrified as she looked at the man on the altar. "Roberto!"

All Sam could do was hold her. No way could they
stop this from happening. Again, bile rose in his throat
as Beaufort Montgomery plunged his oval-shaped
knife straight down into his victim's chest. Blood
spurted, splattering on the white clothing of the men
surrounding the altar. A shriek such as Sam had
never heard echoed through the canyon and reverber-
ated off its walls. He forgot to breathe. His knees
quaked.

Another, weaker shriek.

A gurgling groan.

Then Montgomery roared, cutting, stabbing, until
he held a dripping red piece of meat aloft—Roberto's
heart.

The crowd cheered and streamed toward the tem-
ple. A rumble came from deep within the earth and
the very ground beneath their feet shifted.

El Tigre screamed and rose on his rear legs, nearly
ripping the reins from Louisa's hands. Her shocked
gaze met Sam's even as the earth settled. The tremor
had lasted no more than a few seconds. Sam saw that
Louisa was stunned, somewhere between dazed and
wanting to be sick. He grabbed the reins himself and
jerked the horse's head down, then slid an arm about
Louisa and led both the woman and the animal down
the side of the pyramid, against the crowd. He had to
be strong for her, no matter how helpless and weak
he felt.

Though he could offer no comfort for the atrocity
they'd witnessed, no more than he could offer an explanation for it. They seemed to have traveled backward
in time, to have entered a realm where Aztecs still

reigned, a kingdom that existed before the Europeans invaded.

"Hold on, Louisa, hold on. I'm with you," he whispered, knowing his words were of little solace.

He became aware that guards accompanied them, men with weapons who kept them in sight. At one point, a guard stepped forward and motioned for them to turn. Louisa paused and glanced over her shoulder.

"Don't look. There's no use," Sam said, smoothing her hair, leading her forward again.

He didn't want to look himself. Was Roberto's blood streaming down the long flight of steps? If so, he didn't want Louisa to see it. She was softhearted, if courageous.

So courageous that Montgomery had said she could have whatever she wanted. Too bad she hadn't asked for the lives of all the captives. But who could have known . . .

They passed Monte Ryerson standing stone-still, eyes bleak, expression shocked.

Concerned for what might happen to the rancher, Sam told Louisa, "Tell these guards you'd like your friends taken care of."

"What?" Her eyes were wide, her lips almost white.

He motioned to one of the men who shadowed them. "If you tell these men the other captives are your friends, we might be able to ensure their safety."

"Yes." Finally, she understood. She addressed the guard. "The other men are my *compadres*—"

"*Sí*, Señorita, you will see them," said the guard. "They will be staying near you, if you so desire."

"I desire." Louisa exchanged glances with Sam, who kept his arm tightly and protectively about her shoulders.

They kept walking until they'd traversed half the length of the canyon. Several low houses were built on a slope below the canyon wall. Hardly in the mood for observation, Sam had nevertheless noticed canals, crops and animal pens as they passed by.

"Stop here," said the guard, indicating one of the houses. "This will be yours."

The man wanted to lead *El Tigre* away but the horse refused to settle down. Sam didn't blame him but tied him to a small brushy tree. Then he led Louisa inside the house, a one-room affair with the basic comforts of a low makeshift bed set on a platform of stones, a table, a bench.

The guards stayed outside.

Sam took Louisa in his arms. She clung to him, holding him tightly, as if she never wanted to let go. He felt her shoulders tremble and realized she was crying. His own eyes filled.

Eventually, she sobbed openly, brokenly. "I-I saved Roberto's life. He was wounded by a bullet and I made some medicine for his shoulder."

Sam mumbled comforting, murmuring sounds as he cradled her tenderly.

"M-maybe I should have let him die," Louisa mourned. "It would have been less painful. Less horrific. How could one human being do that to another?"

Sam couldn't think of anything that would make her feel better. As for himself, he was haunted by terrible deeds of his own. He sighed, stroked her back, kissed her forehead.

Louisa took a deep, shuddering breath. "If only I could forget that scream—"

"You have to forget about it." As he'd been forced to do in so many instances. "There's no other choice."

Not if a person wanted to live—wanted to keep his reason. Sam laid his scarred cheek against the warmth of Louisa, his hope and mainstay in a violent, insane world.

16

Tezco feared he was going insane. He awoke sick, sore and exhausted in the small mud-brick house he shared with Xosi. Quetzalcoatl—no, Beaufort Montgomery, the crazy gringo—had assigned the dwelling to them after sharing a meal with him and his band the night before.

But Montgomery did not rule them.

Not any more than nightmares would rule him, please God. He'd had the worst yet. He planned to talk to Xosi today about seeing a *bruja* or a priest. Tezco did not wish to be possessed by a demon.

And possession was the only explanation for the vivid visions—first, the snarling face, then the flying on the wind. Lastly, he had become the demon himself and stood atop a great mountain clad only in a jaguar skin as he fought with a plumed serpent. The contest had been closely matched, but the serpent eventually won and made peace by assuring him there would be other women, all that he wanted, and that they should celebrate their divine association by feasting on mortal flesh and blood.

Tezco shuddered as he recalled the second meal of the night, the table in his dream—the bowls of gore he and the serpent had sat down to. He must forget that!

Just as he had to forget the horrific murder he had witnessed the day before.

He wanted to leave this canyon now, just as soon as they found and robbed the legendary *tesorería*. And because he could not stomach more such murders, he somehow had to set his captives free. Especially Louisa Janks, whether or not she wanted him. He'd never meant to put her in such danger.

Needing to talk to his sister, he pulled himself up on the low bed and glanced about the room.

"Xosi?"

The blankets on her narrow bed were rumpled, proving she had slept there at some time during the night. Dishes lay on the table.

"Xosi!"

Shouting only made his head pound. He ran his hands over his face, feeling beard stubble. His Indian heritage made it unnecessary for him to shave every day, but it had been some time since he had shaved at all. Perhaps cleaning himself up would make him feel better.

A sliver of mirror hung on one wall and Tezco dug a razor out of the saddlebag he had set at the foot of his bed. Looking for a vessel to fill with water, he picked up a cup and glanced at the mirror in passing.

Only to stiffen.

The same fierce face he had seen in his dream

gazed back at him. Handsome but ruthless beneath its headdress of gold and feathers. Red-eyed. Ancient. Evil.

"Demon!"

Tezco threw the razor, then the cup, shattering the mirror into a hundred pieces. He backed away, nearly jumping out of his skin when someone suddenly appeared in the doorway.

Xosi. Her golden hazel eyes were wide. "Tezco! What is the matter? I could hear your shouts across the canyon."

"A demon wishes to possess me," he babbled. "The mirror. You saw it, too."

"My little mirror? I admit it may be touched by *brujería.*" Looking concerned, she came and placed her hand on his shoulder, attempting to soothe him. "But there is no demon—"

She didn't understand. "I tell you there is a demon and he is in every mirror!" He brushed her hand away, pointed at the silvery shards on the floor. "He is in every dream—he wants my soul, Xosi!"

"Dreams?" She looked startled.

He told her of the visions that had been haunting him since they'd broken into the kiva in New Mexico Territory, told her about the plumed serpent, the feast of blood.

Fear glistened in Xosi's eyes. "All this talk of Aztecs. The captives. Sacrifices. That is what has brought the dreams. We must remember our purpose, and that a dream is only a dream."

But Tezco remained uncertain.

"You may be assured I am right, brother." She led him to the bench by the table. "Sit down. Rest. I will get you something to eat."

"I am not hungry."

"Then I will make you some tea. That will soothe you." She started to clear the clutter of pottery on the table, then frowned at a shallow bowl of congealed, bloody meat. "What is this?"

Tezco raised his head. He knew exactly what the bowl contained the very moment she asked the question. Knew the taste of the raw organ—the heart Beaufort Montgomery had ripped out of a living man the day before.

Xosi also knew then and dropped the bowl, her face suffused with horror. Blood splattered with a spray of broken pottery. Tezco's gut convulsed and he leaned forward to vomit. He could not stop until his stomach emptied. When he was able to get to his feet, his sister slung an arm about him and helped him stumble out of the house.

"We must leave this place, Xosi," he said with fervid passion, "as soon as possible."

"But the *tesorería,* the gold—"

He no longer cared about the tainted treasure. "Riches are not as important as our souls. You will lose me if we stay. I will lose myself."

Imagining the room around her was shaking, Louisa awoke. The room stilled but a warm heaviness enveloped her. She forced her eyes open. Sam. He was mumbling in his sleep and sweat stood out on his brow. He must have been thrashing. . . .

"Sam?" When he didn't respond, she gently touched his cheek. "Sam, wake up."

Finally, his eyes opened, startled.

She caressed his cheek again, tracing the scar with

a gentle finger. "I'm here, Sam. I don't know what you were dreaming about, but we're not in danger, at least not at this moment." Though God only knew what the day would bring.

His face was drawn, his expression haunted the way it had been in New Mexico. "I was reliving old battles." He raised his head to look around.

They had the simple house to themselves, though the vile bearded man—Beaufort Montgomery—had assigned them servants. Last night two women had offered them food and bowed low before gliding away. A curtain of heavy cloth hanging in the doorway afforded the house privacy—not that Louisa and Sam had done more than take a few bites before falling, fully dressed, into an exhausted sleep.

"Are you hungry? I'm sure one of the women will bring us something." She had already seen one of them pull aside the curtain to peek through the doorway.

"I'll take anything that's edible. We need to keep up our strength."

Some time later, while wolfing down the tortillas and eggs the servants had brought, they stared out of the building's one open-air window. The residents of the barranca were busy, tending fields, erecting more houses, baking, weaving. Cattle and goats grazed. And, except for *El Tigre,* who was staked out near the house, all the horses were being kept in a big ramada at one end of the canyon.

The scene looked peaceful. Only the sinister loom of the ancient tiered pyramid suggested anything awry. Louisa's blood ran cold remembering what had taken place there yesterday.

"What is Montgomery trying to do?" Sam mused, no

doubt also thinking of Roberto's sacrifice. "Trying to re-create some ancient city? Revive the Aztec culture?"

And were Tezco and his band part of it? Louisa wondered. Though Tezco bore the same serpent brand as the men in the valley, his bandits hadn't participated in any strange rituals on the journey into Mexico.

When some familiar figures appeared at the bottom of the slope, she leaned forward. Monte, Jake and Shorty were obviously looking for her and Sam. She waved.

"Thank God you're still alive and well," Louisa said as they came inside.

"So far." Jake's mustache bristled. "But we ain't gonna live long if yesterday is a sample of what we can expect."

"You can expect it. Maybe worse," Monte said grimly.

"They're going to sacrifice everyone, aren't they?" Louisa asked. Even her. Despite the strangely respectful treatment she'd received yesterday, she felt doom deep down in her gut. So much for ensuring everyone's safety.

"I know Montgomery from years and years ago," Monte said. "He wants to bring back the dark spirits. He thinks he's Quetzalcoatl, the plumed serpent."

"Where did this madman come from?" she asked.

"It's a long story." Monte sat down on the bench, leaned on the table. "Captain Beaufort Montgomery of the Confederate Army was a wealthy scholar from New Orleans. He was studying the Mexica, the Aztecs, long before the war began. He made trips to Mexico, brought back some codices—Aztec writing— with secret information. Supposedly, he figured out the location of the wheel of life and death. It was said to be made of pure gold, to have belonged to Quetzalcoatl himself, and had been broken apart when the Spanish came. If it gets put back together and bathed in sacrificial blood, the old gods will return."

"Is that the information you were supposed to tell the army?" Sam asked. The most educated of anyone there, he was probably also the most skeptical.

"Can only tell them what I know," Monte said. "When I got back from the war, I asked my grandfather to teach me to read. Had to find out everything I could; even took a trip to New Orleans. Found plenty of books and papers." He paused. "I served under Montgomery—saw him cut a heart out right on the battlefield. Never forgot it, any more than any of us can forget about Roberto."

Louisa swallowed the lump in her throat.

"It's the dark spirits," pronounced Monte.

She raised her brows. "Evil spirits, you mean?"

"If death is evil—and I think it is if you worship it long and hard enough, serve it, place it above everything else," Monte told her. "That's what my people believe, my Comanche half. The people here—Aztecs, Mayans—served evil spirits time out of mind. Fed them lives and blood through centuries of war. The Aztecs were very strong. They traveled as far north as the Rocky Mountains to take captives."

"You're talking like these spirits and wheels and bunk is real," remarked Shorty, who rarely said two words.

Monte nodded. "There are things that exist beyond the white man's reality. I can say that, having lived both kinds of lives, being both white and Indian."

When he gazed at Louisa, she wanted to shiver. She hadn't lived as an Indian, but she'd heard of unusual things. "Some friends of mine were tracked by a skin-walker, a woman who walked as a wolf. I never saw it with my own eyes, but I believe Chaco and Frances told the truth."

Monte continued to stare at her, his eyes very deep and black. "You're Indian, aren't you?"

"Half-Comanche." She thought his expression changed almost imperceptibly.

"One of the southern bands? The Penateka? The Tenawa?"

"I know very little about the Comanche," she said quickly. "My Anglo mother raised me. She only told me my father's name and that he treated her well."

Jake cut in. "So these death spirits is supposed to come back, eh? Soon as they bathe a gold wheel with our blood?"

"The wheel must be blessed with the most courageous heart. The rest of us will be side offerings. Maybe they'll flay our skins and wear them for a while, practice a little cannibalism."

Both Jake and Shorty looked sick.

Sam moved closer to Louisa. "What did you say about 'the most courageous heart'? Does that mean—"

"Courage is as valued by evil as by good." Monte sounded carefully indirect.

But Louisa knew better. So did Sam, who grasped her hand and held it tightly.

"Well, I'll tell you one thing," said Jake. "I ain't gonna get split open without fightin' back. I'm getting me a gun some way or the other—take a few of 'em with me."

"We need more than guns. We need a plan," Sam said. "Tactics."

Louisa's eye was drawn to a slight movement at the curtained doorway. A hand drew the material aside, revealing Tezco's face. His eyes seemed to burn and she felt a thrill of fear. How much had he heard?

"Uh, let's talk about more pleasant things, shall we?" she suggested. "We might as well try to rest while we can."

The group got the hint, she thought, everyone immediately silencing. Sam stared at the door . . . where Tezco let the curtain fall back into place. Had he come to drag her away? Well, she wasn't going, she thought, clasping Sam's hand for all she was worth.

He lowered his voice. "Take a look outside. See if anyone's still out there."

Shorty shuffled over to the window. "A coupla guards, right outside the door. They's close enough to eavesdrop if they're of a mind to."

"Not that we have any big plans to hide," said Monte.

"Not yet," Louisa added.

"Still, might as well continue this conversation when we have more privacy." Monte got up and headed for the door, halfway there turning and looking at Louisa. "I want to talk some more about the Comanche with you."

As the other captives left, Louisa gazed out the window at the guards, wondering if the men were going to make a move or haul someone else off to be sacrificed. She sighed with relief when Monte and the two cowboys passed by unmolested.

She turned to Sam and sank into his arms, praying he could drive everything from her mind but their love.

Sam's thoughts were heavy, his mind bogged down by war, death, destruction, Indians. He couldn't even worry about Montgomery and his madness. The night before, he'd relived insanity of his own—re-envisioned battles, especially that last time he and his men had been ambushed by the Apache.

Both physically and spiritually fatigued, distracted by the thought of coming up with a plan of escape, he wasn't certain he could offer Louisa the comfort she sought. But he kissed her anyway, closing his eyes, caressing the silkiness of her skin and hair. Making little murmuring sounds, she moved her lips over his and explored his mouth with her eager tongue. His arousal grew when she undulated her hips against him. But before he could cup her breast or back her toward the bed, she suddenly drew away.

Her face was stormy. "What's the matter? Don't you want me anymore?"

"Of course I want you," he said, wondering how she could even question his love for her.

"You don't act like it. You're not even breathing hard."

"It's difficult switching from death to life so fast, Louisa." And while he was feeling so sick inside. "Life is what making love is all about. Maybe we should wait for a little while—"

"Wait? We could die tonight—or this very day!"

"I know. Any minute, any hour. I got used to living like that in the army." He reached for her.

She stepped back. "The army? That's all you can think about. And your *duty.*"

For some reason the very word always made her see red. "I didn't mention duty."

Her dark eyes flashed. "Maybe you're upset because you failed your duty this time, Mr. Soldier. You didn't manage to rescue me, did you?"

True, if rather cruel of her to point out. He was reminded that he hadn't really saved her from that lynching party six years ago, unless one counted accidentally getting her lost in the mountains as a strategy.

He hardened his jaw. "We aren't dead yet."

"Meaning you're so busy thinking about how to get out of this canyon that you can't lose yourself in a kiss?"

"You have to admit the possibility of escape is important." He tried to touch her again, only to have her jerk away.

"Don't! And after you finally told me you loved me."

Behind the angry expression, he thought he caught a flash of sadness so bleak that he couldn't stand it. "I do love you, with all my heart."

"Ha! Don't say that again unless you're prepared to prove it!" With that, she turned on her heel and strode for the doorway, whipping aside the curtain.

"Louisa." Thinking she shouldn't be wandering around on her own, he strode after her. "Louisa!"

She surely heard him calling, but she didn't even turn to look. Her back ramrod straight, she headed down the slope on which the house sat and off toward a rough path leading past some lean-tos. Angry himself, Sam thought about chasing after her, then decided she would only fight him and attract attention—though, as prisoners slated for sacrifice, they could hardly get into any more trouble than they already were.

Which was why he should be completely honest with her.

He'd told Louisa about some of his experiences in the Apache Wars. But he'd left out the worst part.

If there were dark war gods, death spirits that fed on

savage battle fury, on bloodlust that knew no boundaries of age or sex or whether an opponent was armed or not, he'd personally visited their altar.

As soon as she got her emotions under control, Louisa decided to pay Monte Ryerson a visit. Talking about the Comanche should help her forget her disappointment with Sam. Maybe she'd been unreasonable by expecting him to lose himself in passion, yet she couldn't help thinking that if a man truly loved a woman, he'd want to spend what could be his last hours in her arms. But then, he'd waited six years before looking for her and hadn't known whether she was married, dead or living as a nun.

Attempting to ignore the old pain that made her hurt, Louisa glanced about. Last night the guard had said her *compadres* would be staying nearby. Several lean-tos of brush and canvas stood some yards from the house and she spotted Monte sitting cross-legged on the ground outside of one of them.

Pleased that he seemed to be alone, she paced toward him and, without preamble, demanded, "I want to hear about the Comanche."

"Have a seat." As she eased herself down, he asked, "Where did you get that bear claw you wear?"

She fingered her necklace. "My ma gave this to me . . . as my only inheritance from my father, I guess. It's—"

"Comanche," he finished for her. "Warrior's medicine." He opened his shirt, drawing out a similar arrangement of claw and feathers and beads on a cord. "What was your father's name?"

"Red Knife."

"You're sure?" He was gazing at her so strangely,

his lips set in a straight line below his hooked nose, his eyes unrelenting.

"Is something wrong?"

"You might find this hard to believe, but I'm your brother."

Now it was her turn to stare. "Ma didn't say anything about having another kid." Not while living with the Comanche.

"Half brother. We shared the same father."

Louisa felt both awed and touched. Never having had a sibling, she examined Monte's face. His features were stronger and harsher than hers, but their stubborn, squared off chins were similar. "Are you sure?"

"Red Knife had several wives, two white. Mine was the runaway daughter of a Texas rancher."

Louisa objected. "Ma didn't say anything about her either."

"Because she was long gone by the time your mother came around—what's her name?"

"My ma? Belle."

He looked thoughtful. "Hmm, blue eyes, reddish hair. Yeah, I remember her. But she had a Comanche name then—Talks Loud."

Louisa would have smiled if she weren't so stunned. "Ma can talk up a storm all right. You lived in Red Knife's camp?"

"Until I was thirteen." He explained, "My own mother went back to her people when Old Man Ryerson, my grandfather, lined up a white man and paid him to marry her. My stepfather didn't like me much. I was a little too dark-skinned for his taste."

"I know what you mean." She'd never gone unnoticed, either.

"So I went back to the camps of the Penateka when

I was six. Learned to ride and steal horses and go to war the Comanche way."

Amazing. Her heart told her to believe him. *Her brother.*

"Red Knife was hanged as a horse thief when I was thirteen, along with some other important warriors. His people took off; most got hunted down, and what was left got sent off to reservations. I went back to my mother and stepfather."

Her brother. Though Monte was nearly fifteen years older. Louisa had so many questions to ask, her mind whirled. "We had the same father. It's so hard to believe, I mean that we would meet on a journey like this—"

"You do believe in things your eyes can't see?"

"Spirits?"

"And ghosts of ancestors. We rode a trail into Mexico that our father and his people used to take. We both wore the bear claw so we'd recognize each other. Perhaps he came with us."

Louisa thought it would take more than a ghostly ancestor to get them out of Beaufort Montgomery's clutches. Still, destiny had thrown them together, surely for a purpose. Surely not so that they would meet, then die.

"Red Knife had a thousand horses, but not being able to keep his mouth shut about where he got them got him hanged. Horses were the key to Comanche freedom."

Louisa stared off into the distance at the clouds floating above the craggy peaks. Though it seemed long ago, she'd loved nothing better than galloping across New Mexican mesas with her hair flying behind her. "I like my freedom, too."

"Uh-huh. You're damned good with horses and have the courage of a warrior. Our father would have been proud of you."

"Think so? I guess your saying that is the closest I'll ever get to him and the Comanche now." She sighed. "I grew up in an Anglo world. I was persecuted because of my Indian blood and never even came close to leading an Indian life. Half of me was missing, like I belonged nowhere and with nobody but Ma."

"Now you also belong with me, your brother."

Louisa swallowed, feeling tears at the back of her eyes. Though the thought still stunned her, she wasn't going to get all emotional. When Monte offered his hand, she clasped it tightly.

"I wasn't joking when I said a good spirit may have brought us together," he told her. "We should pray to God, to every spirit that fights against death and nourishes life."

Pray. Worship life instead of death. Though not particularly church-going religious, Louisa nonetheless firmly believed in an all-around great spirit, a wise creator with many faces and names.

"Praying sounds good," she told Monte. "Maybe there'll be a miracle. Or we'll figure out some way to pull one off."

Miracles certainly didn't seem impossible, not after finding out she had a brother, someone who seemed to be a link between herself and her Indian heritage. Gratefully, she half rose to hug Monte, not certain whether he'd like it. He responded warmly.

When he released her, she smiled into his eyes . . . until his gaze slid away, focusing on something or someone behind her.

"Must you have every man in the canyon?"

Xosi. Surprised, Louisa rose to face the Mexican woman. Her thick mahogany hair long and loose, dressed in a clean skirt and white *camisa*, Xosi was attractive, though as petulant as usual.

"Were my brother and the soldier not enough?" Xosi went on, taking a puff on a *cigarillo*.

Louisa frowned. "You don't know what you're talking about."

Xosi made a threatening motion, but Monte intervened, stepping between them. "Louisa is my sister."

"Sister?" Xosi's expression changed.

Uninterested in Xosi, Louisa caught sight of Sam watching her some yards down the path. Knowing she'd said cruel things to him, Louisa swallowed her pride and went to meet the man she loved.

Xosi had always taken pride in her beauty; now, she wished to entice Monte Ryerson. Anxious for her brother, she had longed for distraction and been furious to see Louisa Janks taking up the intriguing captive's attention. Spooked by Montgomery and the strange aura that hung over this canyon ruled by the blood-stained pyramid, Xosi needed a way to make herself feel better.

She looked over the big, handsome man standing before her. "That girl is your sister? You have never said this before."

"Didn't know until today when I realized we had the same father."

"For truth?"

"Why would I lie? Got no reason to dodge your jealousy. You're not my woman."

Xosi raised her brows and took another drag of her

cigarillo. Ignoring his insightful remark about jealousy, she lowered her eyelashes and asked, "Would you like me to be your woman?"

"You wanta take up with a prisoner?"

She liked the way he was staring at her breasts, naked beneath her *camisa.* "You are not my prisoner any more. These are not my people. I do not hold their religious beliefs."

"Then why did you bring us here?"

She hesitated for a moment before deciding Monte Ryerson could not tell tales to anyone who mattered. "We came for gold." Which they might never get now. She could not give up hope for the riches, no matter that her concern for Tezco was great. "The crazy gringo promised us the contents of a rich *tesorería.*"

"Uh-huh, the lost treasure of Quetzalcoatl. There actually might be one, you know. I've read about it."

"You are a wise man," she said flirtatiously.

"And are you cruel, like an Aztec goddess? Xosi—doesn't that come from Xochiquetzal, the one who rules love and flowers?"

She became uncomfortable. "Perhaps my parents knew about such ancient names. But do not compare me to goddesses." She did not want to start having dreams and visions like Tezco. "Though I must say I prefer love and flowers to death."

"All Aztec gods are death spirits when it comes down to it."

She felt a chill. "I am not a god. I descend from Moctezuma but I am a human being. A woman." She stepped nearer, gave him a sultry smile. "Would you like me to prove that?"

He ignored the blatant invitation. "You don't crave blood?"

She placed a hand on her hip. "I would kill someone to protect myself or my brother. But I could never tie a helpless victim to an altar and cut out his heart." Which reminded her of the bowl her brother dropped, the way he had become so sick.

"You look like you're afraid."

Was she so transparent? She tried to deny her feelings. "I am not afraid, at least not for myself."

"Then for who?"

Again, she hesitated. But Tezco's problems were like a weight about her neck. She fingered her little mirror, noticing the warm smile lines around Monte Ryerson's eyes, the strength that went far beyond his powerful flexing muscles.

"I fear for my brother. He is being haunted by a demon."

17

Sam still wore a haunted look as Louisa approached him. She said, "I'm sorry about the mean things I said." Monte had given her a more centered, peaceful outlook, even in their awful circumstances.

Sam slid an insistent arm about her waist and told her grimly, "Let's get back to the house. I'm going to make love to you until you can't see straight."

She couldn't help feeling a little thrill at the very thought, but she said, "That isn't the real problem."

"Then what is?"

"I guess I'm never sure if you really love me or not."

"Because of the six years I was gone?"

"And . . . well, there's this distance about you. This look you get on your face like you're somewhere else." The expression he wore right now. "I can't be sure you really want to be with me." Which brought up her own long-standing uncertainty about people's acceptance.

He loosened his hold on her and slowed. "We have to talk. There's something else I need to tell you."

She felt some trepidation. "About the Apache Wars?"

"About one particular incident."

Something even more terrible than the massacre in the caves? She swallowed. "I'm ready to listen." She wanted to bridge the gap, to be able to touch him deep inside.

Just then, Beaufort Montgomery came toward them, an entourage of a dozen men in his wake. Most wore unusual, brightly colored cloaks, necklaces and expressions of importance. The rest were guards . . . wearing loincloths and carrying rifles.

Montgomery halted, his smile focused on Louisa. He must be fifty or so, she thought, though his beard and shoulder-length hair were completely white. He wasn't an ugly man, but his blazing blue eyes made him frightening. Was he here to order his next victims escorted to the pyramid?

"Here is the lovely brave one," he said. "I have come to invite you and your consort to a feast tonight . . . in your honor."

Only a feast, not an execution. But though she was relieved, Louisa didn't return the man's smile. "To hell with honor."

Montgomery laughed. "How defiant—like a cornered jaguar. Ah, you are most certainly the *one.*"

Sam scowled, keeping Louisa within the curve of his arm. "The one what? The bravest heart?" He looked Montgomery up and down. "You're full of bull, and you're no damned Aztec. You're a white American. I don't know why these Indians or Mexicans don't kill you—you don't belong here."

At that, some of the men surrounding Montgomery bristled.

The leader himself kept smiling, his eyes brilliant but cold. "I am Quetzalcoatl."

"Then I'm Napoleon," Sam said. "What happened, Reb? Did you go crazy because your side lost?"

Montgomery laughed again, but Louisa thought the sound hollow. He waved to his entourage, who were still restless.

"How he raves! This one is brave, too. We are blessed." Then he again addressed Louisa. "There is a warm spring some way up the mountainside above your house. You may have your servants take you there and bathe you if you wish."

"I'm not cleaning myself up for your stupid feast."

"As you choose. But you will be bathed one way or the other before the sun reaches its zenith tomorrow."

"That's when you're going to cut out my heart?"

"The gods will welcome you." He straightened his already erect posture, appearing taller. And more threatening. "You will dwell in the eastern paradise beyond the clouds, and we shall bury your remains in great state, your brave horse at your feet."

She shivered but stared him in the eye. "Don't count on that. You're the man who worships death spirits. They'd rather have you. Except I think you'll be burning in hell after you're buried, not floating around on clouds."

Finally, Montgomery's smile wavered. With one angry gesture and proud grace, he started to move off, his entourage in his wake. "I shall look forward to your presence tonight."

As soon as the group was out of earshot, she let herself relax, her knees nearly buckling.

Sam caught her, letting her lean against him. "Are you all right?"

"Yes." Thinking of Monte's explanations, she said adamantly, "I serve life, not death."

They walked up the slope to the house, Sam looking at the ground. He took a deep breath as they paused at the door. "For myself, I've served both life and death. I paid a terrible price for the last. Even if they cut my heart out, part of it is already dead."

"I don't believe that, Sam." And she wanted his heart for herself. "What could possibly be so terrible? Tell me."

Monte listened patiently as Xosi told her wild tale—the meeting with Beaufort Montgomery in El Catorce, the journey to New Mexico, the taking of captives, the face she and Tezco had seen in her mirror.

"Do you believe a terrible spirit is possessing my brother?" she finally asked.

"If the story about that ancient Aztec wheel of life and death is true." In his gut, where the Comanche in him still dwelled, he did believe. His skin had prickled when Xosi told him about the gold in the kiva and the haunting of her little mirror. "The dark gods want to return, to live in the flesh."

She shuddered and lifted the silver chain from her neck. "I saw you the night we found you in the cave—*brujería*."

Monte had wondered how the bandits located him.

"I am no witch, but simple things like that do not frighten me," she went on. "Fierce demons do."

"I hope you've seen frightening visions."

"You wish terrible things for me?" she asked, her eyes wide.

Sometimes she seemed childlike. "Don't you under-

stand what you've done? You and Tezco have brought
people to their deaths, even men of your own band.
How many so far? I know at least one was shot on the
way. Then Roberto was cut up like a steer yesterday.
That's no way for anyone to die."

She lowered her head guiltily. "It was not my fault."

"You have no conscience? You traded lives for gold."

"I did not kill anyone myself," she insisted, agitated.
"I did not wish death on them."

Good; at last he was making her feel guilty. There
was a heart behind the pretty, pouty exterior. "Because
of you, I'm going to die on the altar myself. I wouldn't
mind so much if I wasn't leaving three children
orphaned."

"Orphans?"

"Two girls and a boy. Their ma's already dead. I'm
all they have."

Xosi glanced at him quickly, then looked away,
playing with the silver chain in her hand. "My brother
and I were orphans. He is several years older than I.
He was all I had."

"You're close. That's why you care so much about
what's happening to him."

She sighed. "Even though he's changed—I do not
know if he will ever be the same again. It began with
that Louisa. When he took her, he withdrew from me."

She hadn't told Monte anything about the kidnap-
ping, but he'd heard details from Sam on the journey.
"My sister?"

Again, Xosi gave him a quick glance.

He'd play on the relationship she held dear, a relationship he'd like to live to enjoy. "I'm the only brother
Louisa has." He pointed out, "You're not going to
blame her for your brother's problems. They started

when you two took up with Montgomery. Greed brings about its own bad end."

"You do not know how it was with us," she said defensively. "We were so poor as children, we ate insects when we could not steal tortillas."

"Yeah, I've eaten some grub myself. I spent part of my childhood in Comanche camps—after the buffalo were long gone. And I got by on what little swill the Confederate Army dished out at the end of the war."

She held the little mirror before her, chain hanging down.

He placed a hand on her bare shoulder, an unbidden question suddenly coming to mind. "You know Montgomery . . . Quetzalcoatl pretty well, don't you? Have any influence on him?"

"Why?" She asked sarcastically, "Do you think I could change his mind about the sacrifices?"

"You're beautiful enough to turn any man's head."

A smile flickered on her full lips and she arched her spine so that her nipples stood out against the thin material stretched over them. Despite the situation, Monte was aroused.

"So you think I am beautiful."

"So does Quetzalcoatl, I bet." He remembered another old legend. "He's supposed to be a celibate god—never has sex. But he must have a hard time resisting you."

She laughed. "What do you suggest?"

"Sex is supposed to destroy him. . . . if he really is a god." Which Monte sometimes believed was possible, sometimes not. He could never forget that Montgomery had once saved his life. Ironic that the same man was now trying to take it. "If nothing else, a beautiful woman's body might give the old man something to think about other than killing people." Some romantic involvement with an exotic female like Xosi might distract Montgomery enough to let the captives escape. "Maybe he'd even quit calling up the death spirits that are after your brother."

"Hm-m-m." Again she played with the silver chain. "The madman is powerful," she admitted. "Have you seen the plants that are growing? Grain, flowers—the peasants say he brought them forth magically with drops of blood and holy words."

"So you're afraid to approach him."

"I am not afraid of him. I fear the face in the mirror." She lowered her voice, her tone husky. "But why should I want to lie with an old man anyway?"

The way she was staring at him told Monte that he was going to have to do some influencing himself. He couldn't say that the work would be unpleasant.

"What would you prefer?"

"A strong man, dark . . . like you."

She ran her hands up his chest, then stood on tiptoe to slip the chain and mirror about his neck. Then she arched and rubbed herself against him like a cat. He could feel the hard pebbles of her nipples through their layers of clothing.

"The mirror necklace is a token from me," she whispered. "You are wise. Perhaps you can see good things, rather than evil."

"A token? I'd rather have my life."

"You shall have that, too, if I have anything to say about it." She made a little mewling noise as he slid a hand down her pliant spine and over the curve of her hips. "Let us go somewhere where we can be alone."

She led him away from the lean-to through a copse of mesquite trees, her hips swinging. They climbed some rocks and ended up in a grassy area sheltered by low shrubs.

She took off her *camisa,* let her skirt fall to her feet. Her naked voluptuousness caused Monte's blood to race. He was already achingly hard.

"So sex will destroy Quetzalcoatl, eh?" Boldly, she felt his arousal through his denim trousers, her nostrils flaring, her breath coming faster. She undid buttons quickly. "Luckily, it will not destroy you."

"Destroying those Apaches with a rockslide wasn't the only atrocity I took part in," Sam told Louisa as she sat next to him on the bench. He stared at the packed earthen floor. "I killed Indians with my bare hands, laughed in their faces as they died."

Somehow, she couldn't see Sam laughing as people died, no matter what he said. "You must have been caught up in the heat of battle."

"Maybe. And maybe I was just plain tired." His eyes had that tormented, faraway look. "We were chasing renegades near the Mexican border. I'd lost several men to belly wounds—the worst. The Apache dipped the iron tips of their arrows in snake venom and took pains to aim them at a man's middle." He licked his lips nervously. "It was the day of the ambush that made me resign my commission."

Prepared for gruesome details, Louisa sat quietly, not touching Sam, simply letting him talk.

"That last day, we rode by a small isolated ranch," he went on. "At first I thought the people who lived there were all right. Smoke was rising from the chimney. Then I noticed a trail of something dark on the ground outside the barn—blood. We went in and found the whole family—parents, several children—hanging from ropes strung up in the hayloft. What was left of them, that is. They'd been mutilated so you couldn't tell what they really looked like."

Louisa didn't want to imagine the scene any more than she wanted to remember what happened to Roberto. But she couldn't quite block it out of her mind and chewed at her lip.

Sam continued, "We buried the remains and set up camp that night a few miles away. We had some friendlies traveling with us, a couple of scouts and a woman I thought belonged to one of them. Seems she didn't, since I woke up to find her crawling into my bedroll with me."

"So you slept with her." Though she didn't like the idea, it had happened so long ago. She and Sam had been through so much since that Louisa wasn't jealous.

"We had sex. We didn't make love. I don't know what got into me. I guess I was lonely."

"You are flesh and blood," she pointed out, "no matter how perfect you always want to be." Something she would do well to remember about him.

Only a quick glance told her he'd even heard her. He was caught up in his story. "It was later in the night that the renegades ambushed us. I woke up, thinking I was dreaming. Then I heard shouting and scrambled to my feet to see an Apache brave scalping one of my men right in front of my eyes. I went crazy."

"So you fought back."

"Like an animal." He looked old all of a sudden, far older than twenty-nine. "I wrestled the knife from the brave and slit his throat, then scalped him." He paused, the memory obviously painful. "I picked up a gun. . . . I have no idea how many Apaches I shot."

Another pause. "But somehow I ended up knife-fighting again, got someone down and sunk my blade into his belly. Except it wasn't a man. I realized that when she screamed." He took a deep, painful breath. "I gutted that Apache woman, Louisa, ripped her apart, the same woman I'd slept with."

Despite her resolve, she felt chilled. "It was war and you made a mistake." *Her* Sam, the one sitting beside her right now, could never do such a thing. "You were out of your head. The Mexicans call it getting the *coraje.*"

Sam rubbed his forehead. "Yeah, I already said I went crazy. But a mistake? My commanding officer didn't think so. He commended me—told me the woman was a spy, that she tried to distract me on purpose so her friends could sneak into camp."

"Was that true?"

"That's the horror of it, Louisa. I'm not sure. The Apache scouts agreed with my officer, but then the woman may have been from a rival band, one they hated. I think I remember her attacking me. But I can't be certain that I didn't simply savage her in my rage."

"I don't believe you would have attacked someone who wasn't intent on attacking you. And you were crazy, if only temporarily. I've been crazy at times since Tezco carried me off. I think I would have shot him a long time ago if I'd had a gun. I poisoned his bandits. I'd probably shoot Beaufort Montgomery right now if I got the chance."

"But I killed a woman." Sam shook his head. "Brutally. I'm afraid of myself. I can't forgive myself. I . . . I can hardly take you in my arms without thinking about it sometimes. If there are death spirits, I worshiped them that night."

Louisa felt her heart swell. Haunted as he was, she could imagine Sam flinching if he woke up to bronzed skin and black hair in the morning.

But she refused to let the dark spirits have him. She would fight them. "I'm not afraid of you, Sam." She touched his shoulder and let her hand rest there. "Remember that enemies come in both sexes and all colors. You're too good a man to keep carrying around a burden like this. I'm certain that woman was a spy like everyone said. You don't have an uncontrollable temper; never did. And you're not at war anymore. You must forgive yourself. Choose to worship life."

He couldn't meet her eyes. "Can it be that easy?"

"Maybe not, but you can make a start by saying you *will* forgive yourself. We all fight back when we're cornered and scared. It's only natural." She pointed out, "And you didn't do something cold-blooded like decide to cut somebody's heart out in front of an audience."

"Perhaps Montgomery is only crazy, too."

She hadn't thought of it like that. "If so, he's too far gone to ever come back. He's called up the death spirits and let them live through him. You haven't. You wouldn't. You're not that weak." She urged, "Choose life."

For a while, Sam remained silent. Then he reached up and placed a hand over hers, his eyes sliding toward her, his lips softening. "I think I did choose life after I saw you again, Louisa."

"And I you." She told him, "In a way, before you came back to New Mexico, I was dead inside." She'd worshiped death spirits, too.

"I wasn't worth it."

"You are worth it, Sam. Not that I didn't have other

problems. You leaving me was merely the last straw. I was hiding out, running away from years of shame over what my mother did for a living, years of being treated like I was less than human because I was a breed."

"You were always proud and wild and beautiful," he insisted. "You followed your dreams."

"I tried to act like it, like I was having a real good time. But I didn't always feel good deep down inside. I wasn't certain whether I refused to become the lady Ma tried to make me because it wasn't what I really wanted or because I knew other people wouldn't allow me that choice."

"I've known plenty of ladies. Living that kind of life would bore you."

"Think so?"

He leaned back and let go of her hand to slide his arm around her shoulders, pulling her against him. "Ladies follow stacks of rules. You're far too exciting for that."

She loved to hear him say so, but she made a face. "I'm exciting to you."

"And that had better be important, more important than other people's opinions, because you're my woman."

My woman. Sam's saying those words thrilled her to her core, as did the expression in his blue-green eyes, an emotion deep and pure as the New Mexican sky.

"You're so lovely . . . inside and out." He ran a finger along her cheekbone, then gently touched her mouth. "What a fool I was, letting myself get so wrapped up in my confounded duty. How could I have gone off and left you for so long? The only excuse is that I was young, had to prove my manhood, uphold my family's military tradition." He took her chin in his hand and tipped her face up. "But then, you were young, too, barely a girl."

"Sixteen. Some people get married even younger."

"I had a sister your age."

Sister? Louisa realized she hadn't told Sam about Monte.

Not that doing so was very important at the moment, not with Sam leaning closer, getting ready to kiss her. She let her lips part, her eyes drift closed, her head lean back against the hard muscles of his arm. "I'm not a girl anymore."

"Sure aren't." He trailed kisses down her throat, found the pulse point, moved lower. . . .

Louisa sighed and ran her fingers through his tousled hair. Her skin felt hot wherever his lips touched her.

"Don't stop," she moaned, when he raised his head a few moments later.

But something was wrong. Stiffening, she opened her eyes, slid them in the same direction Sam was staring. Tezco stood in the doorway, having rudely pulled aside the curtain.

She sat up straighter but refused to break Sam's embrace. "What are you doing here? Can't you leave us alone?"

The bandit leader glared. "I have come to speak to Sam Strong, as well as to you."

Sam scowled but loosened his hold on Louisa. Still, she could feel the tenseness in his muscles, as if he were getting ready for a fight.

"We must get away from this madman," said Tezco.

Surprise replaced Sam's scowl. "What?"

"You heard what I said, soldier. Will you join me or will you not?"

"Join you? We can't even trust you," Louisa protested.

Sam added, "What is this, some kind of double-cross?"

"I do not play a trick. I speak the truth." Tezco asked Louisa, "Did I ever hurt you?" Then he looked at Sam. "I could have killed you, but I did not."

Sam remained disbelieving. "You didn't have to kill us. You waited to let Beaufort Montgomery have that privilege."

"Because the madman promised gold to my sister and me. Even so, I thought I could take what he offered and let my captives go."

"I find that hard to believe," said Sam.

"Believe it or not, as you choose. I am a thief, I admit it. I am no killer." He turned, went to the window and glanced out nervously. "I did not know Montgomery would gain so many followers. This is a cursed place. And now even the gold is not important. I cannot allow this devil to spill more blood . . . to consume flesh."

Louisa and Sam exchanged glances and drew apart.

Tezco turned back to them. "The things that this man does in this canyon are sins against heaven and earth. And they are on my head!"

The bandit leader was so impassioned, Louisa tended to believe him. "I don't think this is an act, Sam."

Tezco's amber eyes widened. "An act? The madman has called up a demon to possess me—Tezcatlipoca. He has forced me to—"

"To what?" Sam asked.

"I do not wish to speak of it." Tezco tightened his

jaw. "I have eleven men, you have three. And then there are my sister and Louisa—nearly twenty of us. I can give you guns. You have experience with battles and can help decide our tactics. I heard you speaking of such not so long ago."

"So you want to pull off a surprise?" Now Sam sounded interested. "We'll have to fight our way out."

"Yes, that would be best at the ceremony tomorrow."

Louisa exchanged another meaningful look with Sam. "All right, talk." She rose to go to the window. "I'll keep watch."

Was Tezco actually coming over to their side? Was this the miracle she'd hoped for? Or nothing but a cruel lie?

18

"*There are truly fresh* chilies growing in this valley," remarked Xosi at the feast in Montgomery's quarters that evening. She took a liberal helping from a bowl and smiled sweetly at the madman. "And flowers out of season. It is not a lie."

"There are no lies or liars in my kingdom," the madman pronounced, sounding smug and pompous.

His eyes burned a little less intensely at the moment, but he still appeared plenty crazy.

At least in Louisa's opinion. Montgomery also wasn't too quick in recognizing Tezco as being a danger to him.

From her place further down the long, low table lit by numerous candles, Louisa watched the interaction of the serious-faced bandit leader, his sister and the madman. Before the feast, Tezco had said that Xosi intended to charm Montgomery into letting down his guard, but her fawning and flirting was so convincing, it made Louisa distrust her. She only hoped Tezco knew what Xosi was about and could guarantee that she actually intended to throw her fate in with the captives.

Not that Louisa and Sam could back out now. After talking to Tezco, Sam had brought in Monte and the others to speak with the bandit leader. Now they had a plan completely worked out. As a show of good faith, Tezco had turned over a rifle and a handgun, promising that more weapons would be delivered that night.

While the men had discussed tactics, Louisa climbed the steep slope in back of their house to hide the guns in a rocky outcropping. Nearby, she'd discovered the warm, spring-fed pool Montgomery had spoken of. She had plunged in for a quick bath and brought back a bucket of water so Sam and the other men could clean up.

It had felt good to wash away the grime of the trail. Though she certainly hadn't done so for Beaufort Montgomery.

Sam nudged her elbow. "Like a spot of lizards and seeds?"

She made a face at the contents of the bowl he handed her—chopped-up newts and squash seeds—before passing it on. "No, thanks, I'm not that desperate."

"You're so particular." His tone was light.

That he could find humor in anything was a credit to their renewed hope. She smiled at him and laid a hand on his thigh beneath the low table at which they sat on blankets spread out on the packed earthen floor.

"Um-m-m." He kept his voice low. "Only wish you'd brought me up to that spring—I would've enjoyed washing your back."

That she felt aroused by the remark was also a credit to hope. She whispered, "Maybe we can visit the pool later." She wanted to make love and would find some way to do so. Simply thinking about it made her grow warm. Heat crept outward from her center.

Meanwhile, like the other captives, she ate heartily of the best meal they'd had in weeks. There was plenty of food, most of it served in odd three-legged brown bowls that were decorated with ancient black designs—Aztec pottery, Monte had said from across the table. Louisa filled her plate with fresh tortillas, corn, tomatoes, yams, chilies, beef and turkey.

Montgomery's dwelling was much larger than Louisa's and Sam's, its main room long enough to accommodate the table, which was formed of planks set up on bricks. Besides Louisa, Sam, Monte and his cowboys, there were at least a dozen other people present, mostly men, all dressed in bright cloaks and white cotton tunics that contrasted with their brown skin. Obviously Montgomery's right-hand men, his Aztec nobility, treated him with deference. On the other hand, the servants refilling the food bowls and pouring wine were peasants who prostrated themselves if Beaufort Montgomery merely looked at them.

Louisa thought that disgusting, though she admitted Montgomery exuded power. That's why she nearly flinched when she suddenly realized he had fastened his eyes on her.

"Ah, my brave one." Montgomery smiled. "You look lovely tonight."

Sam slid his hand over Louisa's and gave it a comforting squeeze, urging her without words to be patient and to have faith.

"I have gifts for you," the madman went on. "Quetzal-coatl honors you, just as you will honor Quetzalcoatl."

Louisa forced herself to keep her mouth shut. Earlier, she and Sam had decided passive reactions were best; they might arouse less suspicion.

Montgomery nodded to a male servant. "Bring the trinkets now."

"Yes, O Great God." The man fell to the floor, crawling backward out of the room.

Louisa scowled. She refused to act grateful when the servant came back to lay fresh flowers beside her plate, then present her with a couple of exquisite gold bracelets, some crude bars of chocolate and a fan made of exotic green feathers.

Montgomery smiled ferociously and lifted his wine cup. "Tokens for your courage and your beauty, Louisa."

She hated hearing her name on his lips. And without thinking, she broke her promise of silence. "Are these gonna be buried with my remains?"

"If you wish."

She did a slow burn that someone could be so callous in the face of his victim. "I'm not making plans for any funeral . . . unless it's yours."

Sam squeezed her hand in warning, while Beaufort Montgomery's followers stared at her, a couple of them making shocked noises. Montgomery himself simply laughed at Louisa's veiled threat and spoke again of her brave heart.

Then he changed the subject, discussing the contents of a *tesorería* that would yield jade and gold ornaments for the next day's ceremony.

Louisa noticed that Xosi seemed very interested in that information. Tezco, seated on the madman's other side, picked at the food on his plate and rarely glanced at either Montgomery or Xosi. The bandit leader, a handsome man when Louisa had met him at the fiesta in New Mexico, now seemed a shadow of himself. He'd lost enough weight to put hollows under his cheekbones and enough sleep to create dark circles under his unnaturally bright eyes. She wondered about the demon he claimed was trying to possess him.

And she remembered the spooky legend Monte had relayed about the dark spirits of the Aztecs returning and wanting to inhabit human flesh. Tezcatlipoca, whoever that was, obviously had his sights set on Tezco.

All of the death spirits supposedly wanted her heart.

Thinking about that, Louisa felt less hungry and lifted her cup of wine. Taking a sip of the bitter red liquid, she met Monte's dark gaze. She swore she could feel strength flowing from him. She smiled, so grateful she'd found her brother, that he was a powerful, intelligent man. Sam had also been impressed, if at first surprised, when she'd told him.

Monte, Louisa and the other captives conversed in low voices as they finished the meal, with Louisa learning more Aztec myths as related by her brother. Supposedly there had always been a great rivalry between Quetzalcoatl and Tezcatlipoca, stretching back to the times when the Aztecs conquered the Toltecs, a rival and more advanced tribe, whose ancient gods Tezcatlipoca represented. Louisa wasn't sure she could keep all the details straight.

She was more interested when Monte mentioned he had three children; she had a nephew and two nieces. Intrigued, she nearly forgot where she was until Montgomery boomed a loud order to the servants, requesting dessert.

"The favorite sweet of the Mexica," Montgomery announced as his guests were served cups of frothy chocolate mixed with honey.

"Really? I thought that was organ meat washed down with blood," Sam muttered, very low.

Louisa shuddered and did a little praying. And it wasn't to the Aztec gods.

Beaufort Montgomery finally signaled more servants. "Escort the brave one, her consort and her companions to their dwellings." As they passed, he rose himself to hand Louisa a bundle wrapped in a swath of cotton. "Some clothing—finery for the festivities."

Sam looked like he wanted to stuff the bundle down Beaufort Montgomery's throat. Thank goodness he didn't try. There was no use in insulting Montgomery again and getting his nobles all stirred up.

Now was the time to get ready for battle.

And to cherish Sam in case they didn't win it.

Xosi hoped to win all.

A little tipsy from the wine, she approached Tezco as they walked away from the feast. "Get me the bundle of clothing that was given to your woman."

Her brother frowned. "She has never been my woman, Xosi. And now she has chosen the soldier."

Xosi wasn't about to argue. She was happy to have her brother's full devotion once more. And she would do everything in her power to save him from the demon he feared . . . and to save Monte's life. If Tezco thought shooting their way out of the canyon would work, she would do what she must to make the plan feasible.

Now if they could only take some gold along as well.

If nothing else, she thought, Montgomery's precious wheel would be lying on the pyramid's altar tomorrow.

Aware that she was both desirable and clever, Xosi was hoping she could influence even a madman.

Even a god.

For hadn't Monte Ryerson said she was Xochiquetzal, a goddess herself? She smiled, then hiccuped. Too much wine.

"I had already planned to take the clothing from Louisa," Tezco was telling her. "One of our men will be wearing it tomorrow, along with a gun beneath the skirt."

Xosi shrugged. "Whatever you think best. You should choose a small man, perhaps Juan or Eduardo."

"Juan has a softer face."

"Yes, he could pass for a woman." Actually, he'd done so during one of their robberies in the past. "Give the clothing to Juan."

Tezco went on, "We will use whatever means we must to leave this place. These terrible gods cannot live again—they will take away our souls."

He sounded so worried. And looked so thin.

Worried in turn, Xosi slipped her arm about his waist. "I will not allow them to take you, my brother. But you must help yourself as well. Eat. You are skin and bones. You need your strength."

"I cannot eat until we have escaped. I am not hungry."

"Not even one tortilla? We will regain our freedom tomorrow. Please eat, for me."

He sighed.

"I will send a servant for a plate of food." Which she would inspect herself to make sure no more bloody raw meat appeared. "Eat, and then try to rest, at least for a little while."

For they would have a day from hell tomorrow.

Though Xosi was considering a plan that could also buy them heaven.

Stars filled the heavens and a bright crescent of a new moon had risen in the east. Louisa leaned against Sam as they climbed the slope in the semidarkness.

"The pool's only a little farther—it'll be nice and warm."

"Not that we'll be able to see much." He tightened the arm he'd slung about her shoulders. "Since we're taking off our clothes, I'd like to fully appreciate you."

Again, heat spread from her center. "We can see with our hands."

She'd been afraid to bring a candle from the house. Most people were asleep in the middle of the night but the *barranca* was heavily guarded. Earlier, Tezco had taken pains to sneak the guns he had promised to the captives, along with some *serapes* under which to hide them. He said a couple of his men would have some horses ready the next day, but Louisa had suggested she fetch the mounts for her own group. She knew the Indian method of stringing several horses along on a rope and would feel safer, in case the bandits decided to ride off and let them fend for themselves.

Thank God, she wouldn't have to make an appearance at the pyramid. Tezco had lined up an imposter.

She mused on that. "Beaufort Montgomery is going to be very surprised tomorrow."

"Let's not talk about him. I don't want to ruin this night."

She knew he was thinking the same thing as she—

that either or both of them could be hurt or killed tomorrow. It made each word and touch bittersweet. She glanced back at the narrow valley where campfires blazed here and there in the darkness. How many followers did the madman have? How could so many honor a leader who worshiped slaughter and death?

At least the love she had for Sam paid homage to life. She wanted him to live to be an old man and she wanted to be around to see that herself. She wanted to obtain a little immortality for both of them by having children. . . .

She would require a wedding ring for that, however.

She realized Sam had never said anything about marriage, though surely that's what he planned if they managed to escape. Surely he would be able to forget the horrible experience that had soured the army for him.

Not that she had time to worry about that now.

The soft gurgle of water told her they were nearing the spring-fed pool. "Wait." She halted. "To the left."

He took a couple of steps in that direction until she could see the glimmering reflection of moonlight on the pool's surface. Then she threw down the blanket she carried and started taking off her clothes—first the boots, then her trousers, then her shirt. Sam did the same, emerging pale against the darkness surrounding him.

She realized she'd never seen him completely naked. They'd made love partially clothed six years before and then again at *El Tigre*'s corral. She wouldn't see him naked tonight either, though she hadn't been joking about letting touch stimulate their imaginations.

Louisa considered approaching him and running her hands over his chest, his arms . . . exploring every inch of flesh. But a cool wind whispering down from the mountains made her shiver and drove her toward the water.

"Come on in. The pool slopes gradually and isn't very deep."

"There's no problem. I can swim." He followed her with soft splashing sounds. "Um-m-m, this is warm."

But his skin felt hot when he took her in his arms. She slid against him, catching her breath in pure unadulterated pleasure at the sensation. He was at least half a foot taller but in the buoyant water, she easily stood on tiptoe, grazing her breasts against the hair-roughened hardness of his upper chest. His expulsion of breath told her she was having an effect on him, too.

She clasped his arms, taut with muscle, then slid her palms up and over his shoulders, his neck, into the thick, curly silk of his hair. She touched his face, feeling the long scar that stood for such terrible inner pain. He'd never told her how he'd gotten it, but she suspected some Apache had sliced him with a knife.

"Louisa," he murmured softly, and pressed her closer, covering her mouth with a fierce kiss.

She gloried in the taste and feel and smell of him. Beneath the water, he was fully aroused, rock-hard. She grasped him and caressed him until he groaned.

"Damn it, not so fast . . ."

He took her hand, moving it away, and angled his head to kiss her again. She bit his lips, made little moaning sounds as his tongue invaded. He cupped her breasts, brushing her aching nipples with his thumbs. Then he replaced his fingers with his mouth, sipping at one breast, then the other. The heat of his mouth made her insides quake.

Water rippled gently around them but they were alone in the vastness of the night with its wheeling stars and glowing moon. Sam lifted her in the water, let her slide back down. The friction of skin against skin was exquisite, as was the way their legs intertwined.

He kissed her again and played with her long braid. "I wish I could undo this and let it fall to your waist."

She started to say her hair would just get all wet and that they could let it down next time . . . until she remembered there might not be a next time.

She turned in his arms. "Go ahead, undo it."

Her back pressed against Sam's front felt equally titillating. Quickly, he unwound her long braid, letting her hair float around them. Then he nibbled her throat and slipped his arms about her, weighing a breast with one hand while the other slid lower to find the silky thatch between her thighs. Instinctively, she parted them, allowing the invasion of his insistent, exploring fingers. He quickly drove her crazy with desire. He stroked her over and over, invaded more deeply, made her slippery with wetness, made her burn. His shaft lay hot and heavy against her inner thigh.

She undulated her hips, moving with his fingers' rhythm. Pressure built within her so quickly and suddenly she couldn't stop it. She panted, shuddering with intense release.

"Louisa," Sam whispered near her ear, simply holding her.

When she came to her senses, he lifted her again and turned her in the water to face him. She opened her legs, wound them about him as he brought her back down to impale her. He filled her soft, tight folds so deliciously she cried out and writhed against him. Hands on her rounded hips, he rocked them, thrusting. But he kept up the rhythm for only a few minutes before he started moving back to shore.

"I want you under me, on the blanket," he said hoarsely.

He carried her out, reluctantly breaking their union to let her down. She lay back on the blanket and he loomed over her and knelt to part her legs with thighs hardened by years of riding. Positioning himself above her, he rubbed himself against her, teasing her nether lips with the tip of his penis.

Arching, Louisa grasped him and pulled him inside. His arms trembling, he groaned and thrust hard, once again filling her. Her legs wrapped around his hips; she gripped his back as he began moving, rocking back and forth . . . and the ground moved beneath her.

Sam rode her hard with a strong, driving rhythm. Sweet, yearning pressure building within her again, she swung her hips, sank her nails into his shoulders. Indeed, the very earth *was* moving, the tremors sharper, harsher than those that had come before. Then she lost herself in the harshness of Sam's breathing. He lifted her hips, plunged deeper and faster . . . until her need spiraled into white-hot rapture.

"Oh, Sam!"

At the sound of his name, he stiffened, shuddering with his own release. Then he collapsed on top of her. They lay there, breathing slowly returning to normal, even as the ground stopped rumbling beneath them. What did they mean, these tremors? Were the old gods angry at being summoned? Gooseflesh on her arms and legs, Louisa clung to Sam as if this might be their last moment on earth together.

"I love you, Sam."

"And I love you."

Louisa also loved life. After years of sorrow and separation, she longed to be with Sam, to embrace life with him. Surely the good spirits would realize that, look kindly on them tomorrow and let them escape those who would take everything away.

The powerful took what they needed from the weak.

Having been bathed and combed and dressed for bed by several servants, Beaufort-Quetzalcoatl found he couldn't sleep.

But then, his excitement for the coming events didn't make for a restful atmosphere. He would soon feel the full power of the greatest, highest god. Simply thinking of that made his heart beat faster, his breath come faster and the organ between his legs grow hard.

Shifting uncomfortably in the bed, he tried to keep his mind on higher issues. He would soon hold complete dominion not only over quaking humans but also over the lesser deities.

A great responsibility.

Tezcatlipoca could be a particular problem.

For Beaufort had long sensed a disturbance coming from Smoking Mirror's direction. He would have to make sure that the sun's fiery rays kept the god of night and shadows in his place.

Fire. Beaufort stared at the flame of the candle flickering nearby, envisioning it as a holy glowing serpent. A gust of wind from the open window only added to that effect as the flame danced.

The wind also brought the soft sound of someone moving about outside. Thinking a servant had dared to walk near his private quarters unbidden, Beaufort rose on his elbows, ready with a rebuke—only to be startled by the shadows outside gathering, darkening, taking shape . . . a voluptuous shape.

Wearing only a light wrap about her waist and a flower in her long, loose hair, Xochiquetzal came to the window, smiling. She dropped the wrap as soon as she crawled over the deep sill.

"What are you doing here?" Beaufort asked, mesmerized by the swing of her full breasts and curvaceous hips, the enticing sight of the nest of dark hair between her legs.

"I have come to amuse you."

"Quetzalcoatl is—"

"A great god who may have anything he wishes," she finished, approaching the bed, wafting enticing feminine scents.

Before he could think to protest, she delved beneath his robe to find him turgid, nearly bursting. Raising the garment, she quickly knelt atop him.

He groaned.

"Anything," she repeated, before showing him exactly what that meant.

19

Sam would give just about anything to have the day over with. Standing with Shorty and Jake O'Brian near the back of the crowd gathered for Beaufort Montgomery's big procession, he couldn't help worrying about Louisa. He hoped the *sombrero* and *charro* suit would adequately disguise her. He could only pray that she'd appear with the horses as scheduled when he and the two cowboys opened the gates at the end of the canyon, allowing both the bandits and their former captives to escape.

Sam himself wore a *sombrero* pulled down tight to cover his light-colored hair, as did Shorty and Jake. All three men made use of the *serapes* Tezco had provided, under which they carried both rifles and handguns.

People in the crowd probably wouldn't notice them anyway, caught up as they were in the festivities. Many of the men wore cloaks or *serapes* over white cotton tunics and pants, while the women wore shawls and brightly embroidered white dresses. Flowers nestled in elaborately coiled hair, earrings dangled and toothy smiles gleamed on nearly everyone's faces. From their sometimes vapid expressions and glassy eyes, Sam imagined many had been indulging in pulque, an intoxicating Mexican drink made from agave plants.

The captives, on the other hand, were cold sober and alert, even if they'd lost a few hours of sleep.

Thinking about what had kept him awake brought a smile to Sam's face. He and Louisa had made love half the night.

A nudge from Shorty drew him out of his reverie. "Hey, I think the parade's starting."

Sam straightened, glanced at the other men and shifted the rifle held tightly against his side. The crowd cheered, some playing the flutes and little drums he'd last heard the day Tezco's bandits had arrived in the canyon.

Led by a band, the participants wore costumes that looked plenty exotic—women with finely worked gold-and-turquoise headbands, embroidered tunics, fringed skirts and thick-soled sandals with squared-off toes; men with legbands and quilted tunics that resembled armor over their loincloths, feathers sprouting from their hair.

As one, the crowd suddenly hushed. The people bowed, prostrating themselves to the gods. Resentful, Sam nevertheless dropped to the ground as well.

Shorty and Jake followed, the former grousing, "Look at Montgomery all decked out like some kinda king!"

The madman sported a magnificent towering head-dress of gold and feathers, a gold snarling face flanked by jade snakes around his neck, and an intricate

feathered cloak trailing the ground. Behind him came
Tezco, a jaguar skin fastened at one shoulder and a
gold ornament with long blue-green quetzal feathers
holding back his long hair. Tiny silver mirrors sparkled
on his heavy gold neckpiece.

"Look at all that gold outta the treasury," Jake muttered.

"I can understand why the bandits wanted to pull
off a robbery," Sam said in a low voice. "What I can't
fathom is why Tezco wants out now."

"Maybe them death spirits Monte talked about really
are trying to possess him."

That would mean those spirits had actually lived
during the Aztec culture. West Point–educated and,
like any good Anglo, taught to accept only what he
could see—other than matters surrounding the
Christian God, of course—Sam said, "I find that hard
to believe."

But Tezco obviously believed. Serious-faced, the
bandit leader revealed his unease only by his darting
eyes, which locked with Sam's in passing. Sam gave a
subtle nod, noting the guards accompanying the gods,
one of whom was Monte Ryerson dressed in a white
loincloth and embroidered cloak. Black-haired and
dark-skinned, he blended in with the rest.

To ensure the escaping band's safety, Ryerson would
force Montgomery himself to come away with them at
gunpoint. With Ryerson, Tezco and Juan, who was playing the sacrificial victim, all in league, that shouldn't
be impossible.

A series of gunshots would notify the men bringing
the horses. And Louisa.

Worrying about her again, Sam watched the long
procession split, flowing to either side of the steps at

the base of the great pyramid. Then the gods ascended, guards on either side.

At the top, Montgomery raised his arms. "Rise, children! The gods have come!"

The crowd rose from the ground and cheered as the madman started jabbering in that language Ryerson called Nahuatl. A fire burned behind Montgomery at the big altar. Feathered cloak sweeping about him like the wings of a giant bird, he turned to pick up something shiny and held it aloft.

"Behold a portion of the wheel of life and death! Today, I shall join the broken pieces, make it whole once again! The sun will live forever! The eternal gods will bless you! Quetzalcoatl has returned!"

When a cloud suddenly drifted over the canyon, blotting out the sun, Sam thought it seemed strange. Whether he willed it or no, the hairs on the back of his neck stood at attention.

The crowd around him buzzed, voices low.

Montgomery himself seemed to hesitate. But only for a second. "The bravest heart of all shall feed the gods!"

Dressed in a white tunic and skirt of finely woven cotton, wearing gold jewelry and a huge fan-shaped headdress of feathers, the sacrificial victim marching up the steps of the pyramid, surrounded by guards, seemed a little unsteady.

And sure resembled a woman. Sam narrowed his eyes, thinking that the bandit named Juan must have stuck some pads of cloth under the tunic to give himself the illusion of breasts. At the top of the pyramid, the guards paused, holding on to the victim while Montgomery turned his back to speak to the fiery altar again.

More clouds drifted overhead, thickening, turning the sky gray. Gooseflesh rose on Sam's arms as he thought about the small warning quakes the night before. Determined, he tried to focus on the scenario before him . . . when the victim suddenly removed the tunic, revealing a pair of lovely rounded breasts.

Breasts? Sam was stunned. That victim sure wasn't Juan. Something had gone very wrong.

Had the guards gotten hold of Louisa, after all?

Panicking, he took off, trying to fight his way through the tightly packed crowd, completely forgetting his tactical plan, paying no attention to Jake calling after him. He was going after the woman he loved; he'd climb the pyramid with guns blazing.

Sam was determined to save Louisa this time, even if he had to trade his own life for hers.

Xosi had felt more than a little dizzy as she climbed the pyramid. She feared there had been more than pulque in the cup the guards had given her. She should have known better, should have realized it contained a drug to keep her quiet.

Still, she would prevail, she told herself, despite her vision being slightly blurred, her thinking muddled, her hearing strained. There seemed to be a low drone in the air, a rumble that sounded like faraway thunder. She glanced up at the suddenly overcast sky. A wind slapped her cheeks as if a storm were rising. But she was not afraid, not of anything. Beaufort Montgomery would be shocked, but he would not be able to kill her after having made love to her the night before.

Quetzalcoatl had been conquered.

To remind the oh-so-earthly man of her identity, she

had stripped off the tunic part of the costume she had collected from Juan that morning. Montgomery would recognize the full, firm breasts he had held in his hands. Not to mention that the tunic could be used to carry away the gold lying on the altar, gold she would share not only with Tezco and their men, but with Monte as well. For Xosi knew she loved the man and would not see him die. That was why she'd needed power over Montgomery. And no use letting the gold go to waste . . .

Xosi's eyes were drawn to the intoxicating sheen of the great wheel. Montgomery turned from the altar. She watched his expression change from arrogance to surprise . . . to rage.

Rage?

For the first time, Xosi was afraid. She looked to her brother, whose expression was also shocked, his eyes wide, his posture frozen.

Montgomery's hands shook, his lips trembled. Then he shouted, "Sacrilege!"

The booming voice rang through the canyon. Blue fire blazed from his eyes. Tezco jumped forward, only to be caught and held by Xosi's guards.

Montgomery turned his ferocious glare on her brother. "Once more you have betrayed me, Tezcatlipoca!" Just as quickly, he ordered, "Prepare the gift for the gods!"

"No!" Xosi screamed, even as she was lifted bodily and laid on the great sacrificial stone, her hands and feet tied down.

Montgomery approached, an oval knife raised. Teeth of shell decorated the wicked blade. Xosi's heart felt cold, yet hot blood pulsed through her veins.

"No!" she screamed again. "I took away your power, Quetzalcoatl. You cannot kill me!"

* * *

Monte couldn't find the power to move. Sweating, heart pounding, he tried to make sense of the spectacle before him, a scene that should not be—Tezco held by the guards and Xosi tied to the sacrificial stone. What the hell was she doing here?

Would Montgomery really plunge the knife into her breast?

He pulled the rifle from beneath his cloak, aimed it at Beaufort Montgomery, only to be distracted by the sound of thunder.

Thunder. The guns of the battlefield. The earth had trembled with their roar and the air had burned from their smoke.

Thunder rumbled now. Smoke rose, as did the moaning winds surrounding them. Shaking away the distant memory, Monte placed his finger on the trigger.

As if sensing this, Montgomery turned to him, met Monte's gaze and gave him a burning expression. Plummeted once more back to the Civil War, Monte looked into the face of the man who had saved his life. His hands began shaking so hard he couldn't pull the trigger . . . not even when Montgomery turned from him, raising the knife higher . . .

"No, please, no!" Xosi was sobbing.

Deaf to her pleas, the madman plunged the toothed knife down, burying it deep in Xosi's beautiful breast as lightning split the darkened sky, illuminating the scene.

"E-e-e-e-e!"

Her scream shattered the air, overwhelming the warning rumble of thunder. Blood spurted like a fountain and her body convulsed.

"Xosi-i-i-i!" came another terrible cry to echo through the valley, this from Tezco, who lunged forward, shaking off his guards like a man possessed with the strength of ten.

Horrified, Monte still couldn't move, not even when the ground below him did, not even when Beaufort Montgomery ripped the bloody, still-beating heart from Xosi's chest and took off at a dead run. He gagged. "Xosi!" And something in him died, too.

Suddenly, the altar toppled. The gold wheel of life and death slid off. The pyramid itself was moving. Vibrating. The guards and the people in the procession cried out, started to run as a crack spread beneath their feet.

Earthquake!

Sick inside, Monte shouted, "Tezco!" If he hadn't saved Xosi, he could at least try to save her brother.

Lost, Tezco had eyes only for the limp, bloody body on the stone. He threw himself on her. "Xosi! Xosi!"

The crack in the pyramid widened and Monte stumbled backward, trying to keep his footing. Lightning flashed through the unnaturally dark sky, while the rumble of the earth grew louder.

He shouted one last time, trying to reach the other man. "Tezco, come on!"

It was already too late. The top of the pyramid split completely open, revealing a deep, dark heart, isolating the bandit leader on the opposite side. The sacrificial stone tumbled, taking Xosi into the darkness below. The last thing Monte saw before fleeing for his life was Tezco clinging to the edge of the splitting stone, still crying his sister's name as she plunged into oblivion.

With the earth splitting toward him, Monte ran, dodging falling stones, aware the ground below him was shaking and that crevices zigzagged out in every direction. When a half-crazed guard confronted him, he froze, remembering too late the gun in his hands. A blast suddenly hit the guard in the chest. He crumpled.

"Ryerson!" It was Sam Strong, a Colt .45 in hand. "Got to save Louisa—"

Monte stopped him. "It wasn't Louisa on the altar. It was Xosi! Get out of here!"

Both men then ran to the base of the pyramid as the world rocked crazily. A sea of humanity surged around them, some falling, getting trampled, toppling into the crevices. Only when Monte jumped a wide crack did he realize he'd left his sister's man behind.

"Strong?" he yelled, looking around.

But Sam Strong had disappeared and Monte could only hope he would head in the right direction.

Meantime, he sprinted off again. Shorty, Jake and Louisa should be waiting at the canyon's gate. If he was going to be buried alive, he wanted to die with people he cared about.

Louisa was riding for the gate when the earthquake struck. Having waited for the gunshots— a signal that had never come—she'd decided to take action herself. She had all she could handle controlling the horses with the electricity of the approaching storm hanging in the air.

Now the earth itself roared.

El Tigre reared, knocking her *sombrero* off. Her hair tumbled down about her shoulders. Louisa firmly reined him in, at the same time trying to keep hold of the other four horses. Defiant squealed and dug in his heels; the other mounts snorted and danced.

She felt as if her arms were being yanked out of their sockets, but she held on for dear life and kicked the black stallion's sides.

"Come on, let's go!" she yelled.

She had to find Sam and the others—had to escape this place of death. Even earthquakes didn't matter.

El Tigre reared again, then came down with a lunge. Guiding him with her legs, Louisa held on to the ropes of the other horses and galloped for the gate.

Chaos reigned. People shrieked, debris flew through the air, huts burned as they collapsed on themselves and the cooking fires within. Hell erupted around her, seeping up from deep, dark bowels to set the earth ablaze. Swerving to avoid a growing crevice, she shrieked when the devil rose out of the trembling ground. Spooked, the horses came to a shuddering halt and screamed in terrified protest.

"Death!" shouted Beaufort Montgomery, gore staining his tunic, the feathers of his torn cape flapping and standing on end. "Sacrifice!" he roared, running toward her with a ragged-edged knife in one hand, a bloody organ in the other.

The madman still wanted to kill her!

Fighting to control the horses, fighting her own urge to throw up, Louisa felt a surge of fear and anger, then something . . . wilder, more instinctive and elemental. The face of a long-haired, bronzed warrior flashed through her mind.

Montgomery was nearly upon her. "You were meant for the gods, damn you, and they shall have you!"

Louisa could ride a horse as if she were one with the animal. And now she used her mount as a weapon, giving a warrior's loud war whoop, "He-e-i!" At the same time, she kicked *El Tigre*'s sides hard to send him and the other horses hurtling at the demonic man. "Go back to hell!"

The stallion hit Montgomery squarely, knocking him to the ground. The bloody mass flew from his hand. Sharp hooves thudded over flesh and cracked on bone. So much for his being some kind of god.

Heart pounding, she rode on, only coming to another dirt-splattering halt when a boulder rolled down the mountainside and rumbled across her path. The gate lay just ahead. Sam was supposed to be there. But he wasn't. The horses spooked again when lightning flashed overhead, and it took all of Louisa's strength to hold them.

"Sam! Sam, where are you?"

Sensing a presence beside her, she hoped to see Sam . . . but instead met Montgomery's insane gaze.

"Die, damn you, die!" screamed the madman, grabbing her leg, tearing her out of the saddle.

He was still alive—despite the blood pouring from multiple wounds and the leg he was dragging at a strange angle, despite the caved-in chest revealed by his torn tunic, the sharp bone of a rib that stuck out, piercing his flesh. Louisa bit back a scream. Perhaps he *was* some sort of god or demon, one who couldn't die.

She fought and kicked wildly as the apparition wrestled with her and finally threw her to the ground. He was so strong, he held her fast; then he raised the knife, his face a twisted mask, red glittering in the depths of his icy eyes.

She saw her own death coming as he said, "Your blood shall make me live! Die—"

The last word was cut off in a gurgle as Montgomery was seized from behind. His arm locked around the madman's throat, Sam pulled Montgomery off Louisa.

She scrambled to her feet, screaming, "Sam!"

With a fierce growl, Montgomery tore away from him and headed back for Louisa. Sam attacked yet again, punching the man viciously, then drawing a gun and shooting. Another bloom of red spouted on Montgomery's chest. He roared with anger and tore the gun out of Sam's hands even as Sam tore a medallion that looked like a wheel from Montgomery's chest. With a display of more-than-human strength, the madman threw out an arm and knocked Sam several feet away. Blood trickling from his mouth, Sam groaned and lay still.

Dear God, was he dead?

Montgomery came for Louisa yet again, his face set into a snarl, his blood-stiffened hair coiling out like snakes.

An evil god.

Though that knowledge wouldn't stop Louisa from fighting for her life—or avenging Sam's. She backed up, snatched the pistol from her belt and aimed it at him.

"Yah-h!"

The shout came from Sam. Thanks to the spirits of life! He was on his feet again, running at the madman.

"Be careful!" Louisa maneuvered the gun as the two fought, looking for a clear shot at the madman. If another bullet could stop him . . .

Montgomery shoved Sam backward with a snarl, then slashed the jagged blade at him. Sam feinted, lunged. At the same time, another crevice split the earth behind Montgomery. Sam charged him and, with the hand holding Montgomery's own medallion, hit him square in the bloody chest. Yowling, Montgomery flew back, teetered on the crevice's edge—and, finally, horrific face wreathed in surprise, fell in. . . .

Louisa stared, gun still in hand.

Until Sam threw down the medallion and grabbed her in a crushing embrace. "Thank God!"

She clung to him, oblivious to the chaos and carnage around them, and watched the earth close around the madman, swallowing him whole, then exploding in a shower of dirt and stone, the sight unlike any she'd seen so far. Montgomery's death bray vibrated beneath her feet and permeated the very air they breathed.

Sam was the first to come to his senses. "Catch the horses! We have to get out of here!"

She sprang into action, finding Defiant with his reins trailing and his eyes rolling, then *El Tigre*. The animals had milled about but stayed nearby, as if they thought the humans could offer them comfort in the upheaval.

Sam caught the others and guided them back to her. Both mounted; then, they galloped for the gate.

"Jake!" Louisa shouted, catching sight of the cowboy as he and Shorty swung the barricade open. "Monte!"

Still dressed in his Aztec costume, her brother bolted up to spring onto a horse's back. Sam, bringing up the rear of the party on Defiant, raised his hand in a cavalry signal. "Let's ride!"

And ride they did.

The quake continued to move outward from the crumbling pyramid. The pass ahead of them was so narrow, they raced single-file. Pounding *El Tigre*'s flanks, Louisa flew, leaning over the horse's neck, only looking back to make sure that Sam was all right and that it was actually him on her heels, rather than a pack of blood-thirsty demons.

20

Sam kept his eyes on Louisa and rode hell-bent-for-leather. The party galloped at top speed through the narrow pass, whose sheer walls seemed ready to crumble at any moment. Small rocks pummeled them; sand sifted down and into their faces.

"Watch out!" yelled Monte Ryerson in the lead.

Sam immediately saw the rockslide near the mouth of the pass. Ryerson and Jake O'Brian swerved, slapped their horses with the reins and jumped the lowest end of the debris. Shorty's mount didn't quite clear it, his rear hooves scraping a small boulder, before scrambling across. *El Tigre* and long-legged Defiant leapt the barrier with ease.

Sam felt greatly relieved when the party finally shot out on the other side of the gorge. But a rumble behind them told him they had to keep riding. He glanced over his shoulder to see a wall of stone crack, break and thunder to the earth in a great cloud of dust. Lightning shot from the four corners of the sky to connect with the mountain in a single spot . . . which Sam imagined to be Montgomery's burial place.

Or was it Quetzalcoatl's?

He kicked the gelding's flanks, urging him on. "Yaah!"

The land they were covering now had flattened out but didn't seem to steady for at least another mile. The horses were lathered and blowing when Louisa pulled in the mustang stallion, dropping back beside Sam.

"Think we could slow down for a while?" she shouted. "We're gonna run these horses into the ground."

Ryerson and his cowboys were already reining in.

Sam glanced around. "All right, let's walk them."

He prayed the quake wasn't coming this far. They surely were going to need their mounts to return to New Mexico Territory, thank God, since they'd made it out alive.

Still, they kept going, plodding along, putting distance between themselves and the canyon of death. Dark clouds sat on the far western horizon and lightning flashed from time to time.

When the ground started to rise again, foothills building toward another range of mountains, Sam called out to the others, ordering them to dismount. His final cavalry command, for he had finished his assignment. Face filled with emotion, Louisa barely hit the ground before she pounced and clung to him, tucking her head into the hollow beneath his chin. He rocked her, made soothing noises and stroked her hair, silky despite a thick coating of dust. He never wanted to let go of her.

"I was so scared when I was bringing the horses," she murmured. "I didn't hear the shots. I couldn't find you anywhere."

"I thought you were dead." He'd just about died himself when he saw the knife plunge into the victim's breast. "I tried to climb the pyramid, but everyone was rushing down and drove me back, nearly trampled me."

Louisa tipped her head to gaze at him. "The pyramid?"

Sam realized she hadn't seen the sacrifice. "It wasn't Juan up there today. Beaufort Montgomery put his knife through Xosi's heart. That's why there wasn't any signal. It took me a while to find out it wasn't you dressed in that outfit."

Louisa's eyes widened. "Xosi? Why?"

"Can't be sure about that." Ryerson stood nearby, his usually taciturn face looking troubled. "Knowing Xosi, it probably had to do with getting her hands on the gold."

Knowing Xosi? Sam absently wondered how close Ryerson had gotten to the striking Mexican woman, having caught them with their heads pretty close together a few times. Not that it was any of his business.

The big man went on, "Whatever her reasons, Xosi's gone now. Tezco, too. Last thing I saw of him, he was hanging on to a piece of that crumbling pyramid by his fingertips. He musta been crushed when the stone fell."

"Tezco's dead, huh?" Louisa murmured softly.

A twinge of jealousy struck Sam, which was stupid, considering the circumstances. Louisa might have come to respect Tezco, but she'd never cared for him. He also reminded himself that the Mexican had come over to their side.

"Tezco didn't have to offer to let us in on the escape plan. But he did."

Ryerson nodded. "Too bad something went wrong. I could tell Tezco was as surprised as I was when his sister sashayed up the pyramid. The guards had to grab hold of him to stop him from taking action." He paused. "And as soon as that madman killed Xosi, all hell seemed to break loose. The very earth quaked."

"The earthquake started the moment Xosi died?" Louisa turned to face the others, but she still nestled into the crook of Sam's arm. "That's strange."

Again Ryerson nodded. "Yeah, real strange."

"All hell breaking loose." Louisa shuddered. "I can imagine Beaufort Montgomery as the devil . . . or some kind of evil god. I don't know how he got off the pyramid, but he tried to kill me."

That got the other men's attention. Sam tightened his hold on her reassuringly.

"He wouldn't die." Louisa's face grew pale. "I ran him down with the horses and he got up again. . . . His chest and his leg were crushed. Even when Sam showed up, he couldn't be stopped—not by fist or bullet. It was like he possessed supernatural strength."

"He didn't weaken until I hit him with that medallion of his," Sam said. "The one that looked like the sacrifice wheel."

"You killed him with his own magic," Ryerson said.

"Is everyone dead?" Louisa gazed toward the dark clouds.

"Nope, a few of them bandits got away." Jake O'Brian had plopped down on the ground in exhaustion. "Some of 'em rode out afore the rest of you showed up."

"And they wasn't lookin' neither to the right nor the left," Shorty added. "They was jest ridin'."

The mention of the bandits, a group of armed men in the vicinity, made Sam a bit nervous. He glanced at a steep slope some yards away. "Think I'll take a climb and see if I can catch a glimpse of the surrounding area."

"Not a bad idea," Ryerson agreed.

In the end, Jake stayed with the horses while everyone else scrambled up the mountainside. Some ways up, they got a clear view of the surrounding terrain and gazed out upon a bizarre sight. The dark clouds roiling on the horizon were partially made up of dust, billows of dirt rising from the steaming, half-filled hollow where the canyon had once been.

"I'll be damned," Shorty breathed. "Them Aztec people and their city has up and disappeared."

Arms crossed over his muscular bare chest, Ryerson looked like some kind of ancient warrior himself. "Either the earthquake destroyed everything . . . or the old gods did."

Including the lay of the land immediately surrounding the hidden *barranca.* It was at least a mile out before the foothills and mountains rolled to the horizon undisturbed.

Very strange.

Sam's neck prickled. Trying to ignore the sensation, he scanned the surrounding countryside. "I don't see anything of the bandits."

"Don't think you will," Ryerson said. "They're headed for home, wherever that is."

"Then we're safe." Louisa slipped her hand into Sam's.

"Safer than we were before . . . in more than one way," Ryerson agreed. "The death spirits went back where they came from. Quetzalcoatl and his fifth sun were destroyed." He fingered a silver chain that he'd drawn from the waistband of his loincloth. "Not that death is really evil, not unless you worship it. It's the natural end for things."

"But Montgomery and his friends were trying to bring about unnatural endings," Louisa said. "They were murdering people."

"And they finally got kilt themselves and by nature," Shorty said. "Kind of justice-like, don't you think?"

Sam remained reflective as he scrutinized the scene before them, simply holding Louisa against his side. A bright streak of lightning zigzagged across the western sky.

"That storm is coming our way." Ryerson gestured. "Coming slow but it'll be here by dark. It's gonna rain— hard. We should take cover."

"You need some cover yourself." Louisa looked him over. "At least a blanket to wear." Then she noticed the silver chain her brother was playing with. "What's that?"

Ryerson quickly pushed the necklace back in his waistband. "A mirror."

"That was Xosi's, wasn't it?"

"Yeah."

The big man headed back down the mountainside. From the way he was acting, Sam could swear Ryerson was covering up some kind of uncomfortable secret. Not that he'd ask about it, being a man who'd had plenty of secrets himself. Thank God he'd finally lightened his conscience a little by talking things over with Louisa.

He helped Ryerson and Louisa secure the horses while the two cowboys built a temporary shelter by laying brush across the top of a cluster of boulders.

The storm was coming, nature's wrath.

Though after what they'd been through with twisted human beings, natural dangers didn't seem so terrible.

All in all, nature had been kind, Louisa decided several days after they'd started the trail back to the Rio Grande. The thunderstorm following the earthquake had made the travelers a mite uncomfortable when it had poured down on them, even leaking into their shelter, but the rain had filled the rivers and the potholes. There was plenty of water available and green shoots for the horses to eat. Even the desert plateau east of the mountains flourished.

The life spirits were celebrating.

Louisa herself had been saying prayers of thanks. Remembering her vision when she'd faced down Beaufort Montgomery, the way she whooped like a warrior before running him over with the horses, she wondered about the ghost of her father. She had shyly shared her experience with Monte. Her brother had smiled and said that Red Knife had been with her, that her actions were pure Comanche.

They'd had quite a few opportunities to talk about Comanches and everything else the last few days. Whereas they'd traveled hard with the bandits before, the party of five now took their time, saving their mounts. They also had to search for food, scouring the terrain for game and roots and edible cacti. Thank goodness Monte knew how to survive in the desert.

"Did you learn about living off the land from the Comanche?" Louisa asked him as they rode along one afternoon.

Brother and sister were relatively alone, Sam and the two cowboys having gone off to hunt some peccaries when they'd spotted a small herd of the wild pigs.

"The Comanche traveled light. They found their food as they went along." Monte pointed out, "Sam knows something about living off the desert, too. He led troopers on plenty of campaigns in Arizona."

"You talked to him about that?"

"What else are you gonna do but talk when you're traveling day after day?"

True. Louisa had enjoyed hearing about Ginny and Cassie and Stephen. "I want to meet your kids." That would have to be in the future, since they'd already agreed they would split up when they reached Texas. "I bet I could teach them a few things, especially the girls."

That brought a smile to Monte's face. "Maybe you could. Then again, they're pretty wild on their own." He sobered. "Hope they didn't get into too much trouble while I was gone. I hated going off and leaving them the way I did."

He probably felt guilty about it, Louisa surmised, certain she saw sadness in Monte's dark eyes. To tell the truth, she'd swear there'd been something bothering him ever since they escaped Beaufort Montgomery's canyon.

"I'm sure you wouldn't do anything you didn't feel was necessary."

The line of his jaw remained hard, his lips tight. "Yeah, I was supposed to bring back Roberto and Shorty. Only got one of them. Don't know what I'm gonna tell Roberto's family."

"None of us could have saved him."

"Maybe not." But he sounded uncertain.

"Guilt eats away at your insides like poison," she told

him. Something she was already dealing with in Sam's case. "You have to get rid of it."

"Uh-hmm."

She could tell he wasn't taking her seriously. So she reiterated, "You have to forgive yourself."

"Already have—at least as far as Roberto's concerned."

She frowned. What else was bothering him? Hoping not to offend, she tried to draw him out. "Do you feel responsible for something else?"

"Real responsible . . . for someone." His haunted gaze reminded her of Sam. "I probably gave Xosi the idea of walking up that pyramid in the first place." Before Louisa could force a further confession, he leaned over to pat her on the shoulder. "Don't worry about me, little sister. Sometimes poisons have a way of working themselves out on their own."

So he felt guilty over Xosi. She'd wondered about Monte's connection to the woman, who'd been very flirtatious with him. Sam and the other two men approaching took her mind off the situation.

Sam waved, grinning. "Pork chops for supper tonight."

Louisa grinned back, the man she loved always a sight that warmed her heart. They may have had a very limited menu for the return journey, but she'd had a wonderful time just being with Sam, cherishing every moment they spent together.

Though what would happen in the future, she wasn't sure.

Brooding a little on that, sobered by Monte's confession, knowing they were within two days' ride of Texas, she decided to talk to Sam as soon as they set up camp.

They stopped early, while the sun was still shining.

Having retraced their steps, following the trail the bandits had taken into the western Sierra Madre, they found themselves in the same valley where Sam had first been captured and Louisa had poisoned the bandits with jimsonweed.

What made things different was the riverbed. Dry before, it had become a torrent, swollen with rain from the mountains. The travelers would have to wait for the flood to go down.

Sam didn't seem worried and took Louisa for a walk along the riverbank. The rays of the setting sun gilded his blond hair, making the curls at the edge of his neckline gleam with gold. His fair skin tanned by years of living in the open, his muscles firm and rippling, he was handsomer than ever. His scar even seemed paler, though Louisa had never minded it.

They stopped in a sheltered, grassy nook some ways from camp. The gurgling sound of rushing water added a refreshing ambiance.

Sam took her in his arms. "We can sleep here tonight."

They'd been sharing a bedroll almost every night anyhow, Sam having sought out privacy for them. He drew Louisa close and angled his head to kiss her. She ducked her head away.

"Something wrong?"

"Just . . . thinking about the future."

"Well, all I can say is thank God we've got one."

Louisa had to admit that was important. "I'm happy we're alive and in one piece. But—"

"But what?"

"Now there are a few other things to consider. We're heading home." She chose her words carefully. "What then?"

"I'm resigning my commission. We'll never be parted again."

"Can you promise me that?"

"I can promise you my love forever."

Which touched her but still didn't erase her doubts. Plenty of women she'd known through her ma had loved men and even lived with them, yet never had a marriage license or a wedding ring. Louisa wasn't willing to do that.

Sam touched her cheek, tipping her chin up to gaze into her eyes. "My love isn't enough?"

Would he marry a woman who reminded him of someone he'd killed? Could he have babies with her, wake up with her every morning?

Louisa's misgivings deepened. She pushed away from him. "I can understand how you feel about . . . the bad things that happened in the past."

"I haven't had a nightmare since I shared those bad things with you."

Which startled her. "Really?"

"Talking it out cleansed me somehow. I want to live, and as fully as possible. I'll die when I have to, but I'm not going to spend my time wishing I was dead before then." His tone tensed with emotion. "What are you worried about? That I'll expect you to cook, scrub floors, wash my clothing? I know you're not that type of woman, that you want to be outdoors. We can hire a housekeeper."

Part of Louisa was thrilled that he wanted to make some sort of commitment, that he accepted her as she was. But she needed even more. She swallowed the lump rising in her throat, fighting against the desire to get her dander up and flounce away.

"I want children."

His expression softened, and the blue-green of his eyes deepened to a smoky color. "That's fine by me. Two, a dozen, however many we end up with."

But he still hadn't said the right words. "You're the only man I've ever loved, Sam, but I don't want to be your mistress."

"Mistress?"

She hurried on. "I won't live with a man unless I'm married to him. And I'm certainly not going to have a pack of illegitimate children."

Sam raised his brows and looked disbelieving. "I would never bring children into the world without offering my name. It's a man's duty—"

"*Duty!*" The word scratched at Louisa. Despite her determination to keep her temper in check, it flared like a torch. "To hell with your stupid duty!" She whirled and stalked off.

But Sam came right after, easily keeping pace. "Louisa!"

"Go away!"

"Damned if I will!" He sounded just as angry as she was. "And I'm getting damned tired of chasing you around." He took hold of her arm, jerking her to a stop. "I've traveled halfway across Mexico, for God's sake."

She glowered and shook him off. "Why can't you damned well ask me to marry you then? And because you want to, not because it's your duty!"

He looked surprised. "Of course I want to marry you."

She was now too angry to do anything but cross her arms over her chest. "I didn't hear any proposal."

"Is that what this is all about?" His expression changed. "Well . . . I guess I just didn't get around to it."

Making a disgusted sound, she started to stalk off again.

"Louisa!" Again, he caught up with her, demanding, "Stop right now! This minute." He grabbed her arm, whipped her around, then fell to one knee. "I'm proposing. Will you marry me?"

If she wasn't so peeved, she would have laughed. He looked so funny, posed against a backdrop of mesquite and creosote brush.

His tense features softened. "I love you, Louisa, with all my heart. I want to marry you. Please say yes."

The emotion in his eyes made her knees go weak.

"I don't have a ring, but I'll buy one as soon as we get back to Santa Fe," he assured her. " Now, answer me—"

"Yes."

His face brightened. "Yes?"

"It's a woman's duty to accept a sincere proposal like yours." She laughed aloud at his sudden scowl. But she went to him and slid her arms about him as he got to his feet. "I was teasing." Then she spoke from her heart, intensely, passionately. "I love you so much, Sam. And I want nothing more than to share the rest of my life with you."

Their kiss was sweet, lingering, but soon spiraled into something far more demanding and fierce.

"Hrrmph."

Louisa stiffened and felt Sam tense as well.

When Monte cleared his throat a second time, even more loudly, she broke off the kiss to find her brother standing nearby, watching them.

"If you two are finished entertaining me and the boys for the evening, I have a suggestion about this marriage thing."

Louisa was appalled. "You were eavesdropping?"

"Eavesdropping? Hell, your voices were echoing off the mountainsides." He turned to Sam. "I'm Louisa's next of kin. You need a marriage gift, not a ring. A few horses will do. That's the usual for a Comanche woman's relatives."

He couldn't be serious.

Sam wasn't acting like it either. A smile hovered about his lips. "I only have one horse. She already took the others away from me a long time ago."

"Yeah?" Monte glanced at Louisa speculatively. "Stole 'em?"

"So to speak," said Sam.

Now Louisa laughed and punched her man's arm. "I didn't steal anything. We bet the horses on some races and I won."

"Hmm." Monte looked thoughtful, finally shrugging. "Guess that'll have to count. You can keep the marriage gift yourself, little sister."

Louisa nodded. "They'll only be the beginning of my herd anyway. I want a thousand head." Just like Red Knife.

"A thousand?" asked Sam, raising his brows, registering some surprise. He glanced from Louisa to Monte, then back again. "I can see we're going into horse ranching seriously."

Monte laughed long and loud. "Come on back to camp and celebrate this deal with a drink. I've got about six swigs of whiskey in a flask in my saddlebags. Both the bandits and the Aztecs missed it somehow."

Celebrate.

Louisa's heart sang, winging high with the flight of a hawk overhead, flying with the wind. Sam loved her and wanted to marry her, and they were headed home. She didn't think she'd ever been so happy before in all her life.

*   *   *

Even Monte's departure at the Texas border didn't seem to dampen Louisa's happiness. She told her brother that they couldn't really delay the wedding but they'd save a big fiesta for his arrival. Monte hugged her and promised to bring along her nephew and nieces. Then he also embraced Sam, who felt touched, if a little embarrassed.

Louisa smiled tremulously as she and Sam rode away, but she didn't cry and soon turned her big dark eyes on him. They were full of love. Sam was so happy about that, he felt like bursting. What a woman she was, and how he'd deprived himself through the years. Well, that wouldn't happen again.

Extra protective, he was the first to notice riders on their trail some time after they'd entered New Mexico Territory. "We're going to need to take cover," he warned Louisa.

She turned in the saddle, sighting the dozen or so men raising dust behind them. "More bandits?"

Sam slid his rifle out of its boot. "I don't know, but we can't take any chances."

They were riding the horses toward a rocky out-cropping when Louisa gave a little cry. "The man in front! It's Chaco!" Before Sam could say anything, she wheeled *El Tigre* around, taking off at a gallop. "And Adolfo!"

Now Sam recognized the approaching figures as well. The men whooped and shouted and rode full-out. He stiffened, fearing there'd be a collision but Louisa swerved the black at the last moment and fairly leapt from the saddle into Chaco's arms. The ex-gunslinger caught her and held her with her feet dangling. Now Louisa couldn't stop the tears from flowing. She was sniffling and trying to wipe them away when Sam caught up. Everyone had dismounted and she was hugging Adolfo, then Ben Riley.

Sam gazed at the latter with pleased surprise. "You're all right! What happened, man? Javier?"

"He's laid up but he'll live," Ben told him. "Took a bullet in the shoulder, but I bandaged him up and we made it back to Texas where we found a doctor. I'm going back to get him when he's ready to travel." The sandy-haired young man looked sheepish. "I was left on my own. That's why I didn't follow or keep tracking you."

"You would have lost our trail anyway," said Sam. "We went deep into the west Sierra Madre. Nobody lives there but a few peasant farmers and Indians."

"Some of whom are now dead Aztecs." To Chaco's questioning look, Louisa added, "It's a long story."

She was obviously far more interested in hearing about Amelia and Luz. Both were well, having recovered some days after she'd disappeared. Chaco and his party had set out after her then, crisscrossing the Rio Grande several times as they struggled to pick up the right trail. Frustrated by washed-out tracks even Chaco had trouble interpreting, they'd come back to Texas one more time where they'd finally met up with Ben.

It had been the insistence of some hombres they'd run into only hours before that had sent them flying north again. A man named Monte Ryerson had claimed Sam Strong and Louisa Janks were free and headed for Santa Fe.

"Monte Ryerson is my brother," Louisa told Chaco. And she laughed and waved more questions aside.

"Another long story. Let's get going. I want to organize my wedding. Sam and I are getting married."

Chaco turned his spooky gaze on Sam. "About time."

Adolfo merely frowned menacingly, though Sam could tell he was joking. "You are marrying this gringo, *chica?* He is scarred and looks dangerous. You must be very brave."

"Brave? She has the heart of a jaguar," said Sam with a huge grin.

And she would never be tamed. Which was exactly the way he wanted her.

Watch for

SHADOWS
~ IN THE ~
MIRROR

OCTOBER 1995

Monte fights Xosi's ghost to find true love
with a flesh-and-blood woman.

The Trouble With Angels by Debbie Macomber

Shirley, Goodness, and Mercy are back and better than ever! Given their success last Christmas in *A Season of Angels,* they're eager to answer the prayers of troubled mortals once again, to ensure that this holiday season is filled with love and joy for all.

The Greatest Lover in All England by Christina Dodd

From the award-winning author of *Outrageous* and *Castles in the Air* comes a delightful romance set in Tudor England. "Settle down for a rollicking good time with *The Greatest Lover in All England.* A sexy, fast-paced romance filled with wry wit and bawdy humor. A winner!"—Kristin Hannah

The Green Rose by Kathy Lynn Emerson

A tale of love and deception in Tudor England. In order to be eligible for a vast inheritance, Sir Grey Neville needed someone to pose as his betrothed; and Meriall Sentlow, a recently widowed beauty, was the ideal choice. But when it was time to call off their charade, Grey wasn't ready to give up Meriall, despite the dangerous secrets that lay between them.

Heart of the Jaguar by Roslynn Griffith

Set in the Southwestern Territory in the 1860s, *Heart of the Jaguar* is a poignant love story that readers will cherish. Beautiful, rambunctious Louisa Jenks was sure that she'd never see Lieutenant Sam Strong again after he rode out of Santa Fe without even a goodbye. But when a series of grisly murders occurred in the New Mexico territory, Sam was back to track down the killer and save the woman he loved from a bloody death.

Knight Dreams by Christina Hamlett

A spellbinding romantic thriller involving a secret from the past which is linked to the ghost of a 15th-century knight. On a mission to bid for an ancient suit of armor in London, Laurel Cavanaugh finds herself propelled into a mysterious chain of events and into the arms of her very own knight in shining armor.

Marrying Miss Shylo by Sharon Ihle

From New York to California, a witty historical romance between a pair of crafty characters who never believed they would fall in love with each other. Shylo McBride was determined to find her mother. Dimitri Adonis was looking for a rich heiress. They wound up marrying, each convinced that the other's "supposed" money and status would come in handy for his or her own purposes.